Jennifer Scales
and the
Messenger of Light

MaryJanice Davidson
and
Anthony Alongi

BERKLEY JAM BOOKS, NEW YORK

THE BERKLEY PUBLISHING GROUP
Published by the Penguin Group
Penguin Group (USA) Inc.
375 Hudson Street, New York, New York 10014, USA
Penguin Group (Canada), 90 Eglinton Avenue East, Suite 700, Toronto, Ontario M4P 2Y3, Canada
(a division of Pearson Penguin Canada Inc.)
Penguin Books Ltd., 80 Strand, London WC2R 0RL, England
Penguin Group Ireland, 25 St. Stephen's Green, Dublin 2, Ireland (a division of Penguin Books Ltd.)
Penguin Group (Australia), 250 Camberwell Road, Camberwell, Victoria 3124, Australia
(a division of Pearson Australia Group Pty. Ltd.)
Penguin Books India Pvt. Ltd., 11 Community Centre, Panchsheel Park, New Delhi—110 017, India
Penguin Group (NZ), Cnr. Airborne and Rosedale Roads, Albany, Auckland 1310, New Zealand
(a division of Pearson New Zealand Ltd.)
Penguin Books (South Africa) (Pty.) Ltd., 24 Sturdee Avenue, Rosebank, Johannesburg 2196,
South Africa

Penguin Books Ltd., Registered Offices: 80 Strand, London WC2R 0RL, England

JENNIFER SCALES AND THE MESSENGER OF LIGHT

This book is an original publication of The Berkley Publishing Group.

Copyright © 2006 by MaryJanice Davidson Alongi and Anthony Alongi.
Cover design by Lesley Worrell.
Cover illustration by Daniel O'Leary.
Text design by Stacy Irwin.

PRINTING HISTORY
Berkley JAM trade paperback edition / June 2006

Berkley trade paperback ISBN: 0-425-21011-1

An application to register this book for cataloging has been submitted to the Library of Congress.

PRINTED IN THE UNITED STATES OF AMERICA

10 9 8 7 6 5 4 3 2 1

WITHDRAWN

Praise for the novels of
MaryJanice Davidson

"A hilarious romp full of goofy twists and turns, great fun for fans of humorous vampire romance." —*Locus*

"Delightful wicked fun!" —Christine Feehan

"Move over, Buffy, Betsy's in town and she rocks! . . . I don't care what mood you are in, if you open this book you are practically guaranteed to laugh . . . top-notch humor and a fascinating perspective of the vampire world."
—*ParaNormal Romance Reviews*

"One of the funniest, most satisfying series to come along lately. If you're fans of Sookie Stackhouse and Anita Blake, don't miss Betsy Taylor. She rocks." —*The Best Reviews*

"*Undead and Unwed* is an irreverently hilarious, superbly entertaining novel of love, lust, and designer shoes. Betsy Taylor is an unrepentant fiend—about shoes. She is shallow, vain, and immensely entertaining. Her journey from life to death, or the undead, is so amusing I found myself laughing out loud while reading. Between her human friends, vampire allies, and her undead enemies, her first week as the newly undead is never boring. . . . A reading experience that will leave you laughing and 'dying' for more from the talented pen of MaryJanice Davidson." —*Romance Reviews Today*

"Chick lit meets vampire action in this creative, sophisticated, sexy, and wonderfully witty book." —Catherine Spangler

BERKLEY JAM titles
by MaryJanice Davidson and Anthony Alongi

Jennifer Scales and the Ancient Furnace
Jennifer Scales and the Messenger of Light

***

BERKLEY SENSATION titles
by MaryJanice Davidson

Undead and Unwed
Undead and Unemployed
Undead and Unappreciated
Undead and Unreturnable
Undead and Unpopular

Derik's Bane
Dead and Loving It

For Liam,
who is always nice to his sister.

PROLOGUE

Emergence

The entire subterranean town of Coober Pedy was dark and quiet when the monster came.

Coober Pedy, self-described opal capital of the world, was a unique place in the world. This opal mining community in south-central Australia evolved partly underground so that the original miners would be sheltered from the brutal elements of the outback desert. With many homes, churches, and even shops underground, the township drew a modest number of tourists every year.

But there was no one near, above or below ground, when the portal opened. It was evening, and too far from town for anyone to see.

Near the Dog Fence built long ago by European settlers to keep dingoes at bay, an unusually bright crescent moon shone down upon the vast expanse of rocky plains. High above this *otherworldly, cracked-stone landscape, a fiery rift appeared in midair with a sizzle. The tear gaped for a moment, revealing a world beyond far darker than the twilit sky. Then the beast emerged.*

Blackness surrounded its head and body. Only six spindly legs and two long, narrow, tattered wings pierced the darkness. The limbs stretched and clawed at the air outside the portal it had created, and then pulled the rest of the shadow through. A tail with a scythelike tip slipped through the rift, and then the portal snapped shut soundlessly.

There was no one around for miles, the thing realized as it hovered in midair. Was this the right place?

It was close. Without sight, sound, or even scent, it could nevertheless feel the beginning of everything. It was just a short flight away.

Once it found the trail, it would be able to pull in more thoughts and memories. Not just those twisted inside its own mind—but of others across time and space. It had taught itself this skill where it grew up. Where you learned quickly or died.

It had been alone when it was younger, and easy prey. Now it was still alone, but as a hunter.

Tattered wings flapped, and the shadow rose to eclipse the moon. It followed the trail of memory north, wings and limbs raging against the thick air of this world. From unseen jaws, a silent howl let loose in a strange tongue, a single word that no one else could hear or understand.

Father!

CHAPTER 1

The Return from Crescent Valley

"That place is so amazing!"

"I'm glad you like it, ace."

Jennifer Scales flew over the surface of the lake on bright blue dragon wings, letting a hindclaw skim the water's surface. The crescent moon slipped away under the horizon and gave way to the morning sun. "I can't wait to go back again!"

Jonathan Scales chuckled at his daughter's enthusiasm, silver eyes aglow and indigo features proud. "That's the third time you've been there in the past two months! It may be a while before we can find time to get there again, with school starting and all."

"I suppose. Soccer season's already—"

"Uh-oh." They were coming up to the shore of the lake now, and could make out the large cabin and farm where

Jennifer's grandfather lived. But it was not Crawford Thomas Scales waiting for them alone on the north lawn.

It was a beaststalker. Beaststalkers were the mortal enemies of weredragons like Jennifer, Jonathan, and Crawford. Unlike weredragons, they did not change shape every crescent moon, but kept their skills and prowess with lethal weapons poised each and every day.

This beaststalker had its sword out and stared at the two dragons with an inscrutable expression as they increased their speed to meet her. Blonde hair swept over cold emerald eyes and a tight frown.

"Your mother looks pretty annoyed."

"You didn't tell her *again*?" Jennifer could not hide the dismay in her voice. "You said you had asked her if we could go!"

"Well . . . technically . . . she wasn't around when I asked. So I left her a note."

"*Daaad!* That never works! She doesn't just get angry at *you*, you know."

"Easy, ace." Her father grinned. "It'll burn off fast once we're back. Just let me handle this."

They reached the shore and touched gently upon the ground. Jonathan strode right up to his wife on his hind legs, stretched his wings out in a welcoming hug, and began to speak.

"Liz, honey . . ."

Before he could get another word out, Dr. Elizabeth Georges-Scales stepped past her husband with lightning speed and shoved him over her leg. With a gasp of smoke the winged beast found himself flat on his back, breath knocked out of him.

"I'll deal with you later. *You*." She pointed right at Jennifer and spoke in calm but clipped tones. "You should know better. I expect this sort of stunt from this idiot. But not you."

"Mom, he told me—"

"Oh, he tells *me* stuff every day! 'I mowed the lawn, honey!' 'My dirty socks aren't strewn all over the living room floor, honey!' 'I have a brain, honey!' I still double-check. And so should you. If you haven't learned *that* about him after fifteen years, you're not as bright as your teachers insist you are."

"Okay, Mom. But there's still time this weekend for beast-stalker training!"

Elizabeth raised her voice. "You had all *last year* to practice flipping your tail and flapping your wings . . ."

"—you know it's more than—"

". . . I asked for just one thing from you this year. Focus! That's all. Focus!"

"That's *all*?"

"And instead, you go off to your secret hideaway, on the moon or wherever. As if I'd know, because your father won't even tell me . . ."

"—we're not allowed to"

". . . and of all the weekends to go! I had planned a surprise for you!" The harsh, clipped tones were gone now. Jennifer could see her mother straining to keep her composure. Dr. Georges-Scales almost never cried—the only time she had done so was last spring, when her family had been in severe danger. But her jade eyes betrayed a bit of moisture.

Although she still felt most—if not all—of the mess was her dad's doing, Jennifer instantly gave in at the sight of those watery eyes. "I'm sorry, Mom." Deflated, she flexed her muscles and shifted back into human form, a teenaged girl with platinum blonde hair, gray eyes, and wiry limbs. As the new incarnation of the legendary Ancient Furnace, she was the only weredragon anyone knew who could change back and forth at will. "No more dragon shape, until next crescent moon. I promise."

After a short sniffle, Elizabeth allowed a tight smile. "Thank you. We should have a short training session this morning, assuming you're up for it. Then, I'd like to give you your birthday present."

"My present? But September just started. My birthday's not for another seventeen days!"

"I received it earlier than expected. I wanted to surprise you. You know, do something nice for you, *if your father has no objection*."

She delivered this last line with a fierce kick to the pale belly of the miserable creature at her feet. With a short *oomph*, Jonathan rolled over and sputtered, "Sorry, Elizabeth darling . . ."

"Not yet, you're not. Jennifer dear, go on inside. Your father and I will finish this conversation in private."

"No, Jennifer . . . don't go . . ." Jonathan reached out weakly with a wing claw as his daughter callously abandoned him on the crisp lawn. He was torn between pain and laughter. "Oh, you ungrateful wretch . . . it's the beaststalker in you! That's it—you're grounded!"

"*Don't stomp your foot, dear.* This isn't like pulling a rattlesnake out of the ground."

"I *know*, Mom."

"You've 'known' for months. But that hasn't helped. Perhaps another trip to your little dragon theme park would help? Or perhaps not . . ."

"Get off my back!"

"Okay, sure. I'll get off your back. And you can fight your battles with a swarm of hapless pygmy owls for the rest of your days."

"Oh, for crying out—"

"It will be stuff of legends. The Ancient Furnace and her trusty band of miniraptors. All field mice will know and fear your name—"

"Okay, Mom, I get it."

Jennifer glared at her mother with fierce gray eyes. Elizabeth returned an even, emerald gaze. Neither of them moved for several moments.

Jonathan, back in human form now with the end of the crescent moon, watched from the safety of the deck chair on the backyard porch. He cradled Geddy, Jennifer's pet gecko, in his left palm while stroking the lizard's green and red markings with his right thumb. Phoebe, the family's black collie-shepherd mix, lolled by his feet. Like both animals, he kept his mouth shut.

Jennifer finally adjusted her tanned leather jerkin, raised a rusty, second-hand sword from her mom's college days, and attempted a deep breath.

"Tighter grip."

Jennifer gritted her teeth, but the point of her sword came up a bit.

"Deeper breath."

The resulting hiss was a bit heavier than necessary.

"Begin."

Jennifer spun around and made a circle high in the air with the point of her sword. It began to glow dimly. In a single, practiced move, she flipped the sword point-down and jammed the tip into the earth right in front of her.

Out of the dirt popped a black-and-gray spotted pygmy owl. It gave a hoot, fluttered over to the backyard porch, and settled down on the railing—at the end of a long line of tiny owls just like it, except all snowy white.

"Well," sighed Elizabeth, "at least you got a different color."

"I *hate* this!" Jennifer plunged her sword hilt-deep into the cool turf.

"Don't do that, it's bad for the bl—"

"Why don't we just go inside already? I'll never get it right."

"Honey, bird calling is not an easy—"

"That bird *sucks*! The other birds *suck*! This sword *sucks*! *I* suck!"

"Jennifer, that's simply not true."

"Which one?"

Elizabeth paused. "Well, *you* certainly do not suck. The rest is up for debate."

Her daughter seized the opportunity. "It's this *sword*!" She kicked the hilt where it stuck out of the ground. "This thing's a disaster! What did you do, leave it in the rain the whole time you attended medical school?"

"The sword is fine for training purposes."

Even Elizabeth herself didn't seem entirely convinced by that, but Jennifer was ignoring her anyway. "And why do I have to learn all this stuff, anyway? I can fight like a dragon when I need to fight! See?"

In less than a second, she was back in her dragon shape, a shimmering blue-winged lizard with silver accents, a severe nose horn, and a long spike at the end of her double-pronged tail. She continued her rant.

"*This* stuff, I'm good at! I can breathe fire! I can disappear with camouflage! I can tear stuff with my claws! I can shock things with my tail!" She pounded the ground with her tail, sending bits of turf sailing. "But best of all—" She finished by punctuating her words with stomps of a heavy hindclaw. "—I can summon any . . . *lizard* . . . I . . . *want*!"

A trio of large, exotic lizards emerged from the earth she had pounded—a black Yangtze Alligator with yellow crossbands, a Galapagos tortoise with moss hanging off of its dark olive shell, and an enormous black mamba that swept the ground under her wings and coiled gently around her left hind leg. Phoebe, up on the porch, whined through her muzzle but relaxed as Jonathan reached down to pet her.

"You promised, Jennifer," he murmured loud enough for all to hear. Jennifer breathed deeply and willed herself back into human form.

Elizabeth looked over the animals and her daughter with an inscrutable nod. "Perhaps you're right. You need to ditch that sword."

"Huh?" Jennifer was startled. "Really? I don't have to use this anymore? Can I have yours?"

"*No.*" Her mother's voice was very stern, and Jennifer recalled last spring, when the two of them had killed Otto Saltin together. Werachnids like Otto were sworn enemies to

weredragons, and Jennifer found their spider shapes terrifying. The werachnid champion had not completely died until
she had taken her mother's sword and chopped the sorcerous
spider's eight-eyed head off. Instead of congratulating her on
a fine slicing technique, however, Elizabeth had snatched the
sword away and yelled at her.

There must be something about a beaststalker's blade, Jennifer guessed, *that's quite special. Either that, or Mom has
sharing issues dating back to childhood.*

"There's something about a beaststalker's blade that's
quite special," Elizabeth said, walking to the porch.

Ah-ha! "Really?" Jennifer asked casually.

Jonathan reached under his lawn chair with his right hand
(Geddy was now sleeping in his left), pulled out a long shoebox
wrapped in foil paper with a glistening bow, and handed it to
his wife.

"Each weapon is unique to its owner," her mother explained. "Over time, beaststalker and blade become almost
like brother and sister. As an only child, you may not understand that analogy. Fortunately, I *do* have a brother. You remember your uncle Mike, who owns that butcher shop in
Virginia? Bladesmithing's a bit of a hobby for him. I con-
tracted his services for this. He sends it with his compliments.
Happy fifteenth birthday, dear."

Jennifer flushed and looked down as she kicked at the
lawn. The mamba slid off her leg and sought a dark, cozy spot
in the weeds by the porch, where its green-gray skin blended
nicely. "Wow. I'm really sorry I wasn't here earlier, Mom—"

"Forget it. As you pointed out, it's early yet, and you
couldn't have known. As for your father, he has paid his

penance by baking an emergency birthday cake. Your grandfather's inside now, putting on the candles. We'll have it in a moment, but you should open this first."

Jennifer took the shiny gift and gave it a soft shake. It didn't rattle much. With a single tear, the paper and bow were off the box and on the grass. Left in her hands was a slender but sturdy box of polished mahogany. The locking clasps were brass, and they made satisfying *clacks* as she popped them open and lifted the lid.

Inside, nestled in black velvet-lined molds, were two long daggers. Their broad blades curved gently from precise steel tips, for well over a foot, to exquisite hilts gilded in bronze. One hilt was in the shape of an angelic woman in flowing robes whose arms hugged the base of the blade; the other was in the shape of a dragon with jaws open, as if devouring the rest of the weapon.

She couldn't say a word. Setting the box on the ground gently, she knelt, reached into the box with both hands, and pulled the weapons out. The hilts seemed to melt into her hands. Flashing the blades back and forth, Jennifer noted they were each longer than her arm from elbow to fingertip.

"Mike made me my first sword as an apprentice when I was in college—this rusty nail you've been using all summer," Elizabeth explained. Her daughter barely heard her. "When I told him last year it wouldn't do for you, he offered to replace it for free. He worked on these for some time."

Jennifer still couldn't think of anything to say.

"As you can see, my brother's technique has improved. I don't think those will rust anytime soon. Now, let's put them to the test."

Without any warning, she drew her own sword and brought it down at her daughter's head.

Jennifer was used to this—all summer long, her mother had tried to find ways to test her reflexes.

But it was hard to surprise the child of a beaststalker and a weredragon. In a flash, the two knives were crossed in an X above their owner's head, and the mother's blow stopped cold at their junction.

The knives twisted as Jennifer stood up and turned, and like that Elizabeth's sword flew out of her hand.

"Well, what do you know," Jonathan said with a grin from the porch. "First time for everything."

On an adrenaline high, Jennifer smoothly swirled around with the knives' points facing up. They blurred and traced a glowing silver halo over her head before she flipped them down and jammed them into the earth together.

In a burst of black feathers, a modest but sturdy eagle with white and red markings arched out of the earth and made straight for the porch railing. The row of owls that had been perched there dissolved into a flurry of hoots and white feathers, and before long the larger raptor stood alone on the railing, cocking its bright crimson face at the serpentine shape that coiled just beneath it.

"Bateleur eagle," Elizabeth identified with an impressed look. "Member of the snake eagle family. Native to the African savannah. Incredibly large specimen, especially for a male of the species—that must be almost a seven-foot wingspan. Nicely done."

"*Snake* eagle?" Jennifer looked in alarm at her black mamba, which had felt the shadow of the bird on its back and was reared up in a warning hiss. The eagle flexed its claws and squawked menacingly. "Um, they wouldn't happen to call them snake eagles because they're *really good friends* with snakes, would they?"

They had just finished separating the combatants when Grandpa Crawford came outside. His gray eyes were bright, but his smile was restrained as he observed the blades in Jennifer's hands. "Hey, Niffer! Cake's almost ready. You get your present?"

She flipped up the knives with a grin. "Check it out, Grandpa!"

"They're nice," she heard Crawford mutter to her mother. "Of course, it's just one more thing to keep her from focusing on her dragon heritage."

"I'm terribly sorry my relationship with my own daughter has crowded your ego. Perhaps we should all leave?" Elizabeth's voice was less dark than her look.

Before Jennifer could react to the sudden tension, Jonathan cleared his throat. "How about that cake, Dad?"

A few moments later, a birthday cake was on the patio table, with fifteen long and thin candles all poking out of a frosted dragon's mouth. Jennifer looked around the table, spotted her mother and grandfather still eyeing each other, and made a silent wish: *I wish they would get along better.*

Of course, she mused as she wiped out all fifteen tiny flames in one breath, they got along a *lot* better than most beaststalkers and weredragons. Dr. Georges-Scales was the only beaststalker anyone knew who had befriended, much less married, a weredragon. And according to her, Crawford Thomas Scales had softened considerably over the years. Maybe Jennifer had something to do with that.

Crawford was smiling at his granddaughter now. "Good job on the candles, Niffer. Reminds me of your grandmother, before she passed on. I'm sure I've told you about the Barn Fire of '52 . . . ?"

Jennifer shook her head, a little warily. As a child she had loved Grandpa's stories, but as a teenager she had grown a bit impatient with the way he could go on about family history and dragon legend.

"This would be back in Eveningstar," he started. "Before the werachnids came, of course. Grandma and I had a place on the edge of town. We used it a bit like we use this farm, as a gathering place for weredragons with nowhere else to go during the crescent moon."

"Like Joseph?" Joseph Skinner was a weredragon without any family in the area; Crawford had let him stay at the farm often last year and help out with the horses, bees, and sheep. Like all new weredragons, he was a couple of years older than Jennifer; but he had been kind to her and helped her with homework.

"That's right. Anyway, we used woodstoves back then, and we stored a bunch of wood in the basement and barn . . ."

"Would you like a slice of cake, Crawford?"

The old man shot an irritated look at his daughter-in-law, but Elizabeth kept a tiny smile at the corner of her mouth as she held out a paper plate with cake on it. Jennifer realized her mother knew full well how much Crawford hated interruptions, once he started a story.

"No thanks, Lizzard. As I was saying, we had a wood-stove, and plenty of fuel all over the place. All it took was an oil lamp and a nervous horse by the name of—"

"Jennifer, sweetheart, will you want a small piece or a large one? I've got a large one here."

Crawford hissed audibly and stared—not at the grinning woman holding out the piece of birthday cake, but at Jennifer herself. It was as if he was daring her to make a choice. Beast-stalker cake or dragon story?

Diplomacy was crucial. Slowly and gently, and without breaking eye contact with her grandfather, Jennifer reached out, took the cake from her mother, tried a bite, hummed appreciatively, and motioned for him to continue.

He nodded and went on. "So the place is all ablaze, and your grandmother, who was always quite the talker— "

"I always found her rather quiet," observed Elizabeth.

"Well, *Doctor*, maybe when you were around she couldn't get a word in edgewise," Crawford snapped. He eyed the woman's leather training armor, as if seeking a vulnerable spot.

"I think it's because she didn't care for me much." The taunting smile never left the woman's face. *Surely,* Jennifer thought, *here stands a brave woman.*

Grandpa Crawford stood up and turned. "I can't imagine why. Jennifer, perhaps we should continue this story inside—aw, hell, Jonathan!" This last remark was directed at his own son, who had appeared in the doorway at the least convenient time possible.

Jennifer immediately saw something was wrong in her father's expression. He was holding a phone and listening intently to whoever was on the other end.

"What's wrong?" Elizabeth stood up and opened the screen door for her husband.

He stepped onto the porch and gave her a hug with his free arm. "Okay, Cheryl . . . yes, Cheryl . . . of course. We'll be there tomorrow. I'm so sorry."

He hung up the phone and sighed. "Remember Jack Alder, Liz? From college? He died last night."

CHAPTER 2

The Best Man's Funeral

Jennifer hadn't really known Jack Alder. According to her parents, he had served as best man at their wedding. He came across state to Winoka once a year or so to reconnect with old friends. Broad and tall, with short-clipped reddish-gold hair and a beard, he had reminded Jennifer of a Norse god— one that drank well and laughed plenty.

Of course, during his visits, she had never talked to him much. He would say dumb things like, "You're in seventh grade already? . . . Wow!" and "You're in eighth grade already? . . . Wow!" but not much more than that. If the Alders stayed for dinner, Jennifer usually excused herself right after eating and retreated to her room.

Although she didn't tell her parents this, she felt bad— because she didn't really feel so bad. She knew they would miss their friend, and she felt sorry for them. But he was *their* friend, not hers.

During the drive to Roseford for the funeral, she wondered if thinking that made her a bad person.

By the time they pulled into the generous Roseford Funeral Homes parking lot, with its neatly clipped lawns punctuated by friendly evergreen trees, she was no closer to an answer. But she forgot all of that when she saw another family walking across the lot.

It was the Blacktooths.

Eddie Blacktooth and his parents, Hank and Wendy, lived next door to the Scales, back in Winoka, on Pine Street East. Eddie and Jennifer had grown up together, and the Blacktooths were beaststalkers like Elizabeth, but the families were hardly friendly. While never exactly pleasant to begin with, Mr. and Mrs. Blacktooth had become positively hostile once they discovered what Jennifer and Jonathan were. At the point last spring when Jennifer most needed her childhood friend, Eddie had turned against her. The two had not seen or spoken to each other since.

As soon as he caught sight of Jennifer, Eddie turned red and looked away. His brown hair was cut shorter, and Jennifer could make out a few scars on the back of his neck—training wounds, she guessed, since she also had a few. But he still looked an awful lot like a sparrow to her, with his gentle beak of a nose and his penchant for wearing brown—in today's case, a chocolate suit that overwhelmed his modest frame.

They walked by, and Hank and Wendy did not bother to hide their disgust when they saw the Scales. Hank looked like a larger, stockier, and angrier version of Eddie, and might have been ready to foam at the mouth on the spot. Wendy had a smooth, calm appearance not unlike Elizabeth, but with sapphire eyes that pierced from beneath shiny black hair. The two women held each other's eyes, and Jennifer saw the mutual distaste. Then they were past, and the Scales all breathed out a bit.

"What are *they* doing here?" Jennifer almost spat.

"Ms. Blacktooth and I went to the same college as Jack. St. Mary's, right down the street from here. The three of us were in the same dormitory our sophomore year."

"Really?" This seemed like a coincidence. Jennifer adjusted her dress, checked her hair in the minivan window, and decided to redo her hair clips. "How did that happen?"

"Wendy and I were roommates, actually. Best friends."

"You're kidding! Ugh, this hair is impossible . . ."

"I don't kid, honey. Here, let me fix that." Her mother's hands worked deftly at the platinum strands and black clips. "We were quite inseparable. Went to the same high school, too. Started our beaststalker training together." Then she shifted subjects as if she hadn't just admitted being best friends with the woman who had almost killed her daughter. "You know, Jack and I even dated once or twice. Didn't last long after graduation, but we parted on good terms. A few years later, Jack introduced me to one of his new business associates in town . . . your father."

"Ewww! You dated *the dead guy*?"

"When he was alive, dear. He was cute. Nice butt. Kissed like a dream."

Jonathan coughed. Jennifer groaned.

"I so *don't* need to hear about your past love life."

"Yes, well, believe it or not, the world *did* turn on its axis—several times, at least—before you were born. And people lived here, and did things. Without you."

"Funny, Mother."

"I just find it amusing that you never took an interest in your parents' lives until this past year. There, all done." Elizabeth's hands stopped poking at the hair clips, and Jennifer checked her reflection in the window again. She looked suitably put together—and quite austere, in her black dress.

"I can't believe the Blacktooths have to be here. Is— I mean, was Jack also a beaststalker?"

"No," Jonathan replied. They were walking into the funeral home foyer, so he lowered his voice to a whisper. "Not a weredragon, either. He was a regular guy, a computer software sales manager. But I think he began to figure some of us out, after our enemies burned down Eveningstar and we moved to Winoka. As for Hank and Wendy, they didn't really catch on to us dragons until last year, of course."

"I can't believe you moved in *next door* to a beaststalker family back then, knowing what they were!" Jennifer tried to keep her voice down, but disbelief made it hard. "How dumb are you guys, anyway?"

Her mother glared at her, but Jonathan breezily pulled his wife along. "Hey, *you* try to find good real estate value in a seller's market someday." That was all her father would say, since they were entering the funeral home.

* * *

After the ceremony and graveside service, Jack's mother hosted a short wake at her house. Jennifer didn't even know the elderly woman's name, and there were virtually no people her age to talk to. In fact, the only other teenager there at all was Eddie. So she stayed close to her parents, waiting out their conversations with people she had never met.

Only one person stood out—a gaunt, middle-aged woman with brilliant red hair and a sober gray dress. She approached Jonathan as if she had known him for years, turned him away from the other guests, and passed him a photograph. "From the crime scene investigator," she said.

"One of us?" Jonathan guessed.

"One of us." The woman glanced cautiously at Elizabeth. *She's a weredragon,* Jennifer guessed. She also guessed this woman, like all weredragons outside of her own family, had no idea Jennifer's mother was a beaststalker.

She saw her father's expression turn white when he scanned the photo, and she shifted position to get a look.

It was the first time she had seen a photo of a murder victim, and she had to force her stomach to remain calm even though there was no blood apparent. Jack was lying faceup on the carpet of his apartment living room, staring just past the camera. Two details stood out to Jennifer. First, he looked thirty years older than she knew he actually was. *How can someone age that fast?* she wondered.

The second detail was a phrase gouged by some sort of sharp implement into the carpet next to his blanched hair:

No friends.

"That doesn't make any sense," Jonathan mumbled. "No friends? Jack had plenty of friends. Women, especially. They gravitated to him. And he had us. And . . ."

He stopped short with a painful expression, as if something unpleasant had stung him in the kidneys.

"Dad?"

He didn't respond. His eyes did not leave the photo.

"Honey?" Elizabeth peered over her husband's shoulder. "What's wrong?"

"Mr. Scales, perhaps we should put the photo away for now. People may begin to notice." The red-haired woman was clearly nervous.

"You've obviously upset him," Jennifer whispered harshly. "Couldn't this have waited?"

Her father suddenly noticed her, which broke him out of his trance. He slipped the photo into his breast pocket. "You're right, ace. It can wait. You shouldn't be seeing this sort of thing anyway."

Jennifer slid away, irritated. Again, guilt at not feeling worse gnawed at her. She felt sorry for Jack, of course, but she was uncomfortable here and wished her parents had let her stay home.

She caught a glimpse of Eddie, sandwiched between his parents as they droned on with some strangers, and saw the same wish on his face. It almost made her smile. Then he turned and caught her gaze, and her face froze in a frown. The relish tray on the buffet next to her had carrots, and she decided to count them until he looked away.

. . . *sixteen, seventeen, eighteen* . . .

"You eating those, or hoarding them?"

She gave a start. Rather than disengaging, Eddie had come

right up to her. His expression betrayed no emotion, but the attempt at a joke felt like a try at friendship.

It was a try Jennifer wasn't ready for. "Hoarding them. Back off or I'll shove one through your eye socket."

"Hey." His palms went up, facing her. "How about a one-day truce? I know you're still angry at me, but—"

"Angry isn't even a start, Eddie. Your mother was ready to dice me, and you stood there like a statue."

"I didn't have—"

She picked up a baby carrot and gnawed on it. "What is that, anyway, some kind of family code of conduct? My mom hasn't had time to go over the full Beaststalker Happy Fun Camp Handbook, yet. Maybe there's a chapter toward the end about how to betray your friends and act like a creep. You must be ahead of me. Star student."

Eddie winced. "I don't expect you to forgive me right now. I'm still working through what happened that day. This is so confusing, Jennifer."

"You know what's *not* confusing? Your pathetic excuse of a friendship. I don't even know who you are anymore."

"I know who I am," he hissed back. "The question is, do you know who *you* are?"

Jennifer bristled, not least because part of her suddenly realized she didn't have a very good answer. "What's *that* supposed to mean?"

"I'm not the only bad friend here. You hid yourself from me last year. It hurt when my parents told me what they'd learned about you. They had to piece it together from what Otto Saltin was doing, but when they figured it out, they knew more about you than *I* did."

"Gee, you're right, Eddie, I'm sorry. I should have come running to you right away, just as soon as I was in the shape of a dragon. Then you could have betrayed me right away to your mom and dad. I mean, they're *sooo* understanding. They probably would have stitched a lovely corsage to my wing before slicing my head off."

"They don't want that," he insisted. "Not if you're part beaststalker. Mom even said the other day there may be hope for you." He was trying hard to look as though he wasn't really talking to her. Jennifer scanned the room and saw the Blacktooths spot them. Their expressions were pure poison.

"Yeah, she seems really delighted to see me. Your dad, too. They probably can't wait to embrace me as the daughter they never had. Listen, I don't want you to knock yourself out trying to make nice. You're already avoiding me at school, so just stay the course. And keep your family away from mine."

With that, she flicked a carrot at him and strode back to her parents.

The Wednesday after the funeral was the first day of tenth grade, with new teachers and classes. High school this year was only slightly less scary than it had been last year. But she was just glad to be experiencing it—last year she didn't think she would be able to ever go to any normal school ever again, since most weredragons had to keep to a strict schedule of changing with every crescent moon.

But as the Ancient Furnace, Jennifer was different—and at Winoka High, "different" could be a harrowing experience. So she stuck close to her best friends, Susan Elmsmith and Skip

Wilson. Skip, son of the late Dianna Wilson and Otto Saltin, had put his life on the line to defend Jennifer against his own werachnid father.

Because of Skip's bravery, she always wore the necklace he had given her, with a Native American wood carving of the Moon of Falling Leaves. Since her father told her that he and Dianna Wilson had been good friends before Otto Saltin came on the scene, Jennifer felt that there was history to build on— and that maybe some weredragons and some werachnids could be good friends instead of mortal enemies.

Right now, however, she just wanted her geometry textbook back.

"Come *on*," she pleaded. He returned a mischievous grin and used his wiry frame to hold the book high above her head while Susan rummaged through her own locker. "Susan and I need to get to math class. Don't make me kick your ass for it. It'll embarrass you."

"All I want is a date to the Halloween dance."

She ignored Susan's resigned hiss and gasped with transparent indignation. "That's blackmail! Are you really that desperate?"

His green-blue eyes twinkled with mischief. "Desperate to hear you say *yes*. C'mon, Jennifer, I've asked you twice and you said you had to think about it. You're killing me."

"And you're killing *me*," interrupted Susan grumpily, slamming her locker shut and twirling her brown curls with a well-manicured fingernail. "Both of you. For heaven's sake, get a room."

"Well, gee, Skippy, I dunno." Jennifer gave a coquettish smirk and rubbed the floor with her toe. "The dance is almost two months away, and it's only the first day of school! I could still get a better offer."

His smile disappeared and the textbook came down. "Are lots of guys already asking you?"

She stammered a bit at the question. "Um, well, yeah. A few. But no one I *like* has asked me yet," she hastened to add.

At Susan's gasp and Skip's fallen expression, she talked even more quickly. "I mean, no one besides you! Ah, geez, Skip. Yeah, okay, I'll go to the dance with you."

"Don't do me any favors," he sulked.

"What do you mean?" Jennifer began to panic. This had started all in jest, but she began to feel a fun night slip through her fingers. What was going on?

"I know you could get better offers," he explained. "If you just want to be friends, just say so. But I don't want your pity."

"Oh, Skip, no! Don't take it that way. I thought we were just playing around. I want to go with you, really! Look, see, *I'll* ask *you*." She cleared her throat and straightened up. Her voice came out throaty and serious. "Skip Wilson, will you go to the Halloween dance with me?"

He paused. Susan stared at him with impatience, and then smacked him on the back of the head with her pocketbook.

"Cripes, loser, say 'yes!' "

"Ow! Okay, yes." His easy smile returned, wider than ever, as he rearranged the chocolate strands of hair at the back of his head. "Cool. Um, here's your math book back. So, um, I guess we'll talk more about the dance later, okay?"

"Okay."

"Okay."

"Okay."

Susan glowered at them both. "*Okay*. Hit the road."

Still sporting a goofy smile, Skip practically pranced down the hallway and out of sight.

"Boys are so sad," Susan commented.

"What the heck was he talking about, better offers?"

Her friend turned and began walking down the hall. "Oh, just quit it."

She scurried after. "Quit *what*?"

"This false modesty . . . it doesn't become you."

"*Susan.*"

"Okay, you didn't know. Whatever you say . . . I mean, you can't be this dim."

Jennifer restrained herself from picking Susan up by the ankles and banging her pal's head on the floor a few times. "What. Are. You. Talking. About."

Susan stopped in the middle of the hallway, causing Jennifer to run right into her. "You're *only* the most talked-about girl at school nowadays. It's irritating beyond belief—you dye your hair platinum blonde and the boys just fall all over themselves."

"I didn't dye it! You know I can't control my hair." This was true—Jennifer's hair, which used to be a darker blonde, had developed more and more streaks of silver throughout ninth grade, as her weredragon nature emerged. Over the summer, the last of her old hairs had turned, and the sun had toned what was left into platinum.

"Yeah, whatever, you're a freak and your life is miserable. Cry me a river. You're all anybody can talk about. Your shiny hair, your perfect legs, the way you're already a starting wing on the varsity soccer team . . ."

"You made the team, too! And you'll be a starter next year for sure!"

"Hmmph. Anyway, it's day one of tenth grade and you're already everyone's favorite person. Good thing no one knows you're really a lizard in disguise." Susan softened her comment with a ruby grin, but Jennifer still panicked.

"Susan, you can't tell anyone what I told you last spring, you swore you wouldn't, please . . ."

"Easy there, camper. Susan Elmsmith doesn't do gossip. I'm not that desperate for popularity."

Jennifer sighed with relief. At Winoka High, only Susan, Skip, and (unfortunately) Eddie knew about her weredragon heritage. Everyone in her family agreed that was dangerous enough. "Honest, Susan, I'm not trying to attract attention. If the dye would stick, I'd color my hair pale green to match these lockers and disappear. I thought freshman year was bad, but in some ways this year is *terrifying*!"

The class bell rang. They hurried, falling naturally into step with each other.

"I know what you mean. Have you seen Bob Jarkmand yet? I hear he's bigger and uglier than ever. Get the net!"

Jennifer giggled at her friend's remark. Bob Jarkmand, a fellow sophomore, had been the class bully in ninth grade last year until a certain girl had laid him out in front of the guidance counselor's office with a single punch. Now he was reportedly large enough to be a starting offensive lineman for the Winoka varsity football team.

"In three summer months he converted what was left of his brain into more muscle," Jennifer commented. "I saw him at the mall a couple of times over the summer. All he does is stare at me now." She shivered. Bob *was* much bigger. Jennifer didn't know many students taller than her, not even juniors or seniors. But this fellow was a tower—a big, unsightly tower (and one missing a few bricks at that). She wondered to herself why she had bothered to pick a fight with Winoka High's hugest denizen.

You did it for Skip, she reminded herself warmly. *Because he was sticking up for you.*

"What's that?" Susan sounded amused.

"What's what?"

"That goofy smile on your face."

"Eh, nothing."

"Sure, right . . ."

Well, Jennifer thought as they slipped through the classroom door together, *if Bob decides to pick another fight this year, I might at least get some exercise in before he floors me.*

"Ladies. Nice of you to join us."

They both flinched. The classroom was incredibly quiet, and they were the only two people standing. Embarrassment clove their feet to the floor.

Whhhrrrt.

A slight man dressed in a sharp black shirt and neatly pressed pants rolled up to them in an electronic wheelchair. The polish on his designer shoes was exquisite. His blond hair was swept to one side and stuck there as if ordered. Beneath it, his handsome, tanned smile did not extend to his piercing black eyes.

His voice was smooth and quick, with a hint of somewhere

in eastern Europe. "When Principal Mouton offered me the position of mathematics teacher over the summer, I wasn't aware that I would have to review curriculum like How to Read Schedules and Tell Time. My naïve hope was that we could skip such harrowing topics and dive right into, oh, say, Euclidean geometry. If you're willing?"

"Sorry," they both mumbled, scampering to their seats through a sea of smirks and titters.

"As I was saying," Mr. Slider addressed the entire class, "My name is Edmund Slider. I will be your geometry teacher this year. Geometry has multiple practical applications. It also has some uses that may seem a bit abstract, but help us answer some big questions. Take, for example, the size of the known universe. Most of you have heard of the Big Bang Theory . . ."

His chair spun to face the chalkboard, which had been lowered before the school year started so the new instructor could reach it. As he talked, he drew circles within circles, and rays that stretched from the innermost circle outward. Everything was labeled with stuff like $z + 1B$ *years* and such. Jennifer thought herself fairly good at mathematics, but that had been in algebra last year. Her parents had encouraged her to keep pushing herself in advanced classes, but geometry was so different from what she was used to . . .

Someone tapped her shoulder. She turned. One of her classmates—a junior girl she didn't know—was holding out a folded piece of paper, with a mixture of boredom and disdain.

"Someone back there handed this up. I guess for you."

"Thanks."

"Eh." Apparently, this girl wasn't in the Jennifer Scales Fan Club that Susan was insisting existed.

Jennifer unfolded the note and read it:

Will you go to the Halloween dance with me? I don't want to tell you who I am in case you say no.

She looked behind her, but there were five rows back there, full of unfamiliar, unfriendly-looking boys. None of them even glanced at her; they were either listening to Mr. Slider or (in Bob Jarkmand's case) staring listlessly out the window.

A bit off to the left, however, was a new sight—a boy she'd never seen at the school. *Angelic,* was her first thought. He had wavy, shoulder-length blond hair, a smooth face with sparkling blue eyes, and soft peach skin. He looked up and caught her staring, so she quickly spun around and felt herself blush.

Glancing to her right, she saw Susan, two desks over, rolling her eyes in a correct guess of the note's intent.

Sighing in exasperation, Jennifer folded the note back up and shoved it in her pocket. *Susan's right. Boys are so sad.*

"This is so sad!" Jennifer pleaded to her father that evening at home. "We just get back from the funeral of this friend of yours I barely know, and now you want me to go to some dumb *dinner party* tonight?"

"Your mother got called into surgery." Jonathan smiled gamely. "And I'm supposed to bring a date."

"I'll be so bored!"

"I don't think so! The hospital here in Winoka wants to build a new rehabilitation center for people with blindness or vision disorders. I'm the architect. Customers will use this center to learn how to live with no sight, and some of them will be at the fund-raiser tonight—including kids."

"So this lame event is at the hospital where Mom works?"

"No, the fund-raiser's up in Minneapolis! Where the money is. I swear it won't be like the funeral at all."

"But I don't know how to act around blind people—and even if there are kids, they'll still be *strangers*! What will we talk about?"

He scrunched his nose. "I dunno. You should find some common ground in agreeing you all have lame fathers."

"That's a start. What will I wear?"

"You can wear the same dress you wore to the funeral."

"Daaad . . ."

"Please, sweetheart. You'll make your father happy. Isn't that what every teenage daughter really wants?"

She glared at him without a word.

He patted his own chest. "Deep down inside?"

Still no response.

"Thanks, peach. You've got ten minutes to get ready."

"Aaargh!" She spun around and stomped up the stairs.

CHAPTER 3

Aunt Tavia

In fact, the fund-raiser was not at all bad. First, it was an excuse to go to Minneapolis, which was lively and elegant at night. Second, the event began with an enormous dinner. As she worked through her roasted pheasant and wild rice with steamed vegetables, Jennifer began to understand why her father thought she might not hate it.

Third . . .

"Skip's here!" She practically upended the table when she saw him sitting across the room. Jonathan did not protest, so she maneuvered through all of the cloth-lined tables until she rested an arm on her friend's shoulder.

Then she saw who he was sitting with, and slowly removed it. Skip looked and sounded nervous.

"Jennifer, I don't believe you've met my aunt Tavia?"

Even before he gave the name, it would have been easy

enough for Jennifer to guess who this woman was. After Otto Saltin died—no one beyond the Scales knew exactly how—his sister had moved to Winoka to take care of Skip. Tavia Saltin, like her nephew and her late brother, had dark chocolate hair and hazel eyes. Her long, maroon-painted fingertips curled around Skip's neck where Jennifer's hand had been, and her face betrayed recognition at this girl's name.

"Jennifer *Scales*?"

"Yes." Jennifer had no idea whether to shake hands, make a grab for the birthday daggers she had strapped under her dress, or run.

"My goodness!" Tavia stood up, and without warning, warmly embraced her startled prey. "I've been *dying* to meet the girl who saved my sweet nephew! Oh, bless you, sweetheart! Thank you so much!"

Jennifer tried to return the hug, but this woman was quite spindly. It was like trying to grab a bundle of sticks. She settled on a shoulder pat. "You're welcome. What are you two doing here?" She tried not to sound too suspicious.

"Oh, I'm an eye specialist. Some of my patients are here tonight. I saw your father's name as the architect—but I didn't realize we'd see *you* here tonight! This is *delicious*!"

Jennifer looked at Skip, who appeared ready to swallow his own tongue. "Skip's told you we're friends, then?"

"But of course!" Withdrawing from the hug, Tavia bared her teeth in an oversized smile. "He talks about you all the time. I keep telling him we must have you over for dinner some evening, but he never follows up!" Now her voice sunk to a conspiratorial whisper. "I think he's afraid you'll say no if he asks you out."

"Yeah. Huh. I'd, er, love to come over sometime. So, um, my being friends with your nephew doesn't bother you?"

"Why should it?" Tavia made the very idea sound like the most preposterous notion anyone had ever offered. "I'll tell you what. Later this week, I'll give you a call. We'll try to set a dinner date for next week, or the week after?"

There was no chance to respond, because Jonathan walked up. Next to him were two people—an elderly man and a teenaged boy. Not just any boy—the new angel face from her geometry class!

For the second time today, Jennifer found herself staring at him. He stared right back.

"Everything all right here?" Jonathan asked tentatively.

"Of course!" Tavia clapped her hands. "You're Jonathan Scales, right? I'm Tavia Saltin, Skip's aunt . . ."

"Nice to meet you. This is Martin Stowe." He bowed to the elderly man, who looked at least seventy. Martin's shoulders were hunched and his frail hands held a white cane. "He and his grandson are new in town. He has severe glaucoma and will likely use our new center's services. His grandson, Gerry, goes to Winoka High. Maybe you've met him, ace?"

Jennifer couldn't quite speak. Those crystal blue eyes! That fluffy blond hair! So beautiful!

She felt Skip's elbow dig into her side. "Well, Mr. Scales, you know, Jennifer and I have actually been spending a lot of time together. You know, talking about the Halloween dance and all. I'm not sure she'd notice . . ."

"I've seen him," she blurted out. Skip's eyes narrowed slightly. "Geometry class, right? I'm Jennifer."

There were handshakes all around. Martin Stowe held his

hand out and turned his blind eyes slightly as different hands shook it. Jennifer was fairly certain she was going to faint, what with beautiful Gerry and irritated Skip and spindly Aunt Tavia and blind Martin and everything else coming together all at once.

In a bit of small talk for which Jennifer, Skip, and Gerry just sort of looked at their shoes, each other, and each other's shoes, Martin revealed that they had just moved to Winoka two weeks ago, a few months after Gerry's parents died in a horrible accident abroad. Austria, or Switzerland, or maybe Hungary—Jennifer forgot the place quickly. What was the difference? And was that too mean a thought to even think? After all, Gerry was an orphan, and—

"Well, I hear them serving desserts now," Martin said, breaking her concentration. He was right: The servers were setting down new china. "Better get back to our seats."

The Stowes said their good-byes, and so did the Scales. Tavia hugged Jennifer again before she would let either of them leave. As they walked back, her father whispered.

"His aunt Tavia, eh? Does she know who we are?"

"I have no idea," she murmured back.

It didn't seem right to bring it up with Skip the next day— after all, talking to him about it might raise more questions in his head. All he and his aunt knew was that Otto had kidnapped Jennifer and Jonathan, knocked Skip unconscious, and then died at the hands of an unknown rescuer. They were grateful the Scales had thought to rescue Skip as well. Why rock the boat?

He didn't seem to want to talk about it either. But that might have had to do more with Gerry, who by scheduling coincidence was in at least three of Jennifer and Susan's classes, to their mutual delight, while Skip was only in Jennifer's history class.

So the week went on in fairly boring fashion. Skip was incredibly attentive and spoke of nothing but going to the Halloween dance, Susan was continually plotting how to run into Gerry, Eddie was barely a ghost they saw in the hallways from time to time, and Bob Jarkmand still glared at Jennifer from across hallway crowds like a distant, horrifying lighthouse.

Jennifer was ducking away from the enormous boy's gaze one afternoon when she almost walked straight into Gerry.

"Whoa!" She almost dropped her backpack. "Um, hey, Gerry."

The boy stared back at her, but said nothing.

"Sorry I almost ran into you." An idea struck her—this was an opportunity to help her friend! "Hey, er, you haven't seen Susan around lately, have you? She was talking about you earlier."

Despite her meaningful wink, she got no reaction at all. Gerry Stowe appeared frozen in midair.

She waved her hand in front of his face. "Hello?"

That made him blink, but he didn't smile. Instead, he looked her up and down, wiped the sweat off of his forehead, and bolted in the other direction.

Hmm. She watched him run. *Should I be flattered or insulted?*

"Jennifer!" It was Eddie's voice behind her.

Or warned.

She walked as quickly as she could away from the voice, in

the same direction Gerry had taken. Eddie called after her a couple more times, but the voice got more distant and she soon could breathe a sigh of relief.

"Hey, gorgeous! Whatcha up to?" Skip's voice made her jump.

"Oh! Hey, Skip." She looked around, distracted. "Yeah, I was just looking for Gerry. Did he come this way?"

His easygoing expression shifted into anxious irritation. "I wouldn't know. I don't pay much attention to him."

Sensing his jealousy, she offered a soft smile. "Oh, Skip. Really. I just wanted to talk to him and find out if maybe he'd be interested in asking Susan to the dance."

"Susan, eh?" He surveyed the hallway as if expecting the brunette to leap out of a locker. "She could probably do better."

Jennifer decided to change the subject. "Are you going to take me somewhere for my birthday?"

This worked beautifully and he stammered defensively. "Your b-birthday! Oh yeah, that's, er, coming up, isn't it?"

She pretended to be irritated that he couldn't place the date. "September eighteenth, Skip. Next Thursday. You remember, don't you?"

"Of course! Um, well, I thought we might go to the mall . . ."

"Winoka Mall?" She wrinkled her nose. "We go there two or three times a week already."

"No, no! Um, the Mall of America!" This was at least an effort, Jennifer had to admit. The Mall of America was a commercial landmark in Minnesota, complete with four massive anchor stores, hundreds of stores in between them, and a full-scale amusement park in the middle of it all.

But she wasn't ready to let him off the hook yet. "How will we get there?"

"My aunt can drive."

The expression on her face must have been vivid, because he hurried to add, "She'll drop us off! It'll just be the two—"

"Jennifer!"

"Ugh." She flinched at the interruption. Eddie had apparently not given up as easily as she had hoped. He was jogging down the hallway toward them, gracefully sliding between other students' bodies and backpacks.

"Jennifer, I've got to talk to—"

Skip's hand stopped Eddie short. "She doesn't want to talk to you."

The other boy's sparrowlike features tried to maneuver around the hand to get a glimpse of Jennifer. "Skip, back off! This doesn't have anything to do with you."

"She's not interested. So you either walk away, or deal with me."

Eddie stopped moving and growled at the other boy. "What's your problem, Wilson? You want to fight?"

Jennifer took a deep breath. "Ah, the pungent scent of testosterone . . ."

Both of them gave her a look, but Skip's dissolved into a smirk quickly enough. He turned his back on Eddie and put his hand on her shoulder. "All right, Scales. You made your point. Let's just get out of—"

He lurched forward as Eddie shoved him in the back.

"I was *talking* to you, Wilson! I said, do you want to fight?"

Jennifer bit her lip. Skip knew Eddie and his family were

beaststalkers, because Jennifer had told him weeks ago. But she was pretty sure Eddie had no idea about Skip or his family—or what Skip would become someday.

So why the hostility?

Skip turned with a hiss and straightened up. He was a full two or three inches taller than Eddie, though both of them were wiry enough that height didn't make a whole lot of difference. But there was something in Skip's stance—the way he positioned himself to spring upon the other boy, like predator upon prey—that made Jennifer shudder.

"Please, Skip." She touched his elbow lightly. "Let's just go. He's not worth it."

Slowly and reluctantly, Skip took two steps back. When his opponent didn't move, he allowed himself to turn around again and put his hand in hers. "Okay."

"Jennifer, you'd better listen to me!" Eddie didn't seem to be following, but she didn't turn around as they walked away. "You'll be sorry if you don't!"

Without looking back or slowing down, Skip called out, "If you threaten her again, Blacktooth, I'll flatten you."

They nearly ran into Principal Mouton as he came out of his office to see what was going on. The principal was a good enough man who had acted a bit pompously in Jennifer's only run-in with him: When her family had to get her off the hook for fighting Bob Jarkmand last year.

He squinted at Jennifer and Skip, and then down the hall at Eddie. "Am I hearing a problem out here, gentlemen?"

"No problem, *sir,*" Skip said with a bit of edge. Eddie didn't answer at all. Instead, he turned and walked away.

Seeing the problem resolve itself, Mr. Mouton gave Jennifer

a wry hint of a smile. "Ms. Scales, you'll help me keep these two under control, I hope?"

She chewed her tongue thoughtfully. "I think I can manage it."

As it turned out, Skip was horrifically sick on her fifteenth birthday, so their plans to go to the Mall of America fell through. Instead, Jennifer had Susan come over, and they hung out in her room.

"It's a school night anyway," Susan sympathized as she fiddled with the small portable stereo on Jennifer's nightstand. "Ugh, this radio station sucks. Let's try . . . no . . . how about . . . geez, I'm so *sick* of this song!"

"Yeah, me, too. Like, back in August."

Susan left it on for a while anyway. It *was* a catchy song, by their favorite artist. But they had grooved to it all summer long.

"Okay, that's enough! Just flip it to disc; I've got a good mix in there. I guess you're right about the mall—it'll be better to do on a weekend."

"Of course, your family goes up to your grandpa's cabin an awful lot of weekends," Susan pointed out, flipping the stereo switch. "You sure you'll be able to make the time for him?" There was a bit of regret in her voice, and Jennifer wasn't entirely certain they were talking about Skip anymore.

"We are up at the cabin a lot," she admitted. Her mother preferred to do beaststalker training up there—partly for privacy, Jennifer guessed; and partly because she imagined it bothered her grandfather a great deal. Of course, she couldn't explain this to Susan yet, much less invite her along.

Why not?

Susan interrupted her reverie with a glance out the window. "Oooh, pretty moon! Check it out, Jennifer—"

It was a full moon—dusty red, large, and low on the horizon. Looking at the mysterious orb made Jennifer think of Skip again. She hadn't considered it before, but she supposed if she had been looking at a crescent moon instead of a full one, she'd be wondering right now if Skip wasn't sick at all— just very, very different. In the throes of his first change. Change into . . . what, exactly?

Would he look like his father?

She brushed the thought away. "So anyway, is your geometry textbook in your backpack?"

Susan gagged. "You wanna do geometry homework on your birthday night? Cripes, Jennifer. Didn't your parents plan anything for you? It's not like them to forget."

"They didn't forget. We celebrated up at the cabin a while ago, with cake and everything."

"Huh. What'd they get you?"

Jennifer chewed her tongue again. *This is so unfair.* "Just, you know. Stuff. They're kinda clueless."

"Well, *I* got you something cool." Susan rummaged through her backpack and pulled out a small turquoise gift bag, puffed up with pink and green tissue paper.

"Hey, thanks! But you know you didn't have to get me anything."

"Oh, right. After nine consecutive birthday presents from you, I'm going to blow *your* fifteenth birthday off!"

"I hope you didn't get me anything too expensive," Jennifer mused. She had gotten Susan a lovely coral necklace for *her* fifteenth birthday two months ago. It had looked more pricey than it actually was.

"Just open it and see!"

She reached into the tissue and pulled out . . . a folded piece of paper, which got Susan bouncing up and down with excitement. Jennifer unfolded it and immediately saw the words MINNESOTA DEPARTMENT OF PUBLIC SAFETY at the top. Susan's own name was filled in.

"For my birthday you got me . . . your learner's permit?"

"Isn't it cool???" Susan couldn't contain herself anymore. "I can drive now! My dad or another adult has to be in the passenger seat, but *I can drive I can drive I can drive*!"

"Huh. Well, that's great!" Jennifer struggled not to betray any disappointment as she handed the permit back to her friend. "I'm really happy for you."

Susan looked at her for a second and then burst out laughing. "Oh come on, Jennifer! I'm not *that* self-involved! I just did that to mess with you. Your present's still in the bag."

Jennifer exhaled heavily. "Good. Because I was going to have to kill you."

She reached in again and quickly found a hard surface with her fingers. Some sort of stone. Of course . . . the bag was a little too heavy to hold just paper. How could she have fallen for her friend's joke?

Pulling out the object, she whistled in appreciation.

It was a miniature stone carving—pink marble, Jennifer guessed. The shape was a small dragon standing on its hind legs, with its wings folded tightly against its body and head bowed low. The detail was just intricate enough to make out a thoughtful pair of eyes, and a hint of a smile.

"Oh, Susan. It's gorgeous! Where'd you get it?"

"Actually, um, I did it. My father does sculpture as a hobby, and he's been teaching me."

Jennifer almost dropped it in surprise and then looked it over again, admiring every detail. "*You?* This is amazing! Susan, you're so *good*!"

Her friend blushed and looked at the carpet. "I know I haven't said much about—you know, what you are. Since last spring. But I thought I ought to say—you know. I think it's cool. And I hope someday, you'll feel comfortable showing me."

"Oh!" It occurred to Jennifer her friend had never seen her as a dragon. Simultaneously, it occurred to her she wasn't ready for that yet. "Yeah. Someday soon." She winced. "Not tonight though, okay?"

"No problem. So, you like it?"

"I love it! Susan, it's so thoughtful! Thank you! I'll put it here for now—" She put it on the dresser next to Geddy's tank. "—but later, I'll ask my parents if I can put it downstairs in the living room. It's so classy!"

Sporting a huge grin, Susan reached into her backpack again. "I'm glad you like it. And to make your evening perfect, I did bring my geometry text with me! So we can study the volume of a sphere to your heart's content. Happy birthday, math geek!"

The textbook's explanations of the volume of a sphere certainly made more sense than her mother's description of how a beaststalker's battle cry worked.

"The battle cry is on an impossible frequency," Elizabeth explained at Crawford's lakeside farm the following Friday, while Jonathan prepared dinner inside. "Like an enchanted radio that only magical beasts can hear. Others may hear a simple shout, and see a bright light, but it doesn't hurt them like it would hurt a morphed werachnid or weredragon, or any other magical creature."

Jennifer adjusted her leather armor with an uncomfortable wince. "Hold on, I'm still stuck on that enchanted radio thing. What do you mean, impossible frequency? If we can do it, it's possible, right?"

"Yes, and no. Think of a number."

"Um, okay."

"Multiply it by itself."

"Right."

"Did you get negative one?"

"Of course not. I'm at, like, forty-nine."

"Well, I got negative one, because I was using imaginary numbers. Imaginary numbers are technically impossible; but they still exist, even if it's just in our heads. So beaststalkers have learned to use frequencies that radios and satellites can't possibly find to affect the mystical world."

"So let me get this straight. If I get some answers wrong on a math test, can I go back to Mr. Slider and just say I was using imaginary numbers?"

"Try to focus, honey."

"Sorry. So how do I make light or sound on these impossible frequencies?"

"The key is using your blade—or blades, in your case. A beaststalker's kiss makes the metal resonate, and essentially turns the weapon into a sort of microphone. You shout, and it splits your voice into two parts—deafening sound and blinding light. Both are painful to magical beasts. Observe."

"Wait!" Jennifer scooped Geddy, who had been blithely swinging from her hair, off of her neck and ran across the yard and up the porch steps. She popped open the cabin door, flung him inside (carefully, so he landed on the couch), and then scooted back down the stairs.

"That wasn't necessary." Her mother sighed. "Remember in Otto's dungeon, when I used the battle shout to chase Otto off? Geddy reacted like a typical animal then; he took the trauma just fine."

"You probably stung his tender, magical ears and eyes! He's just too polite to complain."

"Can we get on with it?"

"Please."

Elizabeth raised her sword to her lips, kissed the blade, and let out a long shout. Her daughter watched with amazement—she had never really gotten a good look at how it was done in the dungeon where her mother had interrupted Otto Saltin and rescued her with this very skill.

The beaststalker's breath was almost visible as it passed from lips to sword. There, it split on the edge and divided—a fierce cry that swept across the lake and forest nearby, and a piercing light that rivaled the setting sun. Jennifer squinted and wouldn't have wanted to listen to the yelling all day long, but she found it bearable outside of dragon form.

When the radiance and noise had both dimmed, her mother let her sword down and nodded. "Your turn."

After rubbing and breathing into her hands, Jennifer un-sheathed her daggers and raised them in front of her face. She didn't know which one to kiss, so she crossed them and kissed them both. Then she breathed in deeply and let out the loudest yell she could.

Giving the battle shout was a new experience. The sound and light were surprisingly low from her point of view, but she could tell from her mother's immediate grin that she had it right on the first try. It was almost as if the blades were pulling the air from her mouth and then casting it forward with blistering force. After a few seconds, she closed her mouth.

"Excellent, honey! You're really learning stuff quickly. I told you this summer would pay off."

"Each thing you teach me seems easier than the last," Jennifer said, thrilled.

"We can work on some of the finer points now—"

The sound of the cabin door opening made them both turn. Jonathan came out on the porch holding the phone. His hand was clapped over the receiver.

"Phew, heard that shout! Glad it's not quite a crescent moon yet!" He frowned a bit. "Jennifer, it's Skip's aunt Tavia. She wants to talk about dinner at their house."

"How did she track us down here?" Elizabeth asked.

"Well, Skip has the number." Jennifer shrugged. She bristled at her mother's hard look. "He's my friend, Mom!"

"So you're having a lovely dinner with the sister of the man who tried to kill your father? How quaint."

"You know it's more complicated than that. And I'm as freaked out about this as you are. I'm not sure I want to go. I haven't been to Skip's house since his aunt moved in, and I don't know how many other . . . I mean, I don't know how big his family is."

"Well, if you don't want to go, you'd better come up with an excuse fast," Jonathan suggested. He took his hand off the receiver. "Tavia, she's right here." Then he handed the phone to her.

Thinking quickly, she grabbed the phone and put the best smile she could manage in her voice. "Hi, Ms. Saltin? Yeah, sounds great. Problem is, my family's taking me out of town for a week or so. Sure, I promise to call you as soon as we get back! Yes, I know, I can hardly wait to go to the dance with Skip! Okay, bye!" Then she turned the phone off with a smug smile.

"So how are you getting out of this one?" her father asked. "It's not like you can show up at school Monday like you're supposed to. Skip will know you lied to his aunt as soon as he sees you."

"Who says I'm lying? I could go back to Crescent Valley!"

Elizabeth cleared her throat. "Jennifer, you made a promise to me. Just like you needed concentrated time last year to come to terms with your dragon side, you need dedicated time to grow as a beaststalker. You should come home with me Sunday."

"But you said yourself that I'm really coming along—and I'll be back in a week!" She felt them both weaken and pressed on. "Plus, it was just my birthday, so you should be nice to me. Plus, Dad owes me for going to that boring fundraiser last week!"

She knew she had them then, through sheer quantity (if not

quality) of argument. Her mother sighed through tightened lips. "All right, Jennifer. I could use the extra time at the hospital, anyway. We've been short-staffed lately."

"I need to take a short trip to Jack's old place before I go," Jonathan said. He wouldn't explain further, despite her curious look. "You go ahead tomorrow with the crescent moon, ace. I'll catch up with you in a day or so. Grandpa's already there. Mind him, and stay out of trouble."

"Trouble?" Jennifer couldn't stifle a laugh. "How on earth can you get in trouble in Crescent Valley?"

A corner of his mouth creased. "Get careless, and you'll find out."

"All right!" Elizabeth stood up suddenly and shook off the jerkin that covered her blouse and windbreaker. "That's enough discussion of a place I've never seen and can't ever visit. If neither of you are coming home with me, I might as well leave now!"

She gave Jennifer a quick, almost meaningless hug and stormed off the patio in the direction of the minivan.

"Hey, Liz!"

Troubled, Jennifer watched her father chase her mother down. Despite his valiant efforts, the woman wouldn't engage with her husband . . . until they were almost at the car, at which point she abruptly turned and hissed what must have been a ferocious monologue, given his expression. Jennifer caught the phrases *secret lizard club* and *time with her mother,* at which point she figured this was a conversation best held in private. She went into the cabin and closed the door firmly behind her.

CHAPTER 4

Catherine's First Hunt

"You're going *again*?! That's so unfair!"

Catherine Brandfire was a trampler dragon, with olive green skin and crimson eyes that smoked with impatience once she heard her friend was going to the weredragons' secret refuge. She ripped apart her sheep, the dinner of choice at the farm, as a group of creeper dragons and dasher dragons arrived, circling far overhead. Of course, Jennifer was unusual even for a dragon—as the Ancient Furnace, she carried the skills and shapes of all three dragon breeds in her—but that didn't make the older weredragon feel any better.

"My grandmother is eldest among the weredragons, and *she* won't even tell me where Crescent Valley *is*!" Catherine whistled a tongue of flame onto the porch grill, and then set her meat on to cook. "You're two years younger than me and yet you've already gone a bunch of times!"

"I can't help how old I am," shrugged Jennifer, a sour expression on her face as she laid her own slice of sheep meat next to the other. "I don't even know why I told you I was going. I thought maybe I could find out more about newolves for you, or something. Never mind."

Newolves were a breed of elusive, shape-shifting wolves. Catherine had an infectious interest in them, even though Jennifer wasn't certain her friend had actually ever seen one. Jennifer saw her first last spring, and it had been a brief but powerful moment.

"Oh, I'm sorry, Jen." The seventeen-year-old's scaled face wrinkled. "I shouldn't have brought up your age like that. I really don't think of you as that young, most of the time. But even if you were twenty years old, this would annoy me. I mean, what's the big fuss about Crescent Valley? Why does it have to be so secret? Why do we have to wait? Don't the elders trust us?"

Jennifer nodded sympathetically, accepting the apology in silence. She couldn't blame her friend for feeling this way. Last year, her father and grandfather kept mentioning things like newolves and oreams without explaining what they were.

She struggled to find the right words without giving away too much. "It's not about trust, I think. It's just that it's . . . a refuge. The last one we've got. The elders put all these rules in place to protect all of us. It makes more sense once you see it—"

"Which I can't!"

"Yeah. Um. That logic made more sense in my head, I guess."

Her friend's vermilion eyes narrowed as she checked over

her meat on the grill. "I've put you in a hard spot, Jennifer. I'm sorry. It's just—"

"I get it," Jennifer interrupted congenially. "It annoyed the heck out of me, too. But by next year, you'll be able to go. We'll check out the newolf herds together!"

The student's expression fell. "But next year will be too late! I won't get to use newolves for my senior project this year!"

"Wait a second. You're going to *hand in* a school paper on newolves? Um, Catherine, I don't know if that's—"

"It's okay, my science teacher at Northwater High is a dasher. Hey, you got any steak sauce for this?"

"Hang on, I'll go inside and check." Jennifer flexed herself back into human form—she found it was easier to open the patio and refrigerator doors that way—and got the steak sauce, as well as a bottle of ketchup for herself. As she went back outside, she didn't catch her friend's thoughtful expression. "So, are there lots of weredragons at your school besides you and your teacher?"

"You know, I had you pegged for a brunette."

"What's that? Oh, my hair." Suddenly, Jennifer felt self-conscious. Catherine and she had known each other for a year, and they'd never seen each other as anything but dragons. "Sorry, this is weird, I'll change back . . ."

"No, don't do it on my account! Hey, what're those for?" Her wing claw pointed to the daggers that Jennifer had sheathed on each thigh, outside her jeans.

Her beaststalker weapons. Jennifer went cold. Of course, no dragon here could know about her mother, and her own beaststalker heritage! "Oh. Those. Um, well, I'm taking a self-defense class, and I guess I forgot to leave them at home . . ."

"They're beautiful! Can I see?" Catherine's wing claws wriggled with excitement.

Still wary of discovery, but relieved that the impromptu cover story worked, Jennifer unsheathed both blades and handed them over.

"Wow! Look at the hilt workmanship! So clever, too—one girl, one dragon, it's so perfect for you!"

"Thanks. Here, I'll take 'em back."

"I didn't think you were the type to be so serious about self-defense! Grammie Winona says my mom was like that, but I guess I was always more into hunting, and animals."

"Hunting, eh?" Jennifer smiled mysteriously as she flipped the knives back and forth. "Yeah, you'll get along with newolves. Oh, no, my dinner!"

Her portion of sheep on the grill was burning merrily, absorbing flame and giving off a charred scent. She forgot about the blades in her hands and morphed back into dragon form so that she could handle the fire and meat without burning herself.

"Sorry, Jen. I guess since I always like mine well-done, everybody else—whoa!"

Jennifer looked over herself with similar surprise. While much of her was the same as it always was, there were noticeable differences. First, each claw at the tip of her wings was at least eight inches long now, tapered to a dangerously pointed tip. Second, her nose horn was much larger and sharper and gleamed silver, instead of ivory. Finally, her tail . . .

"It looks like I pooped a giant pitchfork," she observed. "Must be because I morphed with my weapons in hand."

Flexing her deadly claws, she sighed wistfully. "Yet another brilliantly flowered float in the freak parade that is my life."

The trampler's eyes were wide, but then she shut them quickly. "I'm sorry, Jennifer. I don't mean to stare. I know you felt awkward last year because you're different. It's insensitive of me."

"No, it's okay . . ." Now Jennifer felt guilty for seeing her friend react like this. It wasn't just the dragon in her, of course—it was the beaststalker. But she couldn't say that, at least not yet. She reminded herself how horrible it had been, lying to Susan, Skip, and Eddie for so long.

Last year, she and Catherine had often traded secrets they told no one else—about newolves, or the visions Jennifer had. But here was something Jennifer couldn't share. For a moment she was tempted to let everything out. But then she thought of the danger it posed to her mother.

She quickly changed back into human form, sheathed both daggers, and flipped her hair as nonchalantly as she could. "It's no big deal, Catherine. Part of being the Ancient Furnace. I'm used to it."

"I guess your grandpa Crawford's stories about the legend of the Ancient Furnace left out a detail or two, huh?"

Jennifer chuckled. "I guess. So anyway, you didn't answer my question. Are there lots of other weredragons at your high school?"

"Not too many. Three or four. Of course, there are some weredragons nobody knows about. So many went into hiding after Eveningstar, and Pinegrove before that."

Jennifer knew firsthand about the destruction of Eveningstar by werachnids—she had turned five the day her family had to leave her hometown—but the other name was unfamiliar to her. "Pinegrove? My parents never told me about a place with that name."

"I think it was before their time. About sixty years ago. Grandma told me she was almost thirty, so your grandfather should know about it. What werachnids did to Eveningstar, beaststalkers did to Pinegrove. In many ways it was worse. Instead of destroying the homes after driving out the dragons, the beaststalkers moved into them and lived there, as if the past owners had never existed.

"Grandma says some weredragon families couldn't get out of the town in time and had to hide in the shadows of Pinegrove, scraping out an existence while staying out of sight. Many of them starved to death."

Jennifer didn't say much. She figured Grandpa Crawford very likely knew about this. If he had survived a slaughter like Pinegrove, the rocky relationship between him and her mother made more sense. That a beaststalker should then marry his only son . . .

She felt a twinge of irritation that her parents had never told her about Pinegrove. Why not? And were there other things they were keeping from her?

Pinegrove. Crescent Valley. Her being a beaststalker. Her being a weredragon. She was getting sick of all the secrets.

Before she knew it, she had blurted it out. "Do you want to go to Crescent Valley with me?"

Catherine, who had been tearing into her dinner, stopped short with half a flank hanging out of her mouth. "Whad yoo fey?"

"There's a hunt every night," Jennifer explained. "And it's

not like the way we play with sheep around here. If you like hunting, you'll *love* oreams!"

"I've heard that," whispered Catherine, looking furtively about the yard and sky between Grandpa Crawford's cabin and the nearby lake. "But Jennifer, we'll get into trouble! *You'll* get into trouble!"

"Not if we're careful. And it's stupid that it's a secret, just like you said. You'll have plenty of places to hide. Crescent Valley is a big place. Really, it's a whole . . . well, you've got to see it!"

Her friend wavered. "I don't know . . ."

"Dad says he once saw ten packs of newolves within a day's flight."

"Let's go."

She told Catherine they would have to wait another half hour—the autumn sun had barely set, and the crescent moon was barely high enough to cast any light on the water.

"What the heck does that mean?" Catherine asked.

"What the heck does that mean?" Jennifer asked.

"Look down there," her father told her. The large lake beyond Grandpa Crawford's cabin was shimmering.

"Okay, so there's moonlight on the water. Big deal."

"Not just moonlight. Crescent moonlight."

"Yeah, okay . . . ?"

"So that means the gateway is open."

"Gateway? What *gateway?*"

He sighed. "I guess there's only one way to tell you, and that's to show you." And then he dove, head first.

They were at least as high as they had been the first day he had taught her to fly and fish. She wondered what he was up to, and began to follow in a cautious slope.

In a split second she realized this wouldn't do. She was losing the shape of her father against the play of light and shadow below. Best she could tell, he was gathering speed—he was going to hit the lake too hard!

"You're going to hit the lake too hard!" Catherine shouted this out from far above, but Jennifer could barely hear her over the whistling of the wind. Her wings were folded in tightly to her body, and her eyes were nearly closed. Even knowing what was coming, she was nervous. Like a gleaming, moonlit bullet, she pierced the surface of the water and was gone.

He was gone! She couldn't see him in the depths below. It was like swimming through cold ink—all the light was behind them, and even her thick hide was beginning to feel a bit numb as she blew the last of her air out and kept sinking. It was terrifying—and thrilling.

Not only couldn't she see him, she couldn't see anything like a fish or plant or the bottom. There was nothing at all, and she was just about to give up on this game and turn back . . .

. . . when she saw the faint light ahead.

Yes, the water was getting lighter now, not darker. Had she flipped over somehow? She knew she hadn't.

After a few moments, she could make out her father's slim shape against whatever light source was ahead. His wings propelled him as he relaxed and tensed, forcing water over his body. Jennifer decided to try it, too.

It was a great deal faster, she mused, than the claw paddle

she had used the first time last spring. And it certainly helped propel her faster through the disorienting swirl of current that greeted her once again. Gravity shifted along her spine until the bottom of the lake was behind her. Neither she nor Catherine had turned at all, but there it was ahead of them— the surface, and the promise of air.

She glanced back briefly to make sure her friend was still following, and then squeezed her wings one final time. The force propelled her up out of the water and right into the moonlight of a different world.

That much was obvious right away. For a start, the moon was the same shape, but was far closer than would ever be possible back home. It was so large and immediate to Jennifer, she was sure she could reach out and touch the lower point of the crescent. The sharp edge slid through the twilit sky, piercing the first bright nighttime stars with a gentle clockwise motion.

The air here was warmer and heavier, as if filled with the lingering breath of ancient things. The scales on the back of Jennifer's neck crinkled, and her ears flexed. She could hear foreign sounds in the near-darkness around them.

"What are those?" Catherine asked. "They sound like crickets, if crickets could play cellos."

"Fire hornets," Jennifer replied. "There are hives of them throughout the forests and mountains near here."

There was another sound, the tinkling of small streams of water. The delicate sound was amplified on the lake's surface. Following the trickles with their ears, they spotted small, mantislike shapes skimming the water just below them. The water beetles raced over the ripples the two dragons had made when they emerged.

"And those are the portal's guardians," Jennifer explained. "The sound you hear carries up to the moon, and then . . ."

"*Wow.*" *A streak of fire was igniting a circular path around the moon's crescent shape. Like a belt of flame, the fire whipped round and round the fattest portion of the crescent several times before it died of its own accord.*

"We are recognized," said her father. She had nearly forgotten he was with her in this strange new world. "The venerables have sent us a signal of welcome."

"Venerables? Who are they, dragons? Do they know who we are?"

"They're dragons of a sort," he answered mysteriously. "They welcome us. Come on, follow me. It's not far from here to Crescent Valley." With a curl of his tail he made off for the shore of the lake, keeping the moon to his right.

This lake was much larger than the one they had entered by. It seemed a prelude to the sea. But all Jennifer could tell for sure was that before her and to either side were the sturdy shapes of enormous hills. Their twilit outlines were rough with treetops, and soon Jennifer could make out the whistling of the wind through large branches with many leaves.

"Jennifer, we've got to get down to the ground! I can't keep this up for much longer!"

Startled, Jennifer turned around. Of course—Catherine was a trampler, and her wings were not suited for efficient flying.

"Whomping?" she suggested with a grin.

"Yeah, sure, but will we be able to see down there? It's already pretty dark!"

"Oh, we'll be able to see!"

They dipped below the tree line and its thick canopy of leaves, and navigated a network of long and slender branches. Jennifer heard Catherine gasp behind her.

It was still a breathtaking sight—and tinged in violet, different from when Jennifer had last been here.

"What an amazing green!" she exclaimed to her father. "It's like having an emerald sun all around us!"

The lichen was luminescent, and laced the slender stalks of the ninety-foot trees. Moon elms, her father called them. There were no branches on their trunks until they exploded in the canopy above, ending in green-tinted bursts of large, five-pronged leaves. The dark trunks were unusually thin for their height, suggesting no more than twenty or thirty rings of astounding growth.

They were going downhill now, she could tell. The lichen was getting more frequent. She could see the gathering luminescence ahead. It was as if they were skimming the surface of an enormous bowl, and all the light had pooled at the bottom.

A stomp behind her told her that her friend had begun to turf-whomp—a trampler's mix of jumping and flying. Here, the ground was sheathed in layers of moss and dead leaves, and the rebound was powerful.

"Whoa!" she heard Catherine yelp as her friend nearly disappeared up into the canopy. "That's quite a spring in the ground! Have you tried this?"

"Once or twice." Jennifer grinned. "I slammed into a fire

hornet nest. Fire hornets get angry fast. I almost got turned into a gooey, charred mess!"

That got Catherine looking warily about.

"Don't panic. They're not in this part of the forest. The strumming you heard over the lake came from the southern shores. We're headed northwest."

She vaulted in front of her friend with her own whomp. With a deft shift of her left wing and flick of a hind claw, she pushed down off a nearby tree trunk and propelled herself back toward the turf. Another *thump* and she was back up again.

Thump. Whomp. Pumph. Like aliens enjoying a planet with low gravity, the two dragons bounded and glided through the eerie violet world.

"How far to Crescent Valley?"

"It's just ahead, over this hill. Er, since you're not supposed to be here, you'll have to hide. Try to stay close, so you can follow us to the hunt."

"There'll be newolves on the hunt?"

"Absolutely. You might see them, though I've never gotten a really good look. But you'll definitely hear them."

"The herd is scattered across the northern slope of Wings Mountain," Crawford explained. He was speaking to forty-nine other creepers, Jennifer among them. Elsewhere, fifty tramplers and fifty dashers were also making their plans. But this was not for competition. Unlike the sheep "hunts" on the farm, she learned, hunts in Crescent Valley were part of a solemn and co-ordinated ritual.

"It will begin with the newolves," he continued, drawing a rough map in the dirt with his claw. "They will drive the herd down off the more difficult terrain and frighten them into a single unit, so that we can get as many of them as possible in our trap. Once they are off the steeper slopes—"

"I don't get it," a young male creeper called out. "Why don't we just pick these things off the slopes, one at a time, whenever we're hungry? Seems easier."

Jennifer could see her grandfather tense. "You have just passed your fiftieth morph, son, so I'm going to assume you've never seen an oream and that's why you're wasting time planning to pick an animal with the horns of a devil and the presence of a mountain goat off a four-foot-wide ridge at an elevation of seven thousand feet!"

If the younger creeper could have shifted his skin to look like thin air, he probably would have, she guessed from his embarrassed expression.

"Once the herd is off the steeper slopes and in the open," he continued, "Ned and the tramplers will rescatter them across the clearing."

Jennifer smiled at the mention of Ned Brownfoot, the easygoing elder who had taught her and Catherine how to call lizards.

"That won't break them down enough, though—their instinct will be to stick in pairs and families at least, for as long as they can. So the dashers will come in and set up a few fireworks."

Dashers had forked tails that could deliver nasty shocks of sparks in midflight. Jennifer hoped to try that role in a future hunt, but with Catherine hiding nearby, simpler was better.

"That ought to break them up into single units, around the fringes of the field." He looked up at them all. "That's where we'll be waiting, camouflaged, waiting to spring. Our job is the kill. Then we all pull together for the barbeque, so to speak. Any questions?"

There were none. All but four or five of the hunters were experienced and well aware of their role. "Good. Let's get set up. We need to be in position an hour beforehand, so we don't spook the herd. Set out in groups of five, and give Wings Mountain a wide berth until you're around it. You." He pointed at the young dragon who had interrupted him earlier. "You're with me. You, too, Niffer."

Crawford watched all the other groups go before he set out with Jennifer, the young male, and two other creepers. They set out in a diagonal formation, like half of the V a flock of geese might make. Just barely skimming the tops of the moon elms, Jennifer took position just behind and to the right of her grandfather. As they approached a cluster of mountains to the north, he led them sharply to the west so that they would remain a good mile away from the closest one—Wings Mountain, they called it, and its southern slopes were home to most of the dashers in Crescent Valley.

"Grandpa," she asked as they swept over the trees, "what happened at Pinegrove?"

"What's that?" His head whipped sharply to look at her, and then craned over a bit to give the young creeper behind her a stern look. "Pinegrove? Niffer, this is hardly the time for a story. In fact, I don't know that there's any good time at all for that particular tale."

"But Catherine said—"

"Catherine Brandfire would do well to keep her mouth shut," he huffed. "And so would you. Keep your mind on the hunt."

His gaze returned to the dim stars ahead, and Jennifer cruised behind him with a seething stare. No, this business of secrets did not sit well with her, not at all.

She spared a quick glance behind and below her. Catherine would be whomping far beneath the canopy, following the creepers to the hunt site. From there, the young trampler would find a quiet spot to observe the hunt, and if luck turned out right, newolves.

Fifteen minutes later, Jennifer found herself on the western edge of a massive clearing, rolled up between two raspberry bushes at the edge of the forest and looking rather branchy herself. Grandpa Crawford was about thirty feet north of her, with his reluctant protégé close by. Her leg was already beginning to cramp, but she knew she shouldn't move if she could help it. At first the oreams were distant points of gray fur high up the mountain, but they were grazing closer now and had excellent eyesight. Across the twilit meadow to the southeast, she thought she could make out the still shapes of the tramplers, but they were hidden by a stiff ridge of rock that thrust up near the foot of the mountain.

Finally, after nursing a cramp in her calf for at least twenty minutes, she heard the newolves.

Four unseen newolves high upon the peak sounded a hunting chord: D major. Crawford had told her that newolves used these chords to inform the dragons how and when they would move a herd, among other things. D major was a standard drive pattern for a scattered herd.

Sure enough, she began to see small, white, fluffy shapes make their way down the lower slopes of Wings Mountain and away from the howls. The earth trembled slightly with the distant pounding of hundreds of hooves, and her nostrils picked up the growing scent of prey.

It took some time, but once the last ranks of the herd gathered at the foot of the mountain and passed into the vast clearing, the tramplers charged.

Jennifer recalled the first time she had seen the breed on the hunt at her grandfather's farm—thunderstorms in skin, she had thought them. There were ten times as many now, and they were more than ten times as loud. She marveled at how fast they moved: While they were the stoutest dragon breed, with wings that barely worked, their gallop was a spectacular sight, and they plunged deep into the meadow and scattered the herd into terrified pairs and trios.

Now it was time for the dashers. A flood of electric blue silhouettes entered the field from the southwest treetops. As the herd got closer to Jennifer's position, she sensed unexpected movement to her right, about where her grandfather was. It was the young creeper. He was out of camouflage, and edging back! He looked a bit frightened by how close some of the oreams were, and how fast they were still going.

She couldn't completely blame the young weredragon, though he must have been at least two years older than Jennifer. Oreams, after all, were not sheep.

The first few were in plain sight now, but even the sound of their hooves revealed their size as closer to that of wildebeests than mountain goats. Their gray fur and yellow irises shone in the moonlight, but it was their horns that gleamed most brightly. Three smooth and sturdy spikes stood on each head—not pulled back like on a goat or ram, but pointed up and forward, like a *Triceratops*. The unified front of these horns broke apart, sending sharp points with heavy bulk moving in unpredictable directions at great speed.

The horns were probably what had the young guy nervous, Jennifer mused. But moving around was still inexcusable. The oreams were too smart to keep driving into a field that held an obvious and jumpy predator.

Indeed they were. Upon seeing the movement, all of the nearby knots—about a fourth of the larger herd—veered away from her grandfather's position and swept back up the gentle slope of Wings Mountain. Multiple other bands saw their herd's new chosen path and followed.

That fool's blunder was reintegrating the herd!

Several dashers tried to rescatter them, but this did not go well. This herd had plenty of experienced adults with the time and instinct to set themselves protectively at the front and sides of the running formation.

Meanwhile, the tramplers were trying to make a second run. But because the predators were now scattered all over the field, their attack came from multiple sides rather than one. The herd reacted according to a different instinct. Dispersing as before made no sense, so instead the formation stubbornly tightened.

Up the mountainside it galloped, ignoring the half-hearted roars behind them and heedless to the difficult terrain ahead. Several stumbled upon broken rock and were trampled by their brethren. Many dragons backed off in uncertainty, and creepers were letting their camouflage break. The hunt seemed ruined.

But it was worse than that, Jennifer realized as she watched the herd's progress. The leading edge of the herd had in fact turned back down the mountain—not as frightened prey, but as determined defenders. Only fifty yards ahead of them, the quartet of newolves that had started this affair were scurrying away, no match for the collective anger of this sea of horns.

And just in front of them, galloping hard but limping with an obvious injury, was a lone trampler.

It was Catherine.

CHAPTER 5

A Blaze of Dragons

"Catherine!" Jennifer broke shape and texture and bolted into the clearing, heedless of the oncoming threat.

Even from a distance under moonlight, it was easy enough to make out Catherine's terrified expression. Clearly, she had been angling for a closer look at the newolves, had strayed out into the upper slopes of the clearing, and was caught by the sudden change in the herd's direction. Now making for the western woods, her scaled face was desperate with the knowledge that she could not outrun the stampede.

Skimming the grass with her wings at top speed, Jennifer judged the distance to her wounded friend (about fifty yards) and then on to the herd (another forty). Somehow, she needed to scare them off, all by herself. No one else was doing anything. She elevated, sucked in a gust of air, and breathed out a massive column of fire. The flames surged over Catherine's armored back, scattered the newolves behind her, and flooded into the front ranks of the oreams.

The herd did not stop.

This was about the time Jennifer realized two things. First, the pounding of the hooves was very loud and did not sound like the kind of noise that you stopped with a bit of heat. Second, about three hundred oreams times three horns equaled an awful lot of fast and pointy stabbing.

She needed something else to stop this herd. And that something was not available—at least not to a dragon.

Before she landed smoothly, Jennifer was back in human form. Whipping out both knives, she held them up to her lips, kissed them, and reached deep within for her loudest voice. And vitalized by the air of this ancient world, the blades responded beautifully.

The deafening sound shook the clearing, and the blinding rays pierced a world that until that day had only known twilight. The mountain shrunk next to her—as if a newfound sun had suddenly decided to rise to the top of the sky and wash out all the deep, dark colors this landscape thrived on.

Under her own shout, she heard the sound of hundreds of collapsing bodies. The sea of horns and muscle in front of her came to a rolling stop as the assault of light and sound stunned the exotic creatures.

A good ten seconds later, after she was sure the herd had fallen, she closed her mouth and sheathed her blades. That's when she finally took in the scene across the meadow.

The oreams were not the only victims of her battle shout. Virtually every dragon in the hunt lay huddled on the ground, mewling and covering ears with wings. Some were writhing in pain. A stalwart few—farther away than most—had taken up a cry.

"Beaststalker! To arms! Beaststalker! To arms!"

"To wha—?" Jennifer began, but at that moment a large, slender shape closed in behind her like a missile and swatted her on the back of her head with a sizzling shower of sparks. She tumbled to the ground, and her mind went blank.

When she woke up, Jennifer was lying on a stone surface, staring up at the bright crescent moon. Its lower tip was scooping up a handful of dim stars.

She turned to the right and saw the shadow of an unfamiliar mountain. Shifting to the left, she saw what must have been every dragon in Crescent Valley—a few hundred of them—sitting in row upon row in semi-circles, staring at her. Some had expressions of mere interest, some anger. Most were clearly afraid.

There were bonfires lit here and there. At first Jennifer thought perhaps some oreams had been caught after all, and that it was dinnertime. But this didn't seem like the festive aftermath of a typical hunt.

"Owww," she hissed, sitting up and feeling the dried blood covering the lump on the back of her head. "That stung! Who was the dasher that shocked my skull? You could kill someone doing that!"

Her grandfather's voice came quietly and sadly. "I believe that may have been the intent."

She looked up. Grandpa Crawford was sitting, along with about five hundred other very old dragons, on large stone slabs behind her, facing the larger mass of weredragons gathered this night. His expression was not encouraging—Jennifer was reminded of Cheryl Alder at Jack's wake.

Another elder stood up on his hind legs. He was a dasher, with blue scales so dark that he seemed sheathed in black, with a sickly grey underbelly. A rich pattern of gold and silver graced the underside of his delicate wings, and his enormous triple-pronged tail twitched with energy that belied his age. He pointed at her with a trembling claw while snarling in a raspy voice, through spittle-stained teeth, "The Scales girl is a beaststalker! The Ancient Furnace is corrupt! Crawford, you will answer for this!"

There were whispers among the ancients. Jennifer made out a few of the words—"outrage!" and "corrupt!" among them. But the majority in the amphitheater remained silent and anxious.

"Wait a second!" Jennifer called out. "Okay, um, I'm guessing that nobody knew my mother's a beaststalker . . ."

The dark dasher looked triumphant as the crowd murmured. "She admits it!"

"All right, all right," she tried to reassure them, standing up with palms out. "This must be freaking some of you out. But you've got to see that I'm not dangerous to any of you. I mean, I just did that battle shout to save Catherine, not to hurt anyone!" She desperately looked for Catherine in the crowd, but could not find her.

Crawford's voice was just loud enough for Jennifer to hear. "Niffer, sit down, please. Let me handle this."

Given the dubious looks of the surrounding crowd, she had to agree with his suggestion.

"My friend Xavier Longtail is right," Crawford began. "This matter is my responsibility. I'll answer for it. My granddaughter is here under my protection. And my son and I did conceal the other half of her heritage from you all, until we could find a way to introduce the truth to the Blaze of Elders."

Blaze of Elders? Jennifer cocked her head at the expression. Was that like a crash of rhinos, or was it more like Congress?

He turned to face her with a frown. "Unfortunately, we would have done well to remind the Ancient Furnace herself of our people's misgivings toward beaststalkers."

Jennifer's face fell. While she knew he would protect her, she also knew how badly he and her mother got along. Having a beaststalker shape here in front of all these dragons must be an insult to them, even him! She decided to shift back into dragon form, but before she could he turned to the others and raised his voice.

"But what I would have told her after warning her, and what I must tell all of you here at this Blaze now, is no less true for my forgetfulness. Our kind needs to come to terms with our old enemies. It is time we made peace!"

There was a great deal more noise at this than before— exclamations of surprise, with several shouts of "No!" and a few of "Yes!" spotted throughout. It was hard for Jennifer to sort out who felt which way, but one thing was clear: Xavier Longtail did not care for this opinion at all.

"Talk of peace sounds lovely," the dasher spat. "So understanding, so moral. But it ignores one fact—you cannot make peace with a people who are devoted to your destruction. The descendants of Barbara the Self-Righteous worked horrors at Pinegrove, and they are not yet finished. These beaststalkers are all the same—every one of them lives for the chance to do our kind in, like their patron saint."

"That's not true!" Jennifer piped up. Once again, she felt the heat of everyone staring at her. She gulped and continued. "My mother would never kill a weredragon! She married one!"

"You will remain quiet," Xavier commanded with disdain. "You are an abomination, and have no voice here."

Jennifer felt the blood rush to her cheeks. "Oh really? You want to *hear* my voice again, buster?"

The ancient dasher roared, raised his triple-ended tail, and smashed it against the ground. It was like no tail shock Jennifer had ever seen. Three explosions shook the ground and burning rock flew in all directions. She flinched as bits of granite sailed by her ear.

With his roar still echoing throughout the amphitheater, Xavier pounced from his stone seat and landed right in front of her. Spittle flicked off of his sharp, yellowing teeth, and his golden eyes gleamed. "If you think that you are fast enough to raise those pretty knives of yours and try that shout again, go ahead, little girl! But I daresay the breath of this Blaze will roast you before you get the chance. And my fire will be the first to its target, you lying—"

A wild bellow from above interrupted the elder. Everyone looked up in time to see a shadow drop from the sky and crash right between Jennifer and Xavier. The amphitheater shook. Smoke fumed and billowed over her. In the firelight, scales pulsed an angry rainbow of dark colors. With another wild roar, the newcomer raised its head and blasted the gloomy sky with a column of fire. Jennifer had never seen a dragon so furious and reckless before.

Then her jaw dropped as she recognized the creature. It was her father. His right wing lashed out, and the claw gripped shut the dasher's crocodilian mouth.

"Xavier Longtail! Keep that mouth closed and your claws away from my daughter!"

Xavier shook off the other's grip and curled his lip, but did not answer.

Jonathan took in the whole Blaze as his skin settled back into a stable shade of indigo. Vapor still leaked from his snout. "This is not a trial," he called out. "My daughter hasn't done anything wrong!"

"She has broken two serious laws," the dasher said coldly. "She has shown our sacred refuge to an uninvited guest, and she has become one herself! Before this night is through, there will be a trial *and* a sentence—and not just for the beast-stalker, but for her father and grandfather as well!"

The reaction to this statement surprised Jennifer. Instead of support, or even anxiety, disapproval rippled through the crowd. There were cries of "No!" and "Let them speak!" Apparently, she guessed, her father and grandfather—and maybe even the Ancient Furnace herself—still commanded some measure of respect here.

"Peace is not just a dream," Crawford pressed. He had come down from his seat to stand by his family. "I have learned this over the years. Like many of you, I used to hate and distrust every beaststalker out there. And when my son met and fell in love with one, I nearly disowned him."

The crowd stayed quiet. Crawford glanced at Jonathan before he continued. "But over the past fifteen years, I have come to know Elizabeth Georges-Scales. And I have watched her daughter grow up for fifteen of those years. These two are not like those beaststalkers that attacked Pinegrove. Their hearts are true. They may be ambassadors for peace. And there may be others like them."

No one spoke for a while. Jennifer watched thousands of dragon heads across the amphitheater turn this way and that, trying to make sense of all this.

Finally, Xavier stood up again. "This is preposterous! Ambassadors for peace? The Ancient Furnace is corrupt! She cannot speak for us. Neither can the bloodthirsty hellion who spawned her. We should—"

"For the moon's sake, Xavier, hold your tongue!" This was a new voice, impatient at the moment but full of depth and wisdom. An enormous trampler stood, her olive-green skin pale enough to reflect the light of both fire and moon. Her nose horn was brittle, but the red was still bright in her eyes. Jennifer recognized the features instantly—this must be Catherine's grandmother, Winona Brandfire.

"I've heard enough of your hateful prattling for one evening. You act as if the entire Blaze is behind you. It isn't. I'm the Blaze's eldest, and I'll speak now." These words made Xavier Longtail sit down under a cloud of discontent.

"First of all," Winona continued to the entire gathering, "I owe this girl my thanks. So do we all. Jennifer Scales quelled a stampede that would have hurt or killed some of us, my granddaughter among them—"

"Is Catherine okay?" Jennifer knew as soon as she interrupted that she shouldn't have. Winona's hard, reptilian features swiveled to her and took in the platinum hair, the leather jerkin, and the twin sculpted daggers. An uncomfortable silence followed, during which the elder scratched her own jaw with a wing claw. Jennifer caught a glint of metal on a wing claw—she could not quite make it out—and then Winona spoke.

"She's fine. Her leg was injured, and so she is resting now, before her *own* trial."

Jennifer bowed her head.

"As I was saying—because of this girl, we have the luxury of this Blaze, instead of a funeral ceremony. It was a feat worthy of the myths behind the Ancient Furnace, and it does not matter what shape did it.

"Second, her good heart does not excuse the fact that her bravery would not have been necessary at all had she adhered to the rules of her people—*our* people. Revealing the portal of this world to my granddaughter was foolish. This refuge has remained both hallowed and secret from the time our beloved ancestor—Seraphina, daughter of Brigida herself—discovered it and molded it for dragonkind. It is a place where we know our people will survive, even if the worst happens.

"I know how persistent Catherine can be—" And at this the old dragon's eyes almost twinkled. "—but the truth remains: You broke the law of this land."

"I'm sorry," Jennifer mumbled with her head down, trying at once to apologize and avoid interruption. The elder appeared to approve the attempt and went on.

"Third, Crawford and Jonathan withheld the truth from us. Even when done with good intentions, deceit is deceit. Were the Ancient Furnace truly corrupt—and I don't believe she is—the lives of many weredragons would be in danger. This, though, is an issue for another day.

"The discussion we must have now is what to do with *you,*

Jennifer Scales! For while I believe you may be trustworthy, the elders cannot stake the entire safety of our people on a warm and fuzzy feeling. My colleague"—she gestured to Xavier, who was nursing a sneer—"is not alone in thinking we cannot afford to allow you among us ever again. And while your father may not feel a trial is justified, that is not his decision alone. Banishment is not out of the question just yet. In fact, in the old days, death was appropriate!"

This caused the younger dragons gathered in the amphitheater to protest. Jennifer smiled slightly as she recognized Alex Rosespan and Mullery, a dasher and a creeper who served as her tutors last year, among them.

Winona raised her wing for silence. "I didn't say either treatment was *likely*. But neither can we just pretend nothing has happened here tonight. Frankly, we have never had to deal with this sort of thing before. I don't know quite where to start."

"If I could say a word, Eldest?" Jennifer smiled at the steady, Missouri-bred voice and the dragon who owned it— Ned Brownfoot, the aged trampler who had taught her lizard-calling. "There's a way out of this mess, p'rhaps. Takes believin' a legend or two . . . but I reckon it'd work. We could try the Fifty Trials."

This raised some interest in the crowd. Jennifer looked questioningly at her father, who signaled her to hold steady.

"Ned, the Fifty Trials are in tales we tell children," Winona pointed out. "We don't know whether they really ever happened, or if they were accurate. We don't even know what all of the trials were supposed to be!"

"We don't know everythin'," Ned admitted. "But I'll lay

two teh one . . . Crawford 'n' his folks would work it out with us. We could change what we don't like . . . fill in gaps as we go. We're smart enough, ain't we?"

Crawford picked up on Ned's idea immediately. "If Jennifer were to pass trials the Blaze chose itself, perhaps that would allay everyone's fears, Eldest. Even the venerables couldn't argue with that!"

"We should discuss this," Winona agreed.

Instantly, the gathering dissolved into dozens of separate conversations. Elder dashers, tramplers, and creepers all whispered back and forth, turning their heads this way and that. It looked to Jennifer as if each elder was trying to consult with as many other elders as they could, as quickly and thoroughly as possible.

"What are the Fifty Trials?" she asked her father in the midst of this din.

"You remember what your grandfather taught you about Allucina and her fifty children?"

"Sure." Jennifer recalled the legend of Allucina, the first perfect shapeshifter. After her death, there had been an epic fight among her children. Bruce the werachnid, Brigida the weredragon, and Barbara the beaststalker were the only survivors, and their descendants had fought ever since.

"Well, over thousands of years, there *have* been attempts at reconciling the three peoples again. Occasionally, a werachnid or beaststalker approached us with an offer for peace. But weredragons learned to be wary. Too often we found ourselves betrayed. So to weed out the spies and identify true friends, we came up with a series of tests. Of course some of this is bedtime story stuff, but chances are some of it is true. It makes sense that we'd have some way to tell good apples from bad ones."

"So, how do I prove that I'm, um, a *good* apple?"

"That's what we'll have to work out. If the Blaze agrees, your grandfather will help them draw out some tasks for you."

Jennifer wished that she could be part of the conversations, but it wasn't like she got to pick what Mr. Slider would put on her geometry quizzes. Tests were, after all, tests.

"You talked about venerables. You mentioned them the first time we came to Crescent Valley. Will they help judge? Who are they? Will I get to meet—"

Her father had no time to reply to any of these questions. As if on cue, the deliberations ended. Winona stood again. "We will move forward with Elder Brownfoot's plan, and start designing the trials tomorrow. It will take some time. The Ancient Furnace will submit to the trials on the last day of October."

"But that means I'll miss the school Halloween dance!" Jennifer blurted out. "And I already told Skip yes!"

"*Skip?*" Xavier's voice rose once more. "*Skip Wilson?*"

The entire amphitheater hushed. Once again, Jennifer experienced the cold feeling the brain brings as it catches up with the mouth. Out of the corner of her eye, she could see both her father and grandfather glaring at her. "Um . . . yeah . . ."

Xavier seemed beyond indignation. "The very same boy your father claims deceived your family and nearly caused a ruin worse than Eveningstar . . . is your *boyfriend*?"

"He's not my *boyfriend*," Jennifer protested. "We're just, um . . ."

Jonathan jabbed her in the ribs with a wing claw. "While

what Xavier says is true, Skip Wilson's actions in Otto Saltin's lair ultimately saved us, and he has expressed regret for his betrayal. He and my daughter have forged a friendship that may, in time, advance the cause of peace."

"Oh, the sneaky spider-boy is friends with the sneaky beaststalker-girl," the veteran dasher deadpanned. "*That* makes me feel better!"

"The spider-boy, as you call him, is the son of the late Dianna Wilson. Some of you assembled today know that this werachnid and I were good friends, years ago. I can vouch for her integrity—"

"We know of your association with the eight-legged witch," Xavier taunted. "It seems that you have always had trouble finding a home among your own kind, Jonathan Scales."

Jennifer's ears pricked. What did *that* mean?

"Perhaps, Xavier," Jonathan offered in a thin voice, "I seek friendship and truth wherever I can, in an effort to counter the bigotry and idiocy that—"

"If we could simply set that issue aside for now," Crawford pleaded, stepping between the other two. "My granddaughter will submit to the Fifty Trials, as Ned has wisely suggested. If and when she passes them, we can deal with the issue of whether or not her relationship with Skip Wilson is wise. Eldest?"

Winona sighed, and motioned for Xavier to sit down. "Very well. Such complicated times require patience. We will deal with each matter separately, as you suggest. The Blaze will convene tomorrow to begin preparations for the trials."

Jennifer started to protest again—the Halloween dance!—

but her father's firm wing claw landing on top of her head suggested silence.

"If I may, Eldest," he called out, "I would like to take my daughter back through the lake with me until the week of her trials. Before my father sent word for me tonight, I was already on my way. There is an urgent matter that requires our attention."

The elder trampler seemed relieved at the request. "Very well. Take the Ancient Furnace home. She is to return by the morning of the last day of October."

Jonathan bowed to the gathering, nodded to Crawford, and then yanked Jennifer up into the air. She barely had time to morph into dragon form before her feet left the ground.

So much had just happened—the hunt, the Blaze, Xavier and her father's confrontation, the way her tongue had slipped about her mother and then Skip—she did not know what to say. But her father spoke first anyway.

"Sweetheart. Apple of my eye. Fruit of my loins. Remind me to go over Blaze etiquette with you, someday."

"I'm sorry, Dad. This is all really confusing. Just as I was finally getting comfortable with who I am, everybody else starts freaking out about it!"

"I understand. But you have to learn when to stop talking and listen! Thank goodness Ned and your grandfather came up with the idea of the Fifty Trials. Things could have gone a lot worse down there."

"Thanks for coming."

"You're welcome. I'm glad I got there in time to face down Xavier! But as I said earlier, I was coming anyway."

"Why is that?"

"I heard from Cheryl Alder."

Jennifer shook her head a bit as they whistled over the elms. What did Cheryl Alder have to do with anything that had happened tonight?

"Detectives on Jack Alder's case shared some interesting news with her," he went on. "Apparently, there was a tiny bit of fluid left at the scene. It resembled blood or spittle, but was unlike anything they had ever seen. However, it does contain DNA. And as you know from science class, DNA evidence can help tell us who was there with Jack Alder before he died."

"So whose DNA is it?"

"They can't pin it down exactly, but since the Alders have known about me, Cheryl asked if I would supply a blood sample for a discreet species comparison. We used an investigative lab near Roseford with weredragon connections. I was happy to help, but we found out something disturbing."

"What's that? Does your DNA match their sample?"

"Not exactly." He turned to look at her. "But whoever was with Jack Alder when he died *is* a weredragon. And that person *is* related to me."

CHAPTER 6

Logic Puzzles

For the next month, Jennifer tried to put her father's news about Jack Alder out of her mind. It was, after all, preposterous. The only two weredragons alive related to her father by blood were herself and Grandpa Crawford—and both of them had been here in Winoka the entire weekend in question.

But the idea of a killer in her family consumed her. How was this possible? She became distracted at school, which bothered her friends. In class, which bothered Mr. Slider. And at home and the cabin . . . which bothered her mother.

During beaststalker training at the cabin, during a chilly Friday afternoon under a late October wind, she lost her concentration repeatedly. Three times her mother disarmed her with simple maneuvers she had learned back in June, and the best bird she could summon was a screech owl—better than the pygmies she managed before, she admitted, but nothing like the snake eagle she had gotten that one day, or the pair of golden eagles her mother could call. They circled overhead now.

"Okay, enough," Elizabeth finally said. She couldn't hide the impatience in her voice. "It's a good thing it's a new moon tonight."

"Why? All the dragons already know you're a beast-stalker now."

"Because if there were any around, they'd laugh you out of this place. You're about as scary today as a hamster to a dragon. We'll try again tomorrow."

Jennifer slipped her daggers back into their sheaths. "Doesn't Dad's news about Jack Alder still bother you, too? And how about these trials, whatever the heck they are, which are next week? I still have no idea what they'll ask me to do! Not even Dad knows!"

"Of course all that bothers me. The difference is that I don't let those emotions detract from my performance. It's a lesson you need to learn."

Once again, her mother's ice-cold demeanor bothered Jennifer. "If being a beaststalker means I have to squelch my emotions, then perhaps I'm happier just being a dragon!"

Elizabeth sighed. "I did not say I *squelch* my emotions. I said I do not let them trip me up. Instead, channel them. Passion is a gift, but so is focus. At our best, we beaststalkers use both in balance. At our worst, we let one dominate."

The thought of beaststalkers at their worst reminded Jennifer of her conversation with Catherine. "Mom, what happened at Pinegrove?"

The color drained from her mother's face. "What do you mean?"

"Pinegrove. There was an invasion of beaststalkers. Lots of weredragons were killed, or driven from their homes. Right?"

"Perhaps your father should—"

"I'd rather hear it from you. Is it true?"

Elizabeth searched the yard as if seeking help, and then looked right at Jennifer. "It's true."

"Was Grandpa Crawford there? Is that why you and he don't get along so well?"

"Jennifer, this is really not—"

"That sounds like a yes to me. So what happened to Pinegrove after the weredragons left? Werachnids razed Eveningstar, but Catherine says the beaststalkers—"

"*I won't discuss this with you now!*" The vehemence in her mother's voice stopped Jennifer cold.

Without another word, her mother sheathed her sword and went inside.

"*You have learned enough* in our first several weeks together for me to reveal a secret," Mr. Slider told the geometry class the following Monday. His black gaze roamed the room as he powered his wheelchair by the front row of quizzical looks. "For the rest of this year, this secret will underlie everything we do together."

Jennifer scanned the faces of her classmates. Most of them, like her, seemed to assume that this was a creative but still ultimately lame attempt to excite their attention for a few precious moments.

His wheelchair stopped, and he held his head up high. "Geometry is not math."

Above average, she graded the effort. *But still a bit lame. Of course it's math!*

The wheelchair resumed down the rows. "There are angles to measure, perhaps, and lengths and volumes to calculate. But that's simple math, numbers plugged into formulas, and you all know how to do that.

"No, geometry is about *logic.*" Mr. Slider's head snapped around fast enough to whip some thin blond strands into his face. "It is about taking certain pieces of information and pushing them together, like a puzzle, until you get the full picture!"

The surly junior girl behind Jennifer punched her on the shoulder and passed her another note from her unknown admirer, which she read:

So you haven't told me yet if you can go to the Halloween dance if you can go to the dance I would like that very much so let me know thanks.

It was, like every note she had received weekly in this room since the start of the school year, unsigned.

This was exasperating. She was just about to turn around and begin interrogating boys one at a time—starting with Gerry Stowe—when she heard Mr. Slider's voice and chair approaching her.

"Let me give an example, class. Assume, for a moment, that Ms. Scales here is a beast of some sort."

She sat bolt upright at that remark and stared at the teacher, but he was smiling congenially. "Ms. Scales, help me out. When I was a boy, all the girls at school wanted to be horses or unicorns, but I don't want to be sexist. What kind of animal do you want to be?"

"Errrr . . . a unicorn would be fine, I guess."

"Very well. Please step up in front of the class. Thank you. Kay Harrison, pick another animal."

The junior in the seat behind Jennifer squirmed uncomfortably. "Um, do I *have* to do this? This seems kinda dumb. Why do we have to be animals?"

"All in good time, Ms. Harrison. I would appreciate it if you just played along. Your animal?"

"Ummm . . . a cat?"

Bob Jarkmand and another boy sitting at the back of the classroom whispered to each other and began snickering. Kay shot them both a venomous look as she got up slowly and walked up next to Jennifer. Standing there, she shifted from one foot to the other and twirled her red, stringy curls with a finger. "This is so stupid," she muttered under her breath. Jennifer tried to give her an encouraging look, but the other girl's dull gaze was glued to the floor.

"We need a third volunteer," Mr. Slider chirped. His gaze passed over the whole class. Susan was the only one not quick enough to look away in time. "Ms. Elmsmith?"

"Ugh. Okay, a shark."

"Terrific! Up you go."

The three girls endured a bit more chuckling from the rest of the class as they waited in a row for Mr. Slider to get on with whatever he had in mind. Jennifer tried hard not to look over at where she knew Gerry was sitting.

"Let's say I want to put you three in a parade," the teacher began. "I want you in order of animal size. Who would be first, second, and third?"

A few hands went up. Mr. Slider motioned to one of the boys in the front row.

"First the cat, then the unicorn, then the shark," the answer came.

The teacher gave no sign beyond a mysterious smile.

Another hand went up. "Cat, shark, unicorn?"

The smile did not disappear.

Jennifer caught on. "You can't know yet," she said. "We don't know what kind of cat or shark. Plus, we have no idea how big a unicorn is since there's no such thing."

"Excellent, Ms. Scales. In other words, to solve this puzzle we need more information. *We need to know what we don't know.*" He let this sink in for a moment. Jennifer liked the way Mr. Slider seemed to enjoy his work.

"We need to know what we don't know," he repeated. "Is the shark a nurse shark, or a great white? Are unicorns the size of kittens, or the size of elephants? Let's try another parade. What if I said I wanted you in increasing order of the number of legs you have?"

The boy in front who had spoken first raised his hand again. "We know the shark comes first now. But the other two could be in either order."

"That's right, Paul! Of course, we need to make an assumption on unicorns based on the way they've always been described—as four-legged horses with a horn. Okay, now let's say we want to put them in decreasing order of how many times we've seen that animal in the last month."

A girl toward the back of the class spoke up without raising her hand. "On television, or real life?"

The corner of Mr. Slider's mouth raised. "Good question. Say real life."

"Cat, shark, unicorn!"

"Not for me!" The boy in front smiled back at the rest of the class. "My dad works at the aquarium!"

"This is excellent." Mr. Slider powered his chair back until he was right next to Jennifer and the other two girls. "Things that we *assume* are an important part of geometry. For the rest of this year you're going to work with what are called *proofs*—logic puzzles that begin with assumptions and lead to an inevitable conclusion. Logic is an amazing tool—it's accurate and ruthless, and sees through lies.

"For example, you could start with a proof with two assumptions: 'There's no such thing as unicorns' and 'Jennifer is a unicorn'—and end the proof with your conclusion that there's no such thing as Jennifer!

"Of course, we know Jennifer exists—we can see that much! So logic makes us go back to our assumptions and ask if either of them could be wrong. If Jennifer exists, either unicorns are real, too, or she's not a unicorn!"

"I swear I'm not a unicorn," Jennifer offered helpfully. This got the class tittering a bit. Mr. Slider looked up at her and the others gratefully.

"Thanks, girls, you can all sit down now. Class, you'll use proofs and logic all year to figure out things where you're missing information. 'What shape is it?' 'How large is it?' 'Will this hold enough liquid?' And so on. But the most important questions are those I mentioned earlier: What do we know, and what *don't* we know?

"For now, let's apply logic to some geometric shapes . . ."

He began working at the chalkboard, but Jennifer didn't pay much attention to the rest of what happened that class. A thought consumed her. Mr. Slider had said logic was accurate and ruthless. And he had said you could use it to figure out things when you were missing information.

And there were definitely some things going on where she was missing information.

Walking home from school alone, she recognized Eddie's voice calling her. She didn't turn around.

"Jennifer, come on, wait up! Just for a second!"

She answered without slowing down. "You want to talk, move faster. And don't expect me to answer!"

His footsteps quickened to a jog, and after a few seconds he was walking next to her and breathing heavily. "You don't have to answer, just listen. It's important. I'm starting to hear stuff, Jennifer. Not just from my mom and dad. People are talking, all over town. They say something bad is coming. Some even say it's already here."

"Must be the horrible Scales family on the rampage," she quipped. "What, you've told every idiot in town that we're weredragons?"

"No, I wouldn't do that," he insisted. "But I don't know if my parents have. It won't take long anyway before people trace trouble back to you guys. At that point, you know full well you're outnumbered. How long do you think it will take?"

She stopped, grabbed him by the collar, and yanked him down and around so that his back was nearly parallel to the ground. "How long do you think *what* will take?"

To his credit, he didn't flinch. "How long do you think it will take for this town to turn on your mother, once and for all?"

Then it clicked. Logic. Accurate. Relentless. She dropped Eddie with a satisfying *smack* onto the sidewalk and began to run. She didn't stop until she had gotten home.

Both of her parents were sitting in the living room, listening to Wagner's *Ring des Nibelungen* at an unnatural volume. She flipped the stereo off and faced the couch squarely.

"When did Pinegrove change its name to Winoka?"

They both blinked in silence.

"Okay, let's try another one. Why the hell are we living in a town *full of beaststalkers*?"

They both blinked again. Phoebe padded into the living room to greet Jennifer, took in the tension for a moment, and then padded away with ears down and tail between her legs.

"How did you find out?" Elizabeth finally asked.

"I used logic. Sixty years ago, beaststalkers invaded a town called Pinegrove. Then they settled there. The Blacktooths are beaststalkers. Eddie talks about more beaststalkers being around, and us being outnumbered, and the town turning on us. Should I go on?"

"That's not exactly airtight—"

"Then tell me I'm wrong."

Jonathan lifted his hand. "You're not wrong, Jennifer. Winoka reincorporated, and changed its name from Pinegrove soon after the weredragons were pushed out. The beaststalkers wanted nothing of the town's old identity to remain, not even its name."

"So after Eveningstar burned down, you guys decided it would be smart to move into a town full of people who would kill Dad and me if they knew what we are?"

"I imagine," he replied carefully, "that for weeks, the entire town has been learning who you and I are, via the Blacktooths."

"Then why hasn't anyone come to kill us?"

"Because of me," Elizabeth answered. She nodded at her daughter's stare. "There is a sacred agreement among beaststalkers which protects each beaststalker's family and friends. Many beaststalkers have used this unwritten law to extend protection to others—people who are afraid of monsters they've seen, or have heard of. They move into towns full of beaststalkers so that they aren't afraid anymore."

"And because we're family, we're okay, even though we're weredragons?"

Her mother nodded. "The idea of a beaststalker wanting to protect a weredragon has never come up before. I imagine the townspeople of Winoka are struggling with that dilemma as we speak."

Jennifer realized something. "That's why Mrs. Blacktooth didn't kill me in front of you that day last spring."

"Yes. Even if she had managed to kill you before I intervened, it would have been hard for her to explain to others."

"Eddie said we might be attacked soon anyway."

"As I said, Winoka is struggling with the idea of our family, and the problems we pose. I'm not exactly a favorite in this town to begin with. I have often disagreed with those in power. I've been excluded from the local church, as you know. What you don't know is that church is run by city hall—and it has many people in it I once counted as friends. Their distrust made my participation impossible. As more people learn about your father, that distrust will evolve into hostility. Fewer and fewer of them will care about beast-stalker law."

"The murder of Jack Alder makes things worse," Jonathan added. "Hank Blacktooth was friends with Jack, just like I was. And just like my sources discovered weredragon DNA on the scene, I am sure his have as well. In fact, he and others may even guess that the murderer is related to me. That will add fuel to the fire."

"Then we can't stay here!" Jennifer couldn't believe they were all still in the well-appointed living room. "We've got to get out of Winoka!"

Her parents nodded. "Your mother and I have been talking about this since you showed an interest in Pinegrove. We thought you might learn the truth eventually—and that you would feel this way. It might not be a bad idea for you to make for the farm again, and stay there for some time. You could relax a bit before the trials, next week."

Jennifer had almost forgotten about the Fifty Trials and the Blaze. In fact, she had never really gotten around to telling Skip that she couldn't go to the Halloween dance. The time, it seemed, was never right—and, anyway, how would she explain the Fifty Trials, and the reason for them? But now none of that mattered.

"Not just me—you and Mom have got to come, too! None of us should be here! We should never have moved here!"

Elizabeth stood and held her daughter's hand. "Honey, your father and I can't go just yet."

"What?" Jennifer yanked her hand away from her mother. "That's crazy!"

"The crescent moon comes tomorrow." Jonathan stood up, too. "Your mother will stay here to protect me. I need a day or so to figure out what happened to Jack, plus my work for the new hospital center—"

"You're nuts." Jennifer spun and ran out of the room. Feeling tears gathering, she shook them away. She didn't want to think about what staying now would mean for her parents. If dozens of beaststalkers came knocking tonight, her mother would be overwhelmed. And her father, without a crescent moon, would be unable to help much. Why didn't they see that?

She knew it was useless to argue. Still fighting back tears, she went up to her room. In a few minutes, she had on her leather training armor and twin daggers. That was all she would need. Without saying good-bye to her parents, she slammed her bedroom window open and jumped out into the cold October afternoon. Moments later, her winged shape slipped up through the clouds.

"*Grandpa, you've got to call* my parents!" She said this as she stormed through the cabin patio doors, reverting to seething girl shape.

From the kitchen, he poked his head back and smiled. "Hey, Niffer! I'm making up some meatloaf. Lucky for you

I've got extra, Joseph's lending a hand at the Green farm down the road again—"

"Grandpa, you have to call them!"

He finally paid attention. "Why? They driving you nuts?"

"No. Well, yes, but—Grandpa, I know about Pinegrove. I know our house is in a town full of beaststalkers, and now that everybody knows we're weredragons, they still won't leave!"

Crawford sighed sadly. "They sent you up here?"

"Yes. Dad said he has *work* to do, of all things! And I know Mom won't leave him. You have to call him and tell him to get up here!"

To her surprise, he actually chuckled. "Niffer, when your parents tell you what to do, do you always listen?"

"Well, no, but—"

"Your father hasn't followed my advice since he fell in love with your mother." This came out wistfully. "He was right back then, I learned over time, and the two of them might be right now. You may know about Pinegrove, but I doubt you know everything."

Jennifer stomped her foot. "I *really* wish people wouldn't keep stuff from me. I'm fifteen years old; I can handle a little family history! Anyway, what could be so important that my parents would stay in that house? It's just a house!"

She caught a flash in his gray eyes. "Not every house is just a house, Jennifer. Especially when you lose one. You should have learned that at Eveningstar."

It took some time to ponder that, but then . . .

"Our house in Winoka used to be *yours*?"

He nodded. "The property did. My mother's farm used to

be where that neighborhood stands. She raised me alone, after my father died in a duel with a particularly powerful werachnid named Motega. She found her revenge on him, but a few years afterward, the beaststalkers came to Pinegrove. There were more of us back then than there are now, but an army of beaststalkers is formidable."

It was a while before he spoke again. Jennifer stared at the white fringe of hair that surrounded the back of his frail head. She knew enough not to press him for details. He opened the oven door, took out a small pan of meatloaf, and began slicing it.

"We hid, of course," he finally continued. "In a secret compartment under the basement. She had dug it long before then, thinking she may need it on occasion. But with the entire town occupied and beaststalkers living literally above our heads, we were trapped. The beaststalker family that moved into that farm never even knew we were there, for several weeks.

"We thought we would just slip upstairs and out of the house some time when they weren't in, but as it turned out, it was a family with children, and the mother stayed home with them all the time. Not only that, many beaststalkers spent time renovating houses and obliterating all traces of their previous owners. Even when she took the children away during the day, they had workers knocking down walls, remodeling, and so on. The best we could do was slip up into the basement and get water from the utility sink. That alone nearly got us caught.

"Having no other option, my mother dug deeper under the basement, making a tunnel that she hoped we could use to escape without alerting anyone. But it was hard work, through bedrock, and we had to do it quietly. I tried to help, but I was little then and couldn't do much."

Crawford had all the meatloaf on a serving platter now. Motioning for Jennifer to get her own dishes, he brought the platter over to the dining table.

"On the verge of starvation, and her claws crusted in her own blood, Mother finally decided her own cause was hopeless. But she didn't give up on me. She made me memorize a fake name that matched up with some friends in another town, and a story I could give authorities about getting lost looking for rabbits. Then she went upstairs one night and distracted them.

"While the family and some neighbors hunted her across her own farm, I slipped out of the house and went the other way. I didn't want to, of course, but I had no choice. I cried the whole time I was running away from her."

Jennifer quietly watched him as he lifted some meatloaf from the platter and moved it onto her plate.

"Somehow, I managed to find the highway and walk to the next town, full of regular folk and not a beaststalker or were-dragon in sight. They accepted my story without suspicion and sent me to my mother's friends, who knew enough to raise me until I was old enough to change. Some years later, I used my savings to buy this farm and build this cabin. As you know, it's here for weredragons now as a refuge, a place where they can come, no matter what. Dragons like Joseph Skinner.

"The family that lived in that house sold off most of the farm to developers, and new houses and neighborhoods sprung up around them. Happens all the time, nowadays. The residents of the original farm house grew old, and their children had children. Among them was a little girl, Elizabeth

Georges. In time, the house and what was left of the farm passed to her."

She stopped with a forkful of meatloaf halfway to her mouth. Her grandfather studied her with a somber gaze.

"I think you misunderstand which of your parents is the more stubborn, Niffer. I have no doubt that my son would rather see his whole family safely up here at this cabin. But your mother made a promise to me on her wedding day, after she learned who I was and made the connection to her own house. She had the beaststalker house razed to the foundation, and swore to me on her own life that she would rebuild a house there where weredragons could live again, for good.

"I was horrible to her in those days and I didn't believe her, but bless her heart, she kept her word. After Eveningstar, as you know, your parents built that new house there, and it will pass on to you in time. So you see, Niffer, I'm guessing there's no way a phone call is going to get her out of that house—or her husband, for that matter."

Jennifer dropped her fork. "They know they'll die! Grandpa, we can't let that happen! We have to go back!"

"And do what? Jennifer, there's no way your parents would want you in that house right now. Your tendency to act like a teenager worked against you. Running away in a fit is exactly what they *wanted* you to do. I'm sure of it. And I'm just as sure that they'd tear my head off if I let you go back. You're staying here, young lady— *Hey!* What do you think you're doing?"

She turned as she reached the patio doors. "Well, right now, I'm trying to imagine how you'll stop me."

His face clouded in panic. "Jennifer, wait! Okay, you're right. I can't stop you. And I imagine I can't convince you to stay—after all, we all know what happens when you decide to rush off and save family."

Despite her worry, she gave a wry grin.

"If I can't convince you to stay," he proposed, "can I at least convince you to go back together with me?"

Her heart lifted at the thought of him helping her. "You promise to break the speed limit?"

"Every sign I see. Just let me go upstairs and get my keys and wallet. And my gun, come to think of it. You pack up this meatloaf with some bread and bring it out to the truck. We'll eat sandwiches on the way there. I don't know about you, but I'm still hungry!"

Visions of her parents in danger racing through her head, she breathlessly stuffed the meatloaf into a plastic container, grabbed the bread from the breadbasket, and carried the food out the back door. Grandpa's truck was parked behind the house, a quick walk from the porch steps.

But it was far enough away that she did not see the dark shape slip into the house through the open door behind her. Nor was she close enough to feel the putrid chill that the thing brought with its shroud of shadow, nor hear the clicking of many legs as they scuttled across the sitting room and into the hall toward the stairs.

She did, however, hear her grandfather's shotgun go off upstairs.

"Grandpa?!" At first she thought he must have set off the gun accidentally, but running up the patio steps into the sitting room, she heard him cry out from the top of the stairs. He sounded very scared, and very old.

"*Grandpa!*" Her daggers were up in her hands instantly as

she bolted up the stairs. At the top, she nearly dropped them in shock.

The thing perched on top of her grandfather was the size and rough shape of a dragon—but it was no beast Jennifer had ever seen before. Dull, rough black scales covered it top and bottom. The scales extended over two long and tattered wings, as well as six insectlike legs whose joints thrust up nearly as high as the ceiling. These legs ended in four-fingered claws that flexed irritably at the walls, the floor, and the prey beneath.

There must have been a head to it, but the entire front end of the thing—as well as the head and torso of its prey—was surrounded by an impenetrable gloom. The darkness trailed back over both bodies in disintegrating wisps, continually replenished by an unseen source. Crawford's hand lay open on the ground, with the spent gun smoking next to it. Sounds of slurping and chewing, and the stench of poison, filled the dim hallway. The assault on her senses made Jennifer reel, and she had to catch herself on the stair handrail.

Suddenly, underneath those senses, another sense of hers perceived words. They were not spoken. They just appeared unbidden in her head, over and over.

no father no father no father no father

"Stop it!" she screamed.

no father no father no father no father

Her terror shifted into fury. Clenching her teeth, she charged down the hall at the thing and leapt on top of it.

Before it could react, she had plunged both daggers into its back.

It gave an awful shriek that shattered the picture window at the end of the upstairs hall. The body heaved Jennifer off and she spilled to the ground, barely able to pull her weapons back out. Before she could ready them for another strike, the monster came about and the black cloud passed over her. The darkness seeped into her eyes and dulled her mind. Its breath lingered over her for a moment, and she felt something slimy probe the skin of her forehead—a tongue, perhaps?

Dazed by the dangerous sensations she felt, she swung up with a knife, but before the blow struck home, the terrible thing gave another ear-piercing shriek, scrambled down the hallway, and surged out the broken window. By the time Jennifer stumbled to the opening, it had vanished into the evening air.

A gasp from her grandfather made her turn around and go to him. What she saw surprised her—despite the horrific sounds the attacker had made in the darkness, Crawford seemed to have no wounds. But he seemed twenty or thirty years older, as if he had vaulted into advanced old age. The white fringe of hair was gone, and his skin clung to his fragile bones. With tears streaking her face, Jennifer gently lifted his skull.

"Grandpa!"

Cloudy gray eyes stared up but did not see her.

"No father!" he cried out with a dry voice that barely sounded like his own. *"No father! No father!"*

For a moment, his eyes cleared and he seemed to see her. A whisper of recognition passed. "Niffer?"

Then he collapsed from her hands and did not move.

CHAPTER 7

Another Dimension's Child

Jennifer remembered very little of the next two hours. She supposed, looking back on that night, that she must have called her parents. Her description of what had happened was urgent enough to get them to the cabin immediately.

Then, best she could remember, she went back upstairs, pushed her grandfather's gun aside, laid his head on her lap, and cried. Eventually, her mother arrived, led her to a bed, and set her down upon it. She must have slept, of course, but she was certain she didn't stop crying.

Her dream was of Crescent Valley, and the enormous crescent moon that lit up that world. It filled the sky, so much so that she could not imagine a way to fly around it. She spread her dragon wings and skimmed its gleaming, rocky surface. What was she looking for?

As if in answer, a stream of flame swept over her head. It circled around the crescent moon like a belt and then passed overhead again, and again, and again. Each time it passed, it was a little farther away, so that the belt of fire became wider and wider. Her path took her right under this growing inferno, but she did not burn. In fact, she felt cool.

"Grandpa?" She could sense him here.

Then she woke up.

Her parents were downstairs. Elizabeth was making breakfast—this almost never happened—while Jonathan stood on the porch, looking northward over the lake. Jennifer sidled up to her mother by the stove.

"Grandpa?"

Elizabeth hugged her.

Jennifer could feel herself start to cry again. "Where is he?"

"We've wrapped and stored the body for now. The crescent of the moon will be prominent later this afternoon. Some other dragons will come, and then your grandfather will be taken to Crescent Valley. There's a ritual there, but your father won't talk about it."

"Can they bring him back?"

She felt her mother's shoulders slump. "I don't think so, honey. It's not that kind of ritual. A funeral of some kind, best I can tell. I'm sorry, Jennifer."

Jennifer started to accept the sympathy, and then broke

away hotly as she remembered what she and Grandpa were trying to do last night. "You weren't here! Neither of you! I was all by myself when Grandpa died, *and you could have died, too—for that stupid house*!" She began striking out at her mother in a rage. "*It's a dumb house! And with Grandpa dead, and you two dead, I would have been all by myself! What the hell were you thinking? Why weren't you here with me?*"

Elizabeth was trying to quiet Jennifer down, but settled for holding her awkwardly as the muffled blows continued. "Honey, we weren't going to die! Grandpa told you about my promise to him?"

Jennifer nodded, sniffling.

"So he told you the story of his mother, and how they hid below the basement?"

Jennifer wiped her eyes and nodded again.

"So he told you about the tunnel?"

"Oh." It seemed pretty obvious to Jennifer now. "You finished the tunnel?"

"As soon as we rebuilt the house and moved in eight years ago. I promised your grandfather I'd hand the house over to you someday. I didn't promise him I'd hold off an endless assault. Your father and I agreed we could hold off a few rogues if any showed up while we finished our business in Winoka, but if it got bad, we'd just slip away and fight another day. I'm sure your grandfather knew."

Her daughter pulled back a bit. "So you weren't going to try to die last night?"

"Honey, the only thing I'm ever going to die for is standing in front of me right now."

Jennifer tried a weak smile. "You mean Grandpa's stove?"

That earned a light punch to the shoulder. "I cook worse on this stove than any other appliance in creation. I just thought I'd make breakfast this morning, so your father doesn't have to. I don't know how much help that is, though." She turned serious again. "He's taking this hard, of course."

"Can I talk to him? I mean, does he want to be alone, or will he talk to me?"

"Honey, you're probably the *only* person he wants to talk to, right now."

Jonathan turned as soon as he heard Jennifer open the patio door. A cold wind blew moist lake air into her face. He tried a smile but it failed miserably. "Hey, ace."

She felt herself crumble right away. "I'm so sorry, Dad! I tried to save him, but it already had him. Before I could hit it more than once it yelled and took off through the window and it vanished so I—"

He stepped over and hugged her. "Ssshhh. It's okay, Jennifer. You don't have to apologize. I know you did your best."

She couldn't keep the tears back. "I should have been able to stop it!"

"Listen carefully. *You are not responsible.*"

"I was just outside for a second to put food in the truck," she started. Before she knew it, the entire story poured out of her—the gunshot she had heard, the dark beast upstairs, and its attack, and the words she heard in her head.

"No father," Jonathan mumbled when she told him.

"And it didn't stop until I stabbed it," she continued. "Then it just screamed and threw me off. I thought it would start to attack me, too, but then it yelled again and bolted."

"It came just for him," he deduced. "It didn't want to fight you. At least not yet."

"But why would something like that come after *Grandpa*? And what *was* it?"

"I have a theory." Jonathan sighed. "But I don't want to share it right now. Later, I promise," he added quickly, seeing the frustration on her face. "We'll be going to Crescent Valley later tonight and there should be time before then. But there's no sense in getting everyone riled up before I think this through. First, I need to call a friend of yours."

With her father on the phone behind a closed door for several minutes, and both parents locked upstairs talking further for nearly an hour after that, Jennifer had a lonely, empty morning. It helped a bit that her parents had thought quickly enough last night to bring both Phoebe and Geddy with them. While the dog and the lizard didn't usually get along, today they seemed willing to share Jennifer—the former resting at her feet with her muzzle over the girl's ankles, and the latter curled up on a shoulder by her left ear.

She tried morphing into dragon shape and blowing a few fire rings for Phoebe to jump through, but nobody seemed to have the heart to do it for long. It was a beautiful, crisp day for flying, or turf-whomping, or even lizard- or bird-calling. Jennifer felt like none of these. It wasn't right. Grandpa was dead, and the world went on—clouds sliding gently overhead, light glistening off the water's surface, insects strumming in her ears.

It wasn't right.

Finally, at about ten o'clock, her father came outside and suggested they take a walk to the end of the driveway.

"Someone's coming and I want to make sure they don't run afoul of your grandfather's bees."

"Who?"

"You'll see." He tried to smile. "He'll be helpful in working this out; and in any case, I thought it might raise your spirits."

All the way walking down the winding gravel driveway, past trees and grazing pastures and sheep and horses and exotic wildflowers and at last the huge hives of extraordinary bees that guarded the borders of the farm, Jennifer tried to think of the person her father could call that could both help them and lift her heavy heart.

Just as they reached the stone pillars that marked the driveway entrance, she saw a taxi come down the highway toward them. It pulled off the road right in front of them, and out stepped . . . Skip Wilson.

"Skip!" She hugged him right away, and he blushed.

"Hey, Jennifer. Hey, Mr. Scales. Thanks for covering my cab fare."

After the taxi was paid and gone, they walked back to the cabin. Many bees swirled around Skip at first, but sensing the presence of an escort, they soon left him alone. He looked uncomfortable anyway.

"Skip, what are you doing here?"

"All in good time, Jennifer." Her father gave her a serious look. "We can talk it all out before our friends arrive from Crescent Valley for your grandfather."

"I'm sorry about your grandpa, Jennifer," Skip whispered in her ear. "Your dad told me some of what happened. I wish I could have been here to help."

She smiled at him and grasped the hand he was offering. "Thanks. I don't know what you could have done, though. This thing was . . . horrible. I didn't even have time to change into a dragon, really. Even that might not have been enough."

He gave a slightly indignant look. "Maybe I could have helped! My aunt says I'm pretty close to—"

Jonathan raised a hand to stop the conversation. "I'm fairly certain that even both of you together would have had your hands full. And once you hear what this thing may be, you may not be so quick to attack it."

"What does *that* mean?" Jennifer murmured to Skip, but he only shrugged.

After lunch—Jennifer caught and prepared a few sheep from the pasture, thinking wistfully of her grandfather and his love for hunting—Elizabeth and Jonathan finally sat Jennifer and Skip down and answered their questions. Jennifer nervously stroked Geddy, who was still curled up on her left shoulder.

"First things first," Jonathan began. "Last year, I told you two that Dianna Wilson and I were good friends."

They both nodded.

"Well," he went on awkwardly, "we were actually more than that. Much more. In fact, Jennifer, before I met your mother, Dianna Wilson and I were married."

"*Married!*" Jennifer nearly fell off the sitting room couch, and she felt her pet gecko leap for the safety of the throw pillows. "You were married to someone else before Mom?" She stood up and turned to her mother. "Mom, did you *know* about this?"

Despite herself, Elizabeth actually chuckled. "Yes, I knew, honey. You don't have to be outraged on my behalf. Your father told me everything he's about to say, soon after I met him. When you were born, we agreed we would tell you in time."

"In time?" The anger Jennifer felt toward her father bled over to include her mother as well. "Like the way you agreed to tell me about Pinegrove? Or how you agreed to tell me about my being a weredragon?"

"You're getting a bit off track—"

"No, this *is* the track!" She was embarrassed that this was all coming out in front of a boy she liked, but there was no helping that now. "It never ends with you two! The secrets, the lies, the long and tortured explanations after something traumatic happens. I thought family members were supposed to trust each other! That means sharing, and telling the truth! You guys are always so big on honesty and integrity, but you can't practice what you preach!"

"Jennifer, I'm sorry." Her father sounded both apologetic and irritated at once. "Perhaps when you become a parent yourself, you will earn the qualifications necessary to critique our own performance. In the meantime, if you sit down and listen, you'll learn all you need to know."

Partly mollified, partly chastened, and completely red-faced, Jennifer sat back down without looking at Skip. Geddy slowly worked his way back to her shoulder.

"As I was saying, we were married," Jonathan continued. "Over twenty years ago, and secretly, of course. Love doesn't hold well to social boundaries, and we both knew the dangers involved. Skip, you may already be aware what your people do to those who consort with their enemies. Whatever you are going through now for associating with my daughter, it would have been worse for your mother, years ago."

Jennifer turned to Skip, who didn't show any emotion. Despite all the trouble she was having with the other weredragons and beaststalkers for her own identity and friends, she never thought about what it must be like for Skip. Was Aunt Tavia really as pleasant and understanding as she seemed at the fund-raiser?

Jonathan continued. "Our plan was to be married for several years, and gradually bring around friends and family so we could forge a loyal core receptive to the truth. For a year or so, we kept our secret. But then disaster struck one day— Dianna informed me she was pregnant."

Jennifer froze. She didn't like at all where she guessed this story was heading.

"We were surprised. And terrified. We couldn't reveal the baby without revealing our marriage, of course. Despite my urging, Dianna wouldn't even go to a doctor, for fear that word would get out.

"But she was a brilliant woman, and she soon had a plan. She arranged to take an extended trip abroad—places far away from Minnesota like Africa, South America, and so on—so no one would see her condition. During that time, she undertook research she assured me would solve our problem, with no harm to anyone.

"As you know, some of the more powerful werachnids have a gift for sorcery, and for seeing across space and time. Dianna was one such woman, and her specialty was exploring other dimensions."

"Other dimensions?" Jennifer felt her ears prick at the

idea. "You mean, like different worlds, where trees grow upside down, or rabbits are twenty feet tall?"

"Sort of," interrupted Skip. Jennifer knew that he was even better with mathematics than she was. "I've been going over this with Mr. Slider during independent study. He says the easiest way to think about it is this: If we were all flat shapes, like squares and circles, we'd only live in two dimensions, right?"

"Length and width," Jennifer agreed. "Like living in a piece of paper."

"Exactly. But if one of us discovered a third dimension—*height*—then that would freak us out. A ball bouncing across the paper would look like a circle that disappeared and reappeared in different places!

"Now apply that to our real world, with three dimensions. If someone found a *fourth* dimension, they could do all sorts of disappearing and reappearing acts. Instead of keeping cars in our cramped three-dimensional garages, they could park them 'up' one dimension, out of the way, until we needed them again." He turned to Jonathan. "So that's what Mom hoped to do? Put this baby someplace out of the way, until you were ready for it?"

"Someplace *safe*," Jonathan stressed. "She was sure she could open a portal to a place where time would stand virtually still, and the baby could remain unharmed, until we could reveal our marriage to family and friends. Ever optimistic, she worked on the mathematics and sorcery the whole time she was away. Seven months into her pregnancy, she sent for me. I can still remember her the night I arrived in the Australian outback.

"She was glowing with the aura of discovery, and triumph. *I've found the perfect place,* she told me, *and it will keep our little Evangelos safe.* The stars had told her the baby was a boy, and that was what she wanted to name him—Evangelos, Greek for 'angel' or 'messenger of light.' As I said, she was optimistic.

"After a few days together gathering supplies and enjoying each other's company, we parted. She told me to return home—I would only be in danger if I stayed—and not to worry. She would remain in a quiet corner of the outback, give birth with the help of a midwife she had come to trust, and then work her sorcery to hold our child safely until the right time came. Wanting to stay but trusting in her instincts, I kissed her good-bye, told her I loved her, and left. It was the last time I ever saw her.

"A week after I left, under the crescent moon, I received a cell phone call from the midwife. Her voice was strangled and I understood only two words—*bad portal.* The call was quickly cut off. Unable to get back in touch with anyone, I took a desperate chance and flew over the Pacific on my own wings. It was days before I got there, and by then there was little I could piece together.

"Here is what I know or can deduce: Evangelos must have decided he was ready early, because there were clear signs in the house of a premature birth. The birth happened under the crescent moon, given the timing of the phone call. But Dianna was gone, and the midwife's body was not far from the house. The cell phone was ruined in her hand. Scratched in the dirt, using the midwife's blood, Dianna had left a brief and gruesome message: *No child.*"

"Yech," Jennifer spat.

"Using blood in writing is an old werachnid custom," Skip explained. "Aunt Tavia told me about it. After battle, a werachnid will often write the tale in the blood of whatever enemies have fallen, so that we pass on the knowledge of what we learned."

"That's gruesome," Elizabeth sniffed.

"It's handy," he countered.

Jennifer decided to change the subject. "So how can there be a child, if it died?"

"There was no body of a child," Jonathan pointed out. "At the time, I saw some evidence of lingering sorcery, which I assumed to be what was left of a portal. While I'm no expert on such things, I could see plainly that it wasn't prepared well. Perhaps Dianna was rushed by the premature birth, or she misjudged the stars, or the midwife who assisted her made some miscalculation. When they attempted to place Evangelos in the portal, I guess it killed him. That would have explained the dead woman—Dianna wasn't normally given to murderous rage."

Jennifer looked at her mother, but the woman's expression was inscrutable. "Why didn't you just ask Ms. Wilson what happened?"

"She wouldn't have anything to do with me," Jonathan answered. "I tried on several occasions to find her, and came close once or twice. But she always anticipated my arrival and vanished. She plainly did not want to see me again and likely considered our marriage a grave mistake. After a month or two, I received papers to end our marriage quietly, through an untraceable stream of lawyers. Since that's what she wanted, I signed them. A few years later, I heard she married another werachnid—Otto Saltin, your father," he nodded to Skip. "And, of course, I met your mother."

"And now it appears Evangelos is alive," Skip said.

Jonathan nodded blankly. "I wouldn't have believed it. When I considered the midwife's words and Dianna's, I came to the natural conclusion he was dead. I know little of sorceries and other dimensions. But 'bad portal' could have meant Evangelos ended up somewhere Dianna didn't expect— somewhere bad or hidden, where she couldn't follow. All this time, Evangelos wasn't dead. He was lost."

"Abandoned in a different world," Skip murmured.

They sat in silence for a moment, until Jennifer couldn't contain herself.

"So that's what this thing is—your *son*? My *brother*?"

"Half brother."

"But how do you know that for sure, if you've never seen him? How did he get back here? What does he want?"

"Even now, we only have pieces of the puzzle," Jonathan admitted. "But put them together, and it's a pretty convincing picture. First, the DNA evidence at Jack Alder's house says that someone related to me was there when he died. It wasn't you, and it wasn't your grandfather. Evangelos is the only other person who could possibly leave DNA related to mine.

"Second, your description of him sounds like something half-spider, half-dragon. While I can't say for sure how the offspring of a werachnid and weredragon ought to look, that's as reasonable a picture as any.

"Third, the words this thing scrawled next to Jack—and the words you heard in your own head—are hauntingly similar to what Dianna wrote in the midwife's blood. Rage and grief have passed from mother to child. Somehow, unlikely as it may seem, Evangelos has survived, found his way out of whatever dimension he was trapped in, and come into our world."

"Okay, so let's say it's him," Skip conceded. "What is he doing here? Why is he killing people?"

"Both victims have had some telling last words," Jonathan answered. "If Evangelos has spent the last twenty years someplace unpleasant, and if he holds his parents responsible, then it's possible he's trying to pass on his grief the only way he knows how—making me experience what he has experienced. No friends, so he finds my best friend and kills him. No father. Thus, last night."

Jennifer swallowed. "This sounds like the beginning of a nasty trend."

Her father nodded. The fear on his face was clear. "I am going to assume that Evangelos does not have a wife or a daughter, either. After that, I assume he will come for me, to complete the circuit."

"So why didn't he try to finish me off last night?" Jennifer asked. "I mean, I was right there, and he was right on top of me. He must have known who I was."

Elizabeth spoke. "He's probably a bit wary of you, dear. He'd want to learn as much as he could first, and it would be hard for him to get close to Winoka. After all, the beaststalkers in that town are a new experience for him. He may be staying on the fringes of town until he can get a measure of them."

It was clear to Jennifer her mother was avoiding telling Skip that the two of *them* were beaststalkers as well. She felt a twinge of irritation—*more secrets!*—but managed to keep her feelings to herself. Her mother continued.

"My guess is that he has started with those people close to your father who don't live near him, and is trying to gain the courage to enter Winoka. Out here, he probably didn't expect to run into you. He might not even have realized you existed until you were on top of him, and it startled him. And since you hurt him, he'll think twice about his next steps."

"Which may make Winoka the safest place to be," Jonathan admitted. "After the funeral, we should probably all head back there and hunker down until we can learn—"

"*Now wait just a minute.*" Jennifer held her hand up. "Yesterday, Winoka was crawling with beaststalkers and it was *too* dangerous for me to stay. Today, Winoka is crawling with beaststalkers . . . so it's the *least* dangerous place I can stay?" She turned to Skip, a pleading expression on her face. *You see what I put up with?*

"We can discuss this further tonight," Jonathan offered. "Skip, I brought you up here because I wanted you to hear the truth as soon as I knew it, because you may be in danger yourself. You are, after all, the closest link to Dianna. Also, I thought you may have insights on Dianna or Evangelos . . . ?"

Skip shrugged. "Most of this is news to me. Mom spent most of my childhood looking for something, but she never told me what—or who—exactly. Her obsession makes a lot more sense now. And then she was gone—" He stopped, plainly upset. "Anyway, I'm glad I finally found out what it was all about. Thanks for letting me know, Mr. Scales."

Jonathan nodded sympathetically. "Since there are dragons coming here soon, Skip, it's best if Elizabeth takes you back now to Winoka. What you do after that is up to you. You're welcome to stay at our house. Or, you may want to go home, and let your aunt know what you've learned. I assume she's aware Dianna and I were . . . friends?"

"She knows," Skip nodded. The others waited for him to offer more information, but he didn't. Jonathan changed the subject.

"The funeral will be later tonight. After that, I expect the Blaze to help Jennifer and me figure out next steps. I imagine we will end up trying to track down Evangelos, though I'm not yet sure how to do that."

"What happens after we find him?" Jennifer shuddered at the memory of the dark, cold thing hovering over her grandfather. The first time, her anger had gotten the better of her and she had lunged thoughtlessly. She wasn't sure how brave she would be in a rematch.

"I won't mince words," her father answered. "Evangelos is my son. He is your half brother—and Skip's, too. But he is a killer, and we have to stop him. Somehow."

CHAPTER 8

The Elder's Funeral

Several hours after Elizabeth and Skip left in the minivan, with darkness settling over the cabin, three dragons arrived. Ned Brownfoot was one of them—he'd come to take his old friend back into another world. Ned and the others helped Jonathan bring Crawford's body from the cabin, out over the lake, and into Crescent Valley.

The first thing Jennifer noticed when they emerged into the ancient refuge was that the large crescent moon, which normally greeted them with a ring of fire, gave no such sign this time.

"The venerables are waiting," Jonathan explained. "They will not signal again, until your grandfather has a proper funeral." The dragons struck out in a path Jennifer had never taken before—due north, with the area of their homes and hunt far off to the left.

Jennifer ignored the additional clue about the venerables, and instead asked a question that had been on her mind since that afternoon.

"Dad, Evangelos attacked last night, right?"

"Right."

"And the moon didn't wane into a crescent until tonight, twenty-four hours later, right?"

His silence indicated that he had not thought of this yet. "This is a mystery."

"You want to know what I think?" She was proud that she had thought most of this through—using the same logic Mr. Slider was so fond of. "I think he's got a bit of Ancient Furnace in him, too. I mean, he's your son, which puts him in the fiftieth generation of Scales, just like me. It makes sense that he'd be able to change at will."

Despite their grim errand, Jonathan glowed with admiration. "It's getting harder and harder to stay ahead of you, ace. I'll admit I hadn't thought that deeply about it. Soon, you'll be giving *me* lectures."

"Count on it. Anyway, a big part of tracking down my brother will be figuring out who he is when he's *human*."

"Of course, it's possible he's always in beast form."

"I don't think so. I mean, I feel pressure to change into dragon form if I stay human for too long—but I also feel pressure to change back. I know we can't be sure, but my guess would be some of the time, at least, he's running around as a guy. How old did you say Evangelos was?"

"He was born twenty years ago. But who knows how fast time passed, where he lived? He could look like an old man to us, or a precocious toddler."

Jennifer sighed. "That doesn't exactly narrow it down. It sounds like there's only one way to catch him."

Jonathan nodded. "We'll have to wait for him to strike again. I just hope we're ready this time."

Looking back on her grandfather's funeral, Jennifer had to admit it passed by her like a surreal dream. Set alongside her experience of Jack Alder's funeral, her grandfather's ceremony felt too strange, too mysterious . . . and far too brief.

After traveling at least fifty miles with their burden, they came to a stout cylinder of a plateau, which broke through the surface of the moon elm forest like an enormous tree stump among weeds. They descended and came to rest upon the unnaturally smooth stone. The northern half of the large circle was covered with etchings, which Jennifer could not decipher. The southern half was bare, and about fifty elders were waiting upon it solemnly. Winona Brandfire was foremost.

Ned and the others laid Crawford's human body down gently where the plateau's designs ended, and Jonathan guided Jennifer back to a place in front of the gathering. She made out some familiar faces, including Xavier Longtail. The prickly dasher did not acknowledge her, but kept his attention on the corpse before them.

Wordlessly, Winona motioned to the other elders, and together they drew closer to where Crawford lay. To Jennifer's alarm, they all breathed in deeply and let out a sustained inferno that rippled over the plateau and washed over her grandfather. She almost cried out, but relaxed at the reassuring touch of her father.

The fire went on for a long time. When it finally ended, she gasped—there was nothing left but a few ashes, and the rock beneath was glowing with molten heat. The smell of sulfur settled upon the plateau.

Winona stepped up and dipped her wing claw into the pool of hot, liquid rock. As her finger swirled a foreign pattern, she called out the words that when cooled would remain etched into this rock forever.

"Crawford Thomas Scales. Elder of the Scales family. Survivor of Pinegrove. Warrior at Cloverfield, White Lake, and Eveningstar. Grandfather to the Ancient Furnace." (Jennifer flinched a bit at this.) "Master hunter, and ambassador to the newolves."

Then Winona looked up at the other elders. One by one, they said other words, and the eldest dutifully etched them into the bubbling plateau surface.

"Shepherd." This came from Joseph Skinner, the young weredragon who kept up Crawford's farm. Jennifer was surprised to see him here before his fiftieth morph; but it made sense given his close relationship to the elder.

"Friend." This came from a slender Ned Brownfoot.

"Guardian." A toneless Xavier Longtail.

"Mentor." Her own father.

Suddenly, Winona's stare was upon Jennifer. She didn't know what to do or say. How could she pick one word to describe what this man had meant to her?

But after a moment, she thought about her fondest memories—sitting on his lap at the cabin as a little girl, while he told her tales about dragons and angels and sea monsters and everything else that seemed part of an impossible world . . .

"Storyteller," she finally managed. Winona nodded, carved the last swirl, and whispered over the new designs.

As the rock cooled, Jennifer spotted a slim, pale violet shadow slip up into the air. It spread two wings as it faced the crescent moon, and then it vanished.

"The elder has joined the venerables," Winona announced. She turned to Jonathan. "You are the elder now, for your clan."

He nodded, accepting the fact without ceremony. "I would like to propose, Eldest, that we postpone the Fifty Trials for my daughter. Not only are we grieving, but it is imperative that we find and stop the killer. No one who knows me is completely safe. Jennifer and I must focus our efforts on stopping any further attacks."

Winona shifted her head just enough to eye Xavier. "Do you have any objections?"

The dasher looked like he wanted to say something, but reconsidered. "No, Eldest. But perhaps a Blaze could advise the Elder Scales on his next steps. He deserves a ceremony of initiation, if nothing else."

"A good idea. Jonathan, do you have time to join us in full Blaze tonight?"

Now it was her father's turn to hesitate. Jennifer wondered herself at Xavier's apparent change of mood—probably in respect for her grandfather, she guessed.

"I have time, Eldest," Jonathan finally answered. "I will need to make arrangements for Jennifer."

"Leave that to me. Jennifer." The ancient trampler's face softened at the sight of the young dragon before her. "My granddaughter can perhaps comfort you in this difficult time. I've let her back into Crescent Valley, and she is waiting at our home. For now, we'll all fly back to Flames Mountain together."

Like a dark flock, the dragons all lifted into the air together and left the plateau. Behind them, they left the sounds of newolves baying a dirge in the wilderness.

Catherine hugged Jennifer with trembling wings as soon as the younger dragon landed in front of the trampler's cave. She insisted on waiting on her guest wing claw and foot, and wouldn't hear anything of going out for training or turf-whomping or anything else Jennifer wanted to do. "At least not until you've had a bit more time to rest. After all, you've gone through so much these last few days! You need to take care of yourself."

After a few hours in the Brandfire household, Jennifer thought a lot better of Catherine's advice. A trampler cave had furnishings most caves would not, such as comfortable straw beds, cream wool blankets, and large rough-hewn fireplaces. Also, since tramplers were lizard-callers, there was always a large alligator fetching water buckets from the nearby stream, or a Burmese python dragging firewood across the cave floor with its coils. All in all, it was a restful place to recover from the recent turmoil.

"So your grandma's not mad at you anymore for coming to Crescent Valley?" Jennifer asked later that night.

Catherine gave a rueful smile. "Oh, I wouldn't go that far. Grammie Winona's not as narrow-minded as Xavier Longtail, but she's still pretty hung up on tradition and loyalty. I've got my penance to do."

"What's that?"

"I've gotta gather wood for the clans' fires while I'm here. Also, back on the other side, I can't drive her Ford Mustang convertible to school for the rest of the semester."

"That doesn't sound too bad."

"You'll disagree after you've ridden in a convertible! Anyway, she's just being Grammie. She was harder on my dad, before he and my mom died. Did I ever tell you about the first day Grammie and my father met? She insisted on meeting him early on. So my mom brought him over to prove he's a proper trampler and all, that sort of thing."

"Huh." Jennifer tried to imagine the kind of boy *she* could bring home who would satisfy her mother *and* her father.

"So the evening's going well enough, but then Grammie puts a pile of venison on his plate. Of course, he doesn't eat it."

"No? Why not?" Jennifer loved venison.

"He was a vegetarian!"

"Oh? Oh." Jennifer giggled. "He was a weredragon? A trampler? And a vegetarian?"

Catherine's violet-crimson eyes rolled. "He told Grammie if bears can make it on berries and nuts, so can we. I've tried the diet myself. Made it about thirty-six hours before I gave it up. Killed about five of your grandpa's sheep on the next— Oh, Jennifer, I'm sorry. That was dumb. Stupid, stupid, stupid!" The trampler smacked herself over the horns with her tiny wing claw.

Jennifer wiped the scales under her eyes. "It's okay. I don't mind thinking of him. And it was a good story. The kind he'd tell."

* * *

As the evening stretched on, Crescent Valley changed. Jennifer generally didn't spend that much time here at once, so she spent some time with Catherine out among the moon elms, gawking at the shifts in nature around them.

While neither the light, nor shape, nor altitude of the moon changed, the crescent did slowly roll end over end around the horizon. Catherine told her it took a full day for it to complete a revolution through the sky.

"I haven't watched it for that long myself, of course," she said with a twinkle in her eye, "but this really cute dasher told me he'd gone to the amphitheater once, when no one else was around, and just laid back and watched it. He told me the moon was in endless motion, like nature, and friendship, and love . . ."

Jennifer started gagging. Catherine laughed.

"Yeah, and he probably would have come up with a few more poetic comparisons, but then Grammie Winona caught him rubbing his wing up against mine and sent him home with a stomp mark on his tail."

"Oh, look at the lichen! It was shifting again. It had changed from lavender to a deeper purple as they first set out for their walk, and now it was moving to a deep crimson that matched Catherine's irises.

As if on cue, some newolves far away howled a midnight chord in A minor, six times, from far away.

"Do you see them much?" A memory of the road not far from Grandpa's cabin, where she had seen her first newolf, made Jennifer sigh.

"Oh, the newolves? Not as much as I'd like. Grammie keeps me on a pretty short leash, and I'm not exactly allowed to go hunting, for obvious reasons."

"I'd like to see them up close someday," Jennifer sighed. "Really, really see them. But even before everyone here freaked out, my dad told me there were dragons who wouldn't look kindly on that. I guess he meant folks like Xavier Longtail."

Catherine hesitated a long moment, then finally brought it out: "Jennifer, do you think he'll—someone like that—do you think he'll ever change his mind? Accept you? Your family?"

"Translation: Will he try to smack me on the back of the head with his tail again before he sees the light?"

"Well . . . yeah."

Jennifer sighed. "I have no idea. I guess . . . I'd like to think . . . he and those like him can accept me if for no other reason than they loved my grandfather. You can't tell me Xavier Longtail isn't capable of love. And if Grandpa Crawford meant anything to him, my dad and I should."

Catherine sighed after a moment. "Sure. That sounds right. It's a logical way of looking at it."

Sure, Jennifer thought. *Logical.*

Early the next morning, as the lichen turned pale yellow, their elders arrived. Neither wanted to talk much.

"It's been a long meeting." An exhausted Jonathan yawned as Winona sleepily offered him an extra patch of straw and wool to collapse on. "Can I fill you in when I wake up?"

"If you think you can get to sleep with a beaststalker

battleshout going off every three minutes, be my guest," Jennifer said with a smile.

"Ugh, all right. Well, it's official: You don't have to do the Fifty Trials."

"That only makes sense!" Jennifer was a bit insulted that it had taken so long for a Blaze of weredragons to come up with that.

"But," he continued, "you are not completely off the hook. As a substitute for that ancient tradition, you have been given a charge."

"Let me guess . . ."

He nodded. "You must find your grandfather's murderer, and bring him to justice. The elders believe Evangelos could be a threat to all weredragons, not just my family. By facing down this enemy, you will prove your loyalty and worth to the skeptics among the Blaze."

"Skeptics like that annoying prig Xavier?"

"Jennifer."

"Dad!"

"Jennifer."

"He totally is."

"Jennifer."

"All right, all right . . . dazzle me. Tell me how he's respected and has had a hard life, blah-blah, I'm already bored."

"Xavier is a respected voice in the Blaze," Jonathan said. "He has had a hard life. His distaste for the unknown, and suspicion of strangers, is rooted in massacres like Pinegrove. It will be hard for him, and those like him, to completely accept you. But they may yet come around."

"If I stop Evangelos."

"If you stop Evangelos. Of course, I'm free to help you. You and I are under the same shroud of suspicion. Many of my fellow elders will feel better about me as well, after this is done."

For some reason, that made her laugh. She startled herself . . . but it felt good all the same.

"You don't have to accept," Jonathan hurried to add. "If you would rather, you can leave Evangelos to me and your mother, and our peers will accept the Fifty Trials as evidence of your trustworthiness. It's your choice."

She sat and thought for a moment. "What do you think I should do?"

Her father's face strained slightly, and his silver eyes bulged. A wing claw clutched at his scaled chest as he tried to keep his balance. "Can't . . . think straight . . . teenaged daughter . . . asking me for advice . . . everything . . . going dark . . ."

She sighed. It was good, at least, to see him joke again. "Really, Dad. I don't know what to do. I'm not sure I can face . . . well, on the other hand, I don't want to leave you and Mom—"

"Whatever you do," he interrupted with sudden seriousness, "do not do it because you're worried about your mother and me. We can take care of ourselves. If you want to face down Evangelos with us, okay. If you don't think you're ready, then you should prepare for the trials instead. And there'll be no shame there. If Evangelos has half of his mother's powers, he will be a force. We can't be sure of his age, as I said before; but he's probably older than you. And you can protest all you want—but you are still technically, legally, biologically, and physically a child."

"Wow. What every teenager loves to hear. Why did I ask for your advice again?"

"Regardless, your reasons must be for *yourself*."

She nodded and realized the decision was easier than she thought. "I'm ready," she said. "I want to face him. With you and Mom."

He examined her face, as if looking for some sign of uncertainty. He didn't find it. "Okay. Let's get back to the farm later today and meet your mother there. But first," he finished as he slumped on a bed, "I need to sleep off that meeting!"

"*Do you think* you can do it?" Catherine's face glowed with amazement when Jennifer told her about Evangelos and the agreement with the Blaze. They were whispering in a corner of the cave, far enough from their sleeping elders to avoid disturbing them. "From what you've told me, your half brother sounds kind of horrifying."

"I don't have a lot of choice," Jennifer pointed out. "He'll be coming for me soon. I'd rather learn everything I can about him so I'm ready when the time comes. You know, the best defense is a good offense, and all that. Besides . . . I want to stay close to my parents."

Catherine grinned. "I bet *that* felt weird to say."

"For their own protection!" Jennifer knew it was more than that, but she insisted. "If our family's going to stay together, that means being outside Crescent Valley. Outside Crescent Valley, Dad's vulnerable. I'd feel better if I were there to help Mom with Dad. Besides, this way I can keep on eye on Skip, too. After all, he *is* Dianna's second kid."

"Skip's your boyfriend, right? I hope I can meet him some-day. I don't think I've ever met a werachnid."

"Well, I don't know if he's my *boyfriend* . . . he's my friend who's, you know, also a boy . . ."

"You talk about him all the time. And aren't you two go-ing to that dance together at your school?"

It occurred to Jennifer that the Halloween dance in two days was back on, since Winona Brandfire and her peers had set aside the Fifty Trials. She supposed she should be happy, but too much had happened recently.

"I guess. But I still don't think of him as my boyfriend. Not yet. It's just so complicated right now."

"Boy, talk about complicated!"

It was the following morning, the day before Halloween, and Jennifer's first chance to talk to Skip at Winoka High since they had learned about their startling ties to Evangelos. The two of them were walking together down the hall to his-tory class.

"Yeah. This is weird. I don't know about you, but I liked the idea of being an only child a heck of a lot better than this."

"You can say that again," Jennifer said fervently.

"Also, I think your mom hates me."

The change of subject startled her. "What makes you say that?"

"She didn't say a word to me on the way home from your cabin. Probably not a big fan of spiders, eh?"

"Oh . . ." Jennifer coughed. *Awkward!* "She's just like that sometimes."

"She could have at least put on the radio."

Jennifer fingered the necklace Skip had given her, desperate to change the subject. "So you think your own mom's trips around the world, studying native cultures, seeking magical artifacts . . . you think she was trying to find a way to locate Evangelos? You know, bring him back?"

He shrugged. "I try not to think much about Mom anymore."

Jennifer didn't know what to say.

He gave an uncomfortable smile. "You're right, this is weird. The two of us having the same half brother."

"Yeah. Weird. It's not like we're related or anything, but . . ." Jennifer stalled at the expression of horror on Skip's face and decided on a rapid change of topic. "Well, it's just weird. Um, do you still want to do the Halloween dance tomorrow night?"

Yes, the Halloween dance! Jennifer was glad now she had never gotten up the nerve to cancel on Skip. "Sure. I mean, if you still want to."

"Okay. What are you going as?"

Skip couldn't stifle a dark chuckle. "Ah, the possibilities! I could win a lot of friends around here, and go as a fanatic warrior bent on killing anything with more than two legs . . ." His expression turned murky. "But I imagine I'll come as something truer to myself."

"Oh, don't!" Jennifer reeled at the thought of Skip coming as a huge spider. It would remind her too much of . . . what? His father? Or who Skip really was, and would be someday?

"What—you want me to be something I'm not?"

She wasn't sure how to answer that at first—he sounded

quite offended. "I guess all I'm saying is, why do we have to be ourselves on Halloween? Isn't the point to be something *else*? I mean, *I'm* not going as a dragon." *Or a beaststalker,* she added to herself. Again, she felt a cold rush as she remembered the secret she still hid from this boy. When and how was she going to tell him the truth about herself and her mother? And once she told him, wouldn't he guess pretty easily how his father had died?

"So what will you go as?" He was still clearly angry. "A faerie princess? A ballerina? Or—"

"Susan!"

Never had her best friend been a more welcome sight. Susan's dark curls bobbed as she jogged toward them both. "You guys will never guess who asked me to the Halloween dance!"

Skip steamed at the interruption, but Jennifer began guessing immediately. "Eddie? Bob Jarkmand? Mr. Slider?"

"No, no, and ewww! No, it was Gerry Stowe. You know, from geometry class? Oh, he is sooo dreamy . . . !"

"Dreamy?" Skip's voice dripped with disgust.

Susan looked him straight in the eye. "Yeah, *dreamy*, as in, 'I'll be *dreaming* about him tonight.' "

"Susan!" Jennifer felt herself redden as she let out a giggle. She could tell Skip was only getting angrier, but she couldn't help herself.

The class bell rang, ending their conversation. Susan skittered away, while Skip walked quickly a half-step ahead of Jennifer as they continued on to history class. An air of discontent hung in the air between them.

She pulled his arm right before they entered the classroom.

"I'm sorry I suggested you shouldn't go as . . . well, as whatever you want. Dress however you like, Skip. I'm just glad we're going together."

"Yeah." He rubbed his temples, not quite ready to end this argument. Finally, he stared back down the hallway. "Okay. I suppose I shouldn't be in a rush. To change, that is. But I'm looking forward to it. Becoming who I am. Aunt Tavia tells me . . ." He paused and seemed to realize suddenly Jennifer was still standing there. "Anyway. I'm looking forward to it."

"Come on." Jennifer took his hand with a smirk. "History awaits."

"*Have you ever been* to a beaststalker trial?"

"No." Jennifer speared a piece of chicken off her dinner plate with her fork, stabbed the fork into her salad bowl to add some lettuce, and jammed the food into her mouth. She spat some of it out as she continued, "Sounds like wild fun. Let me guess: At the end, someone gets executed."

"Six someones, in this case." Elizabeth spoke with clear distaste. "But more likely run out of town than executed. The Winoka city council—which is really a group of beaststalker elders—has called upon some of the town's new residents to answer some questions tonight. Apparently, they are learning about Evangelos, too. A dark shape fitting his description has been seen multiple times, lurking about the fringes of town. They see him as a threat to the town, and they're suspicious of anyone who just got here."

"Hmph." Jennifer swallowed her mouthful of food. "So

much for protecting innocent people, eh?" She turned to her father. Jonathan Scales was uncharacteristically quiet as he ate. "What's wrong, Dad?"

"The Stowes." He ravaged his salad. "You remember Martin? His grandson goes to your school?"

"Sure."

"They're among the suspects." He let some of his exterior calm slip. "Of all the . . . ! He can't see well enough to walk down the street without hanging on to Gerry! And there are others." Her father spat. "There are always others, when beast-stalkers are involved. Always suspects. Always someone to distrust, intimidate, push around. This is what it comes to, with these people."

"You mean people like Xavier?" It was out before Jennifer could stop herself. But she was still sore about her treatment before the Blaze in Crescent Valley.

Jonathan sighed. "You're right, of course. Some weredragons are no better. We need more people who can reach out to other beings. Your mother. You."

"And Skip?"

He sighed again, a gusty wheeze. "I hope so. Did he share anything more about his mother or Evangelos with you? I didn't want to press him up at the cabin, but I was hoping for information more recent than twenty years ago. Where did Dianna Wilson look for her son? Did she say anything about what he was like, what he might be capable of?"

"Sorry, Dad. He hasn't said much. I guess I haven't pressed him too hard."

Elizabeth sighed impatiently and tapped her fork on her plate. "Well, you'll have to start!"

Jennifer fumed. *She really doesn't like him. Why?* Was it because of what his father did last year?

"Elizabeth . . ."

"Fine, Jonathan. Jennifer, I'm sorry. I know this boy means something to you. But you have to realize he may be in danger, too. The more information we share, the better off we'll be."

"Information like: You and I are beaststalkers?"

She slammed her silverware down again. "I don't see how that will get us anywhere, Jennifer, other than to alienate Skip and his family."

"Darling, the flatware . . ."

"We have to tell them eventually," Jennifer interrupted, slamming her own fork down. "He deserves to know how his father died!"

"This is not the best time, honey." Jonathan's voice was steady, but wary. "Maybe after we've taken care of Evangelos—"

"After we've taken care of Evangelos! Sure, and then the next creep will come along, and we'll need Skip's help again, so we'll keep waiting. Then maybe his aunt will go nutty, and we'll have to kill her—so whatever we do, let's not tell Skip again. Then maybe—"

"Please, Jennifer!" Her father was suddenly close to tears, which shocked her. "I know how the boy feels. I've lost my father, too. And I've lost my friend, and I might just lose my wife and daughter if I can't get them to cooperate with me, and each other!"

With that, he kicked his chair back from the dinner table and stormed out of the room. Phoebe, who had been lying in wait for scraps, scrambled to get out of his path.

The two of them sat in silence for a few moments. Then Elizabeth reached out and put her hand over Jennifer's. "Honey . . ."

"I know, Mom. That was stupid. I'll go apologize."

"No, not that. Though that's a good idea. I'm actually glad the two of us are alone for a moment. I want to talk to you about something."

"*Now?* On top of everything else? You have something *new* to share?"

"Well, it's about the trial, actually. I have to go there to-night."

For a moment, worry about herself was obliterated in the horror she felt for her mother's safety. "What, they suspect you, too?"

"No, that's not it. I'm going because I want to. I can't stand this anymore. You see, Jennifer, I keep holding out hope. Hope that we will stop this ridiculous conflict. Hope that beaststalkers will turn to pursuits like medicine and science, focus our energies on killing diseases and healing people. For a while, it seemed like Winoka had settled down, maybe even begun to raise a generation that wouldn't remember the old ways.

"But Evangelos has reawakened something awful. The possibility that something that blends weredragon and werachnid is out there—it's a frightening threat to some, a compelling hunt to others, and a flat-out abomination to everyone else. But just about every beaststalker in this town agrees it must die at any cost."

"So what does this have to do with you and the trial?"

Elizabeth straightened. "I have to try to persuade my order to stop the witch hunt. I have to try to convince them there's a better way to find and stop Evangelos. I must give them *hope* again."

Jennifer could see there was no arguing with the woman. "What does this have to do with me?"

"Well, your father's expecting to change with the crescent moon tonight, and he'll be on his way to the farm. You could go with him if you want, but I'd rather you stayed with me."

"Why?"

Her mother cocked her head. "Why, to help me, of course. In case things get ugly."

Jennifer sighed. "Mom, tell me this. Has there ever been a beaststalker trial that *didn't* get ugly?"

"Probably not."

"Fabulous. Thanks for the heritage, Mom."

"You're welcome. Wear something nice."

CHAPTER 9

The Beaststalker Trial

"You know what I hate?" Jennifer hissed to her mother. They were at the Winoka city hall, a beautiful domed, historical landmark made of red brick with white brick accents. The council chambers were expansive, with intricate mahogany woodwork adorning the doorways, ceiling, and corners. More than a hundred people—all presumably beaststalkers—filled the room from wall to wall. In retrospect, Jennifer was glad her mother made her change into a fabulous crimson and navy wool sweater-skirt combination. It would make reaching her daggers much easier. "I hate meetings. Honestly, who goes to these things, Mom? Dragons have their stupid Blazes, beast-stalkers have their stupid councils. I'll bet somewhere right now there's a dozen or so big old spiders spinning webs together in a musty cave, talking and talking and talking . . ." She flapped her hands at each other like fake mouths to demonstrate.

"Hush," her mother said simply.

"Fine." Jennifer crossed her arms and stared at the ceiling. Some of the mahogany carvings up there stood out a bit. Jennifer had never noticed these before. She'd only been in this building once or twice before, and who examined woodwork? Now that she looked at them carefully, she recognized them as scenes of unspeakable viciousness between soldiers in flowing robes and hideous monsters. In one corner, a three-headed dragon was speared through the belly. In another, a giant scorpion had a lance poking out of one of its wild eyes. In still another, droves of wolves were being driven from a town ablaze.

"Nice decor," she observed.

Elizabeth gave her a gentle but firm pinch on the arm. *"Hush."*

Jennifer tried turning her attention to the seven men and women who sat in overstuffed chairs behind a massive raised, curved table at the front of the room. Every one of them was wearing a ceremonial white robe with black embroidery in a pattern not unlike chain link. Every one of them had a sword on the table in front of them.

And every one of them was glaring at Jennifer—no one more so than the man at the far right end, Hank Blacktooth.

"Mr. Blacktooth is on the city council?" Jennifer had never heard Eddie mention this. She sneered at the large, red-faced man. "Who the hell elected *him*?"

"Hush!" This command, and the subsequent smack on the back of the head, came off a bit harder than Jennifer thought completely necessary.

The woman sitting at the center of the table stood up, sword in hand. She was old enough to be Jennifer's grandmother, but she had obvious strength in her limbs. Her hair was long, white, and flowing. Her irises were nearly as white as the rest of her eyes, giving her dark pupils an unnaturally focused appearance. Grasping the blade of her sword, the woman banged the hilt upon the table in a clear call for silence.

Jennifer didn't know her or any of the other beaststalkers sitting at the table with Hank Blacktooth. Looking around the room, she thought she recognized a parent here or there. Wendy Blacktooth stood rigidly in a back corner. She spared Jennifer a quick, disdainful glance before she returned her attention to the council. Eddie wasn't around—nor anyone close to Jennifer's own age. *But then who in the next generation will carry on this fine democracy,* she snickered to herself.

The woman at the head of the room did not smile as she spoke. "I call this council to order. Bring in the visitors."

Visitors? Jennifer bristled at the word. *They* live *in this town.* Her foot tapped impatiently as six people walked into the room, led by two beaststalkers carrying ceremonial axes.

Well, five people walked. The sixth wheeled in with a gentle *whirr* of a motor.

"Mr. Slider?" Jennifer could barely contain herself. Her geometry teacher looked calm, but she could make out a slight defiance in the way he straightened his back and sniffed at the council. He and the other "visitors"—Gerry Stowe and his frail grandfather among them—all stopped at the front of the room, facing the council and their imposing table.

The woman narrowed her white eyes. "You six are hereby—"

"Excuse me." Mr. Slider's voice came out crisp and clear in the quiet chambers. "I've honored the summons I received for this meeting. A scientist's natural curiosity, I suppose. But first things first. It would be polite to introduce yourself, and then tell me why I'm here tonight."

Jennifer smiled at the man's slightly patronizing tone. *Just like a teacher.*

The older woman was not amused. "I am Glorianne Seabright, the mayor of this town. Tonight, Edmund Slider, this council will determine your true identity and your fitness for residency here in Winoka."

Mr. Slider actually chuckled. "I'm sorry, Mayor Seabright, but I don't see how my identity or residency are really any of your business."

His wheelchair turned toward the exit, but before he could move forward one of the beaststalkers who had led them in stepped in his way and slammed the handle of his axe on the floor.

The geometry teacher slicked back his thinning blond hair with manicured fingernails as he stared up at the expressionless guard with contempt. "You feel mighty brave, stopping a cripple in his tracks, don't you?"

"Mr. Slider," Mayor Seabright's expression hardened. "Our town has a proud history . . ."

Jennifer didn't really hear what the mayor said next, because the blood was swimming in her ears. *A proud history! You came in and uprooted an entire town of weredragons, wiped away any trace of them, and settled down as if this had been your land all along!*

". . . as you can imagine, the emergence of this unknown creature has put quite a stress on everyone here. The process may seem distasteful to you, but it is for the protection of the town. The security of Winoka's residents is our highest priority. If we deem you fit to remain here, you will come to appreciate these traditions."

"That's highly comforting, Your Honor," Mr. Slider managed through gritted teeth. His dark gaze did not leave the guard standing in front of his wheelchair. "I can hardly wait until the proud day when, as a vetted and approved resident of Winoka, I get to watch you humiliate other people instead of me. A fine tradition, indeed!"

Jennifer grinned and chewed her tongue with satisfaction. Mr. Slider had rapidly ascended from "okay teacher" to "hero."

The mayor motioned to the guard, who took a step back. "Mr. Slider, there is no need for rudeness. If our proceedings offend, you may leave. But I warn you, this town faces a serious and mysterious threat. Your words and actions here can only hurt your reputation. A school teacher like yourself—accountable to the public—may want to show more respect."

Mr. Slider's wheelchair, which had begun *whirring* once more toward the exit, stopped and turned to face the impressive table. The geometry teacher nibbled his lower lip as his black eyes bored into each of them. "Your Honor. Council members. I do show you, and the people of this town respect. Every day. When I sit in front of your children and try to teach them logic and reason, better than their parents obviously have."

At this, Jennifer wanted to stand up and cheer. Fortunately, she restrained herself.

Mayor Seabright watched Mr. Slider as he wheeled himself out of the council chambers, then turned to those who

remained. "I do not recommend you follow Mr. Slider's example," she told them. "The town of Winoka does not look
fondly upon malcontents."

Nobody else moved.

"As I was saying," the mayor continued, "you are called
here tonight to account for yourselves. We want to know who
you are—who you *really* are—and how long you intend to
stay here within this town's borders." Her white eyes thoughtfully scanned the prospects. "Mr. and Ms. Cheran, we'll start
with you."

A young couple stepped forward from the rest. Jennifer
couldn't see much of the woman, who wore a long, pale green
flowing robe and veil over her head, face, and body. But the
man was hard to miss—nearly seven feet tall, with a dark
brown complexion and heavily muscled arms underneath a
flannel shirt.

"Angus Cheran here, Your Honor." He was surprisingly
soft-spoken for such a giant, with a slight Scottish accent.
"And my wife, Delores. We don't want trouble. Rumor has it
this town is full of soldiers of some sort, though we haven't
seen anything like that. That's why we came here.

" You see"—he leaned in confidentially, as if everyone in the
room couldn't hear him—"we've come a long ways to get here,
because we thought Winoka might be the safest place to be."

Mayor Seabright squinted at him, betraying no emotion.
"How so?"

Angus looked around nervously. "Well, over the past few
years, Delores and I have noticed some fairly frightening things
around us. Especially when the moon's just right. We checked
around, and there's talk of weird monsters coming out and

breathing fire and sucking the blood out of other people. Delores herself here saw a huge flying beast one night, a bat the
size of a small truck. Gave her a terrible scare. The next week,
something she won't talk about much—she'd only tell me it
had 'lots of legs,' and was the size of a full-grown man—
cornered her in our own house. It shrieked at her like a demon,
she says, and ever since she's been deaf. She doesn't talk much
normally; but if you'll give me a moment, Your Honor . . ."

He nudged her and made motions with his hands that Jennifer recognized for sign language, but the veiled head would
only shake back and forth timidly.

"That's all right, Delores. Anyhow, a friend of a friend
told us, if you're afraid of monsters and such, there's one
town you can go to: Winoka, Minnesota, U.S. of A. So we're
here. If we've caused any trouble—"

"Of course not." Mayor Seabright raised her hand. Her
face remained stoic. "Part of Winoka's proud history is its
legacy of sanctuary for those seeking refuge from monsters
you've seen. I do not believe this council"—she said this without even looking at the other members—"needs to inconve-
nience you any further. You are welcome here. Thank you for
coming out tonight."

Angus Cheran nodded, mumbled some thanks, and gently
guided his wife out of the chambers. He seemed happy
enough, but the woman at his side walked as if she were carrying a heavy burden. Jennifer supposed the sight of a dragon or
enormous spider, to someone not expecting it, must seem
monstrous indeed.

"We shall move on," the mayor announced. "Martin and
Gerry Stowe . . ."

With his grandson's help, Martin Stowe took a few steps forward, tapping his cane on the hardwood floor until he was standing squarely before the council.

"Begging your pardon, Your Honor," Martin began. "I'll speak for both of us, if you don't mind, as my grandson is a minor."

Jennifer noticed some members of the council had the decency to appear embarrassed at the scene unfolding in front of them. At this point, however, no one was willing to do anything to stop it.

Except her mother.

"Your Honor!"

Mayor Seabright stiffened. "Dr. Georges. This council needs no public comment tonight."

"I still must speak."

The mayor turned from side to side, as though gauging the patience of the council members. It was clear from his scowl where Hank Blacktooth stood on the matter, but the others' expressions were more ambiguous.

"Dr. Georges, this council holds deep respect for your lineage, which dates back to Saint George the Dragon Slayer himself. It also appreciates your accomplishments as a warrior in your youth, and as a doctor in more recent years. These facts encourage us to overlook your . . . recently discovered associations."

Jennifer felt all of the faces in the room turn to her. Her muscles tensed, and she was grateful her father was safe in Crescent Valley. Was this where the fight would begin?

Her fingers twitched on her thighs as she stared back at a fuming Hank Blacktooth. *Him first, if I can reach him.*

The mayor continued. "But our patience wears thin. Speak briefly, and be done with it."

"Thank you." Elizabeth raised her chin and spoke to the entire room. "These proceedings must not continue!" There was a restless hubbub about the room, but she continued. "Please, by now you must see the futility of your actions. You drag a public school teacher in a wheelchair in front of you and tell him to watch his back. You scare frightened people who cannot understand the creatures emerging around them, and indulge their fears and encourage their helplessness. You now have marched an elderly man in front of you, who struggles with blindness and the care of an orphaned boy. What more must you do?"

"We must question them," the mayor replied.

"Question them about what? Who they 'really' are? Shall I as a doctor give him medical tests, to be certain he is really blind? Shall I run a DNA test on his grandchild, to be sure he hasn't abducted him?"

"Do not mock the traditions of our people!" This was Hank Blacktooth, who slammed the table with a fist and stood up redder, angrier, and hairier than Jennifer had ever seen him. "You have no standing here! You consort with the very beasts we must extinguish!"

This unleashed a free-for-all of conversation around the room, which the mayor stamped out with the hilt of her sword. "Dr. Georges is not on trial here today," she told the room sternly. "We will hear what she has to say!"

"All I ask is for this council to seize an opportunity," Elizabeth continued. "This beast we all track—this Evangelos, as

I have come to learn his name—is a threat not just to us, but to your so-called enemies as well. While he is a fearsome opponent, I believe we can overcome him—if we seek help, instead of living in fear and suspicion."

"Where do you suggest we find this help?" Mayor Seabright looked like she had already swallowed the answer and didn't care for the taste.

"I ask this city for no more trust than you have already given me for years. End these proceedings. Let me and my family handle this. This Evangelos appears focused on us already, and we're in the best position to handle him. We feel we can help him, rather than kill him . . ."

"What do you mean by 'this creature is already focused' on you?" This question came from a different council member, a younger man with short red hair, freckles on his cheeks, and a skeptical look.

"I mean Evangelos has left messages—messages that appear to target my husband."

A new round of murmurs shot through the room. This time the mayor did not try to quell them. Jennifer could see the surprise on her face, as well as the faces of the other council members.

Hank Blacktooth was the first to speak out again. "So are we to understand that your husband, a demon who shifts with the crescent moon, has attracted a still greater threat to this town?"

"That is not exactly—"

"I have a better proposal," Mr. Blacktooth interrupted. "Let us banish you, and him, and your brood from this town.

Then this thing will not bother us, and it can kill you all quietly, out in the wild, perhaps. We need never concern ourselves with it, or you, or your traitorous ways again!"

This spurred quite a bit of excited shouting back and forth from the other council members, and the dozens of beaststalkers throughout the room. The vast majority of voices clearly agreed with this horrible plan, but Jennifer heard one or two voices argue against it.

She turned to look at the mayor and saw something astonishing: Tears were trickling down the old woman's stern face. The mayor and Elizabeth silently stared at each other while debate raged around them, as if they were communicating without words.

Finally, the mayor had enough. With a single sharp stroke of her sword's hilt onto the table and a piercing look from her mysterious eyes, she brought order to the room.

"That will do. Councilmember Blacktooth, I see your heart is as cold and forbidding as ever. Were it not for your own distinguished heritage, I would remove you from this council for your evil words this evening."

Hank Blacktooth began to protest, but the mayor flipped the end of her sword and smashed the blade into the table. "*I am not done speaking yet.* Plainly, this town has strong feelings about the distinguished Dr. Georges. Too few of us, apparently, remember all she has done for this town. Our forgetfulness is a blemish on our souls.

"That said, we have a duty to the townspeople. We are not all beaststalkers here—some, like the Cherans we just met tonight, are here for protection.

"Therefore, rather than completely reject either Dr.

Georges's proposal or councilmember Blacktooth's, I will accept parts of both. Elizabeth Georges's, you are given the task of tracking down this beast you call Evangelos. Dispose of him as you see fit, as long as he does not threaten this town. Should you achieve your goal by the end of this year, this city will embrace your family. Should you fail . . . we will purge you from this town, as we purged the rest of your husband's kind."

Her simple raised hand was enough to cut short the protests and/or cheers that began across the room. "While you take on this quest, this council will remove itself from the investigation and suspend these proceedings." She turned to the Stowes, and to the last man who had not spoken yet. "Mr. Martin Stowe. Mr. Rune Whisper. You are released from this council's business, for the moment. Do not attempt to speak to others of what you have heard tonight. Please make yourself available to Dr. Georges, should she need to question you. We are adjourned."

With the sound of her sword's hilt hitting the table, a conversation flooded the room, now louder than ever. Jennifer tried to take it in, but she could barely make any of it out. Some people thought the mayor's judgment was fair; others felt it was an insult to either her mother or beaststalker tradition.

The Stowes appeared relieved and made their way slowly through the crowd together. Jennifer heard the rap of the cane fade as they left the room.

Almost unseen, except by Jennifer, was the last man the mayor had mentioned—what had his name been? Rune Whisper? Tall, pale, and gaunt, wearing a pine green suit that seemed one or two sizes too big, the middle-aged man gave a half-nervous, half-arrogant glance about the room before darting out as fast as his legs could carry him. Before he even made it through the doorway, Jennifer lost track of him—had he just vanished?

"Come on," Elizabeth said wearily, tugging on her arm. "Let's go home."

INTERLUDE

Evolution

The outskirts of Winoka, like everywhere else across Minnesota in October, got dark early. A few family farms had tractors with bright headlights working late to finish the harvest. But beyond that, light was scarce in this part of town. Noise was even scarcer deep in the groves and away from the highways.

Exactly the way Evangelos liked it —dark and quiet. A good environment for wrestling with these unusual emotions.

First, fear. It had been a long time, and in another dimension, since Evangelos had felt fear. Before the prey had grown and turned to hunter. But in this world, there was something to fear—these beaststalkers. Going to their gathering had been a huge mistake, and nearly a disastrous one. Unfortunately, curiosity had won out.

The second emotion was relief. Evangelos knew the emotion from the trails of memories traced from Australia, through dozens of other countries across this world, all the way to this town of Winoka. It was a feeling not far from the surge of blood to the head that came with victory, and a kill. Relief. What Evangelos felt when Father's new wife spoke up and halted the proceedings. Up until that time, it was increasingly likely a fight would break out, and too much would be revealed. But now, that moment could wait. If it came at all.

Relief. A gift of sorts. Did that mean this woman deserved some sort of . . . gift in return? Evangelos pushed the thought down deep. Gifts like mercy were illusions of this world, not anything real. There were no allies here.

No friends.

No friends? Then what was a person who did not want to kill you or hurt you? Who wanted to help you?

This unbidden voice brought up the third and most uncomfortable of all these new emotions—doubt. This doubt, this other voice—it was an unfortunate side effect of how Evangelos lived. Learning more about the people who lived here provided a better disguise, and better intelligence—all the better to hurt Father—but it also meant more memories, more thoughts, more voices inside, more of these new emotions.

The girl—the new child of Father, the sister to Evangelos—she brought out the most of all three emotions. Fear, because she had come closer than she probably realized to saving their grandfather, and Evangelos hoped this young stalker-dragon never learned that. Relief, because Evangelos had gotten away, and was assured of greater strength next time they met. And doubt . . . why?

Because she's your sister.

Quiet!

Evangelos craved quiet, wanted the voices silenced. Only quiet could nurture the sorrow, the rage, close the gaping hole where a soul should have been.

This girl was not a sister. This girl was what Evangelos should have been—what was taken away by an incompetent mother and an uncaring father.

Mother was lost. But Father . . .

Father will pay.

So close, now. Evangelos had spent enough time in Winoka now to learn which house was the Scales house. And Father's work took him to the hospital often, near his new wife. But Evangelos still had not really seen him properly, never been close enough to read memories. Father moved quickly and furtively from house to work, and flew quickly to the cabin when in dragon shape. He was being careful, that was for certain. And of course, so was Evangelos.

Spindly claws clenched at the thought of Father. The stench of a twisted dimension swirled off the black scales. It was almost laughable, this name. Evangelos. "Messenger of light."

There was a message, all right. But light had nothing to do with it. Delivery was forthcoming.

Miles away, several farmers stopped cold suddenly in their fields. The scream wasn't something you heard: It was something felt in the blood.

CHAPTER 10

The Halloween Dance

"Oh, Jennifer, you look like an *angel*!"

"I *am* an angel, dork."

"Oh, right." Susan chuckled. "How about me? Is this crown on right?"

"Yeah. I'm surprised you chose this outfit."

"What?" Alarmed, Susan spun around to check herself, making her brown curls dance. "Is there a tear in the gown? Is the color wrong? Do I look fat?"

"No, it's not that. It's just that a princess is so . . ."

"So what?"

"Well, *girlish*." Jennifer tried to soften the blow with a small smile.

Susan frowned. "I *am* a girl. And hey—angels are girlish, too, you know! Look at you, in your girly robes and your pretty platinum hair. Girly, girly, girly!"

Both of them burst out laughing.

Everyone had been more relaxed for some time, Jennifer mused as she admired Susan's makeup job. It had been three days since the beaststalker trial. Her parents had been conducting some initial research—but insisted Jennifer leave this stage to them, so she could focus on school and enjoy the dance. Even her mother, who still seemed ambivalent about Skip, had let Jennifer borrow some deep red lipstick and dark blue eye shadow.

"I just want to look my best for Gerry," Susan explained.

"You do." Jennifer knew how she felt.

"So do you, for Skip. This'll be great! Is your dad ready to take us there?"

"I don't think my dad's ready to take me anywhere," Jennifer guessed.

She was right. As soon as Jonathan saw his daughter in flowing white robes, full makeup, and teased curls, his face betrayed a quick but horrible fright.

"Oh, come on, Dad. It's just for a Halloween dance."

He nodded at Susan as she ducked out of the room for a moment to freshen up. "Well, congratulations. You've scared the hell out of me. Honestly, Jennifer. You look beautiful, but I wish you didn't look so much like . . ."

"An angel?"

"I was going to say *bride*. Honestly, I'm not ready for this. Couldn't you have worn black, or red?"

She cocked an eye. "Red? You want your teenaged daughter to go to a school dance dressed as a devil instead?"

He thought about this for a moment. "Right. Scratch that. In the car."

* * *

Winoka High's gymnasium was decked out with all sorts of spooky and festive touches—cobwebs in the doorways, strobe lights pulsating in the halls, and ghastly winged shapes hanging from the ceiling. While Susan spotted Gerry right away—he was in a businessman's suit, which didn't seem horribly festive to Jennifer—it took a while to find Skip.

After pushing through a few clusters of teenagers, Jennifer finally found him, not far from the punch bowl, and she grinned. He grinned back.

He was dressed as a dragon.

"I couldn't find electric blue," he apologized, turning a bit. "But the store had this nice dark red one. I thought you'd like it." He flapped his cotton-and-wire-stuffed wings, and waved his cloth tail back and forth.

"I love it." She giggled. "You look great."

His green-blue eyes shone. "*You* look great. I mean, really great."

"Thanks." She felt her face flush.

He stepped forward and took her hand. "I'm glad we could do this. I mean, I'm glad the past few weeks have been pretty quiet. I mean, with Evangelos, and your father. I mean . . ."

"I know what you mean." She nodded.

Fortunately, the disc jockey turned on the stereo at that moment and gave them both a chance to talk about something else. They began with music, and then soccer, and then school teachers and classes.

"Art's not so bad, because I've always been into doing charcoal sketches."

"Yeah. The stuff you have up all over your room is really great."

"Thanks. Susan's not too good at it; her trees come out looking like broccoli. She says she likes sculpture better; we start that next semester."

"Our art class began with sculpture. It's pretty cool! You'll like it. Speaking of Susan, why did she pick such a girly princess outfit?"

"I *know* . . . !"

As they talked, it amazed Jennifer how easily the conversation came. They had chatted every day at school for a year, and seen each other on and off during the summer. But it was always easier and easier to talk to Skip.

She felt a brief, wistful air as she remembered this was how she used to talk with Eddie Blacktooth.

Pushing that thought aside, she was just about to ask Skip to dance when she caught his eye straying over her shoulder. She spun around, and her heart sank.

Bob Jarkmand and four or five other boys were standing there, dressed in a variety of solider and knight costumes. Bob, in full camouflage gear and makeup, was in front of them all. Jennifer was startled to find she only came up to his shoulders, which seemed to grow directly out of his thick neck.

Right behind his enormous left arm was Eddie.

Her lips tightened. "What?"

"Your family's brought a lot of trouble to this town," Bob shouted over the relentless, echoing dance music.

Jennifer guessed the other boys here were probably also young beaststalkers in training. She also realized Bob or Eddie could easily spill her beaststalker secret to Skip, right here and now. She needed to change the subject, fast.

"Thanks for the update. How's your jaw?"

Skip snorted at the memory of Jennifer laying Bob out with a single punch last year. The noise got the group's attention.

"You got something you wanna say, *Francis*?" Bob took a step toward Skip. "You know, you've got some nerve coming here tonight wearing a costume like that. My great-uncle died fighting a dragon."

"Yeah? Well, I'm sure I've got an ancestor who died after fighting someone with really bad acne, but you don't see me crying about *your* mask."

Jennifer stopped Bob's punch, grasping his fist in her hand before he even swung. "Don't." She swallowed hard and tried not to show it.

"Come on, Bob." This was Eddie now, who had looked unhappy for the duration of this conversation. "He's not worth it."

"That's a great endorsement of a friend you used to hang out with last year," Jennifer snapped. She shoved Bob's fist back into Eddie's stomach. "Do yourself and the rest of us a favor, Eddie. Stop moping behind stronger people's shoulders. Stand up for something."

The slender, brown-haired boy actually crumpled, his face and posture falling in shame and resentment. When he looked back up, Jennifer barely recognized him anymore. Flushed and snarling with anger, he looked startlingly like his father. The words came out in a flood.

"You never appreciated me! My parents told me you were

no good! They told me there was something weird about you! They told me you'd be a lousy friend! You and your family deserve what you're going to get!"

Nobody even saw Skip coming. Later on, Jennifer realized it must have been because he jumped *over* Bob. Before she could react, his maroon dinosaur shape dropped as if coming down from the rafters, right on top of Eddie. The two of them were a blur of browns and reds as they pounded away at each other.

"Don't you threaten Jennifer!" She heard Skip's voice, high and thin as the two boys rolled back and forth. The soft, fluffy plates along the back of Skip's costume swayed ferociously. "You stay away from her!"

"Get him off!" Bob shouted to the others. They all pressed forward to peel Skip off of Eddie. One of them reached back, and Jennifer saw the glint of a metal blade.

"HEY!"

Before she could even think to control it, the surge of adrenaline had changed her. Even if she hadn't felt the powerful ripple of muscle through her spine and seen the nose horn emerge in front of her eyes, she would have been able to tell her new shape from the sheer terror in the faces of the boys before her. None of them, it seemed, had actually seen a real, live dragon before. *Just stories from their parents,* she guessed.

"Put that away," she hissed with a forked tongue.

The boy who held a dagger in his hand was trembling too hard to do anything. Sweat beaded quickly on his forehead.

Sensing an advantage, Jennifer reared up, spread her wings, let a froth of smoke pour out of her nostrils, and stomped her right leg on the ground hard enough to make the glossy floorboards shake.

The dagger dropped into a slithering bed of black mambas.

"Don't eat me!" Jennifer couldn't tell if that plea came from the boy who had held the knife and was now curled up on the gym floor, or from Bob Jarkmand, who was on his hands and knees as if worshipping an angry god.

Eddie and Skip broke up quickly, scrambling to their feet and backing away slowly from Jennifer and each other. Skip regained his composure first—he had seen her in this shape, once before—but Eddie also soon straightened up, taking in Jennifer's form with a critical eye. It was almost as if he was looking for weaknesses.

Battle training from his parents, she told herself. It occurred to her Eddie looked far braver facing her down as a dragon than he had for months facing her down as the girl he betrayed.

Suddenly, a fire alarm went off and the gym's automatic sprinkler system activated.

"Oh, the smoke!" she muttered. Morphing quickly back to angel shape, she grabbed Skip's hand, shooed the snakes away, and headed for the back door. There wasn't a teacher at this school—not even Mr. Slider, she feared—who would look kindly upon what had happened here tonight.

"Evangelos is ours!" Eddie's voice pursued them through the drizzling water. He had never sounded more like his father. "That beast will die, just like you, your family, and your boyfriend!"

He's not *my boyfriend,* Jennifer thought irritably as she and Skip burst through the fire doors together, and escaped into the dry darkness under a half-moon.

But then again, his hand felt so right in hers.

*   *   *

"*I know, I know,* I'm in *huge* trouble!" She said this as she and Skip burst through the front door, startling her parents on the living room couch. Brass quintet music blared from the stereo system, and a gentle fire licked away at the fireplace. "Just let me explain!"

From her parents' expressions, she could tell two things right away. First, they had been enjoying a quiet evening without their teenaged daughter. *Ew!* And second, they had no idea what she was talking about.

"Never mind," she concluded, spinning out of the living room. "Come on, Skip. Let's go upstairs."

Later that evening, after Jonathan had driven Skip home and Elizabeth had helped Jennifer wipe off her ruined makeup, she told them what had happened at the dance. Their reaction stunned her.

"Okay," her mother said.

"Okay," her father said.

"Okay?!" Jennifer searched the room for a trap, a hidden camera, something.

"Jennifer, revealing yourself tonight may have been a bit reckless," Jonathan explained. "But most of the dangerous people in this town have already learned what you are. It sounds to us like you were protecting Skip. He's your boyfriend. You care about him."

"He's not—" Jennifer interrupted herself with a sigh. Okay, she *did* care about Skip. "So you're not mad at me? I mean, not everyone in that gym was a beaststalker. We were in a pretty dark corner, but I'm sure someone must have seen me when they shouldn't have."

Elizabeth shrugged. "It was a Halloween dance with costumes, the gym was dark, there was smoke, sprinklers were going off . . . who knows what people saw? Ordinary people have seen far clearer evidence of weredragons before and ignored it."

"I wouldn't make a habit of it," Jonathan cautioned. "But there are so many other things happening now, this isn't the sort of thing we can hammer you on. Your mother and I are actually more disappointed that your time with Skip was ruined. We had hoped the dance would help you relax a bit. Did you have any fun at all?"

"At first. After Susan went off, Skip and I— Oh gosh, Susan! Dad, we gotta go pick her up!"

"Yeah, I saw what happened." Susan didn't seem too put off, Jennifer noticed as they sat together in the back of the family minivan. "I figured it would happen one day. I was actually kind of looking forward to it." She smiled at Jennifer. "You're amazing.

"I'm so sorry we had to leave you there!"

"I understand," Susan said. "They were going to hurt you; you had to go. What else could you do? Besides, I was never in any danger. I'm just a plain, ordinary girl." Her smile was a bit more rueful now.

"You're not plain, and you're not ordinary! You're my best friend and you're awesome. So tell me about Gerry! Did the

dance calm down enough after we left so you could have a little fun?"

"Yeah, funny thing. After you left, everyone acted as if you
and Skip hadn't even been there. I tried to talk to Eddie about
it, but he just shrugged it off and told me to go away. He's not
too wild about me and Gerry, anyway."

"He's just sore because he has no real friends now."

"No doubt. It was hard for me to get back in the mood of
the dance, and Gerry seemed pretty preoccupied. He doesn't
talk much. Even when I pressed him about what he likes to do,
I barely got an answer. Running, he mumbled, and archery. He
spent most of his time moping around the gym floor, searching
for any snakes you left behind. He likes snakes, I guess. Thinks
they're cool. This is what I learned."

"I had the snakes disappear as I left."

"Yeah. I told him they were the most poisonous snakes
known to man anyway, so it was for the best. Anyway, we
sort of just hung out until you returned. When I saw your
minivan outside the school, I told Gerry I had to go, and he
didn't seem to care. I guess it was a bust."

"You didn't even kiss!" Jennifer was dismayed. She had ruined her best friend's evening!

Susan shrugged. "It's okay. He didn't seem too much into
me from the start. Never asked me anything about myself.
Pretty boys. Too self-involved. I can do better."

"You bet you can!" Jennifer fumed. "Oooh, wait until I
get my hands on him!" She formed her hands into a throttling
motion.

"Easy, killer. Don't dragon out for my sake. Susan Elmsmith

can take care of herself. You don't have to pull up in the driveway, Mr. Scales; right here is good. Thanks for the ride! See you tomorrow, Jennifer." And just like that, she kissed Jennifer on the cheek and slid out of the minivan.

The next morning at school, Skip was absent. No one acted any differently toward Jennifer than before—Eddie moped, Bob Jarkmand stared, and so on. Better yet, neither Mr. Slider nor any other teacher gave any hint that they were even aware of what had happened at the dance.

At one point later in the afternoon, she snuck out of study hall to get a drink of water. On her way down the hall to the girls' bathroom, she spotted two unlikely figures ahead talking in low voices: Eddie and Susan.

Before they could notice her, she had slid into a dark corner behind a nearby doorway and turned her dragon shape locker green.

". . . don't understand why you have to be so difficult," Eddie was saying. His tone betrayed a hint of impatience—*and arrogance,* Jennifer noted, thinking suddenly of his father, Hank. "You know what she is. You've seen what she *really* looks like. She's a clear and present danger. Doesn't that scare you?"

"I'll tell you what scares me," Susan hissed back. "Jerks like you who try to bully people like Skip and Jennifer—or worse, watch the bullies do their work and don't stand up for their friends!"

"She's not my—"

"How long until you put a knife in *my* back?" Susan asked. "If you're willing to ditch Jennifer and Skip, what's to stop you from bullying *me* someday?"

"I won't do that." Eddie sounded shaken. "I'm sorry about all that's happened, Susan. Including what I said last night. But Jennifer isn't helping herself. She and her family need to consider a strategic retreat—you know, clear out of town."

"That's not your decision to make."

"No, but it's a smart idea."

"What's *that* supposed to mean?"

Eddie paused. "My rite of passage is coming up."

Susan hissed through her teeth. "I'm not exactly sure what that means, Eddie. But it better have nothing to do with Jennifer."

"I'm not sure." Eddie's voice cracked. "My parents get to choose the dragon I will slay. I wouldn't put it past my father. And Jennifer isn't helping herself with the way she's acting!"

"Oh, so if your parents tell you to murder Jennifer, it's *her* fault? You and your family—all of the people in this town— are seriously cracked in the head!"

"You know, Susan, you could show more thanks for someone who lives under our town's protection!"

"Oh, really? To hell with you and your protection. My family came to Winoka years ago because it was scared of shadows. But my mother didn't die of a shadow—she died from a real danger, a real disease! Since then, I've learned more about these beasts you and your parents rant about. And I don't see what the big deal is. Why not get along with the

Scales family? Why not give them a chance? Why can't we all just live on the same block, like normal neighbors?"

"Because she's not normal!" His shout echoed down the hallway.

So did the sound of Susan clearing her throat and spitting. "Well, hot shot, I've got news. Neither are you."

Eddie stormed down the hallway, passing no more than three feet from Jennifer without noticing her. He was wiping something off of his face in disgust.

Susan muttered something inaudible but plainly unflattering, and then went the other way.

Reminding herself never to get on her best friend's bad side, Jennifer morphed back and headed to class. On the way, a voice behind her startled her.

"Hey, Jennifer." It was Skip. "Watchya up to?"

"Oh. Hey, I didn't think you were around today. I was just . . . I . . ."

"I know. I was laying low, too. I saw you listening in on Eddie and Susan."

"You *saw* me?" She didn't know whether to be insulted or impressed. Was her camouflage that mediocre!

"Well, I saw you walking down the hall normally, and then you changed. Since I kinda knew what to look for . . . well, eyes are pretty sharp in our family."

"Huh. So why didn't you go to classes today? I mean, there's laying low, and there's completely disappearing. I was worried about you!"

"Someone's watching us."

"What? Right now?"

He shook his head. "I don't think so. I thought I caught a

glimpse of him outside the gym last night while we were running out, but I wasn't sure so I didn't say anything. This morning, I caught him looking up at my bedroom window from the street. And then again once or twice on the sidewalks on my way here. I thought I'd check and see if he was following you, too."

"Who?"

"Dunno. Older guy, maybe forty or fifty. Really white skin. Fringe of white hair. Dark green suit, maybe a size too big. As soon as he saw me looking back at him, he practically vanished into thin air."

"That sounds an awful lot like a guy I saw at the bea—er, down at city hall a couple of weeks ago. Really thin? Eyes darting all over the place?"

"Sure, I guess. What do you mean, down at city hall? What were you doing there?"

Jennifer tried to make her shrug look offhanded and innocent. "Dad's architect stuff. They're planning a development downtown, and he dragged me along. Anyway, I heard his name was Whisper. Rune Whisper. Funny name."

"Yeah. Funny name." Skip's face was skeptical, and Jennifer felt her insides churn at the deceit. "Anyway, you haven't seen him since?"

"No. Hadn't really thought of him until you brought him up just now. You think we should tell my parents?"

"I guess."

"Ms. Scales. Mr. Wilson." The sound of the wheelchair immediately followed Mr. Slider's voice down the hallway. "You are the umpteeth students I have seen wandering out of class this afternoon. I've seen Ms. Elmsmith slip one way,

Mr. Blacktooth march another, Mr. Stowe glide in late, Ms. Harrison use a water fountain for a makeup mirror, and Bob Jarkmand argue—apparently with himself—over which way the gymnasium is. Does anyone in this school actually *attend class*?"

"Sorry, Mr. Slider . . ."

"Hold on, before you go. Skip, I wanted to talk about your independent study assignment. Have you thought of a topic for your paper on trigonometry in the real world?"

Skip shrugged. "Not really. Things at home have . . ."

"Things at home will always be what they are," Mr. Slider interrupted as gently as possible. "But that doesn't mean what happens at school is any less important. No matter—I have come up with a study topic for you, if you're willing. Construction has begun on a new center for the blind and deaf here in Winoka, as a new wing of the local hospital. In fact, I believe if you ask your girlfriend here, you'll find her father—"

"I'm *not* his girlfriend!" Jennifer barked, immediately regretting it. "Um, I mean, not yet."

Skip's wounded look was unforgettable. "Not yet? What does that mean?"

"Well, it means . . . I mean . . . we just really haven't talked about this."

Mr. Slider's look was inscrutable. "I see. Nothing fascinates me more than the romantic adventures of children half my age, but if I can get to the point—"

"Talked about it? You won't even come over to my place for dinner," Skip pointed out. "My aunt gave you an invite weeks ago, and you never followed up."

"You're right, I'm sorry. It's just that—"

"And we haven't made it to the Mall of America like we planned—"

"I know. So much has happened, and I didn't know if you wanted—"

"—but you never even ask what I want—"

"—you're right, I should do a better—"

"Ms. Scales. Mr. Wilson." Mr. Slider was almost hissing the words as he wiped his palms on his well-creased pants. "If I could get up out of this chair and kick you both, I would. Perhaps you could continue this inane babbling at the construction site for the new rehabilitation center across town, where construction workers will be making considerable use of trigonometry to make sure the building doesn't fall down and take the existing hospital with it. Jonathan Scales is the architect. It would make for a fabulous independent study paper for Skip. That is all I have to say. Good day!"

He wheeled his chair around and set it to top speed. As he disappeared down the hallway, he added one more thought.

"Get back to class!"

CHAPTER 11

Suspicions

"I'd be happy to take you over to the site," Jonathan assured them the next day. He was doing weekend gardening, snipping the brown stalks of several plants—"winterizing," he called it, though Jennifer didn't see the point of "winterizing" plants that looked dead this time of year. "How does next Thursday work for you?"

Skip bent over to pick up the dead plants from Jonathan's hand and stuff them in the plastic bag Jennifer was holding open. "Thanks, Mr. Scales. My family feels pretty strongly about math, and I'd like to ace this paper. I don't want to disappoint them, or Mr. Slider."

Jonathan spoke carefully. "I noticed mathematics is pretty important to your family, and . . . others like you."

"Yeah. Spatial relationships, quick measurement—it's in our blood, you might say."

Jennifer stared off into the bare branches of oaks and maples, torn between boredom and tension. Why was her father picking at Skip's spider family? And did Skip really just use the term *spatial relationships*?

"My daughter tells me she's learning about logic in Mr. Slider's geometry class. I have to admit, I've tried to apply some logic to what Evangelos is doing, and who he really is. I could use another brain on the case, if you don't mind."

"Sure. Where do we start?"

"Well." Jonathan gave Jennifer a quick glance, long enough for her to see his concentrated effort to draw information out of Skip. "Evangelos hasn't been here forever. I'm guessing he showed up a few weeks, maybe a month or two, before Jack Alder died."

"Okay."

"We could look at the most recent arrivals in Winoka—see who's been here only a month or so, and maybe pare down the list of suspects."

"But wasn't that—" Jennifer stopped herself before she added, "*what the beaststalkers were doing at the trial we stopped?*" "Wasn't that what we figured Evangelos was afraid of? Winoka, and all the beaststalkers around here? Why would he be living in this town?"

"I think we need to separate the beast from the person," Jonathan suggested. "In proper disguise Evangelos would have little to fear from anyone. He could walk anywhere, talk with anyone. In fact, it's probably how he's getting acclimated to being around the rest of us. It's just in his other form that he'd be more cautious."

"But how could someone so hell-bent on hurting you

manage a calm disguise of some guy just living in Winoka? Wouldn't he just go nuts if he saw you on the street?"

Jonathan shrugged. "I've been pretty careful not to spend much time out in the open. I pretty much stick to home, the work site by the hospital, and the cabin. Besides, history is full of people who manage to lead seemingly normal lives—but aren't normal at all."

"You mean, like, leading a double life?" Skip's voice was soft, but the words still sounded hard.

"If you're suggesting that Jennifer and I might already know something about leading a double life, then you're right, Skip. What Evangelos does isn't much different in character from what we weredragons do, or werachnids—what you will do someday yourself. We all lie a little to the outside world. We do it to survive, or to make ourselves feel safer. Or smarter. Or better. Or all of these things at once. The difference with Evangelos is not in *what* he does. It's in the intensity."

"So you're saying lying is okay, as long as you don't tell a really big lie." Jennifer knew her father was passing on another opportunity to talk about her mother. She found herself steaming about continually deceiving Skip. And she was most angry at herself, for going along with it.

Her father gave her a level look. "I guess I'm saying we should be looking for what Evangelos has in common with us, rather than what makes him different."

Skip seemed to measure them both. "Okay, what does Evangelos have in common with us? Besides the shape-shifting thing."

"He's intelligent," Jonathan began. "He picks and chooses times and places."

"Sure," agreed Skip. "And if he's smart, he'll pick disguises that would get him close to us. Like at school."

"Or work. And here's something else we have in common: He's curious. He takes the time to learn how to do a disguise right. After all, nobody has shown up in town with clothes or mannerisms that stick out—"

"That's not completely true," Skip interrupted. "There's this guy I've seen. Jennifer saw him, too—Rune Whisper?"

"Huh. That's right." Jonathan wiped his gloves on his jeans and thought for a moment. "We should definitely put him on the list. But we also have to consider the possibility this Rune Whisper is just an eccentric fellow, and Evangelos has taken enough time and effort to learn how people act and talk in this world. That's no small feat."

"Okay." Skip seemed enthusiastic at their progress. "What else does he have in common with us?"

"I've got one," Jennifer offered coldly. "He's got a problem with the truth."

Jonathan shot back a baleful look, but Skip seemed genuinely curious. "What do you mean?"

"Well, it seems maybe he likes circling around the heart of the matter, rather than confronting his problems head on. If he's got a problem with Dad, he could just go after Dad, you know what I mean? Instead of dragging out the whole thing. Dragging it out hurts family and friends."

She and her father held each other's gray eyes for some time, both thoughtfully chewing their tongues. He broke first, returning his attention to the garden.

"Jennifer's right. Evangelos does appear to want to take his time. Sometimes people take their time to draw out the pain. But other times"—and he looked back up at Jennifer again—"it's because they're not certain of what they really want. They try to convince themselves they really want something, but there's a part of them saying maybe it's not such a great idea."

"Huh." Once again, Skip appeared to consider both of them carefully before going on. "Well, it sounds like we ought to start with Rune Whisper. I had noticed him anyway, so I was thinking of following him . . ."

"That's a horrible idea. Not safe at all." Everyone jumped at the voice of Elizabeth Georges-Scales from behind them. She was wearing flowered coveralls and held a dirty spade in her hand. "If you're right and Rune really is Evangelos, then you would find yourself facing this thing alone. I doubt your aunt would thank us for putting you in that position."

"You wouldn't be *putting* me anywhere," Skip objected. "I want to check this guy out!"

"What if I go with him?" Jennifer said, reaching for Skip's hand.

She was certain she actually saw all color drain from her mother's face. "Jennifer, you can't handle this thing on your own."

Skip took a step forward. "She did before. And this time, she'd be with me!"

Elizabeth stepped in herself. She grew taller and more fierce. The spade lifted a little. For a moment, Jennifer was certain she was going to reveal herself to Skip. "And what would you do, young man, if this thing caught my daughter by surprise and got the upper hand? What would you do if it began sucking the life out of her?"

"I'd . . . I'd stop it!"

Her mother's expression shifted between admiration and disdain. "You'd die. And so would she."

His chin lifted. "It's coming after her anyway. Are you just going to wait and let it come?"

Jennifer watched her mother's knuckles whiten around the handle of her spade. "Watch it, kid."

"Watch what? What're you going to do, *fight* me?"

Elizabeth bit her lip. "No. I'll go with you two. So will your father. We stick together."

Skip held his chin up defiantly for a few moments, and then broke into a smirk. "Great. Come along if you want. I'm going *now*."

"*Fine*." The spade clattered on the patio stones. "*I'll get my coat!*"

"Get mine, too, dear?" Jonathan gave a wry grin as his wife steamed off into the garage. "This is going to be a lot of fun."

Jennifer gulped. "I can hardly wait."

"*He's an ass.*"

"Mom! Keep your voice down!"

"We should have left him in his father's dungeon."

"*Mom!*"

"Why couldn't it have worked out with Eddie? Eddie was always polite to his elders."

"Eddie's mom almost chopped me to pieces last spring. Remember?"

"Granted. But there's something to be said for respecting one's elders."

"Skip's nice to Dad. You know why? Because Dad's nice to him!"

"Your dad's an idiot. We've discussed this."

Both males were well ahead of them, far (Jennifer hoped) out of earshot. They were rustling quietly through the woods behind the Oak Valley apartment complex. Apartment 212 was the address her parents had found for Rune Whisper. They weren't sure if he was there or not, nor if they'd catch him coming or going . . . nor, if Jennifer really thought about it, if he was already aware of their efforts and tracking *them* instead.

"So what exactly are you going to do if Evangelos attacks?" she asked. "*Not* be a beaststalker? I mean, Skip will find out, if you're going to be useful at all."

"We'll worry about that if and when it happens."

Jennifer wrinkled her nose. Many of the leaves under their feet were slowly rotting, helped along by the cold rain that had fallen the day before. "My neck and hands are freezing."

"That's because you didn't bring a scarf or gloves. See honey, here's how it works: Clothes keep you warm. The more clothes you wear, the warmer you are. When it gets cold, you—"

"All right, all right."

"You teenagers think you're invincible against the elements."

A thought occurred to Jennifer, and she smiled. "Well, maybe I am."

A moment later, she was a dragon with a thick, electric blue hide. "Ah. Toasty."

"Your windbreaker's going to smell like lizard meat for the next five wash cycles."

"You're just jealous. Hey, this is a good idea anyway: I can see things a lot better now. In fact . . ." She squinted into a window up at the second floor. "I think he's up there. Third window in from the left."

She glanced over at Skip and her father. The boy appeared to be looking and pointing through the same window she had just been scanning.

"What?" her mother asked. "How can you tell? What do you see?"

She renewed her scouting. The shape flitting back and forth past the gap in the heavy drapes was definitely tall and gaunt. Jennifer thought she could detect the fringe of white hair on his head.

"There's too much light reflecting off the glass to be sure. But that looks an awful lot like the guy from the beaststalker trial."

"Does he look like he's staying in for the night?"

"No, he's dressed in that suit. Pretty sure it's dark green."

"Maybe that's all he's got for clothes."

They looked at each other as if to say, "Or maybe it's all he could find for a disguise."

"What else do we know about Rune?" Jennifer asked.

"According to Mayor Seabright, the police don't have much of a file on him. On his rental application, he put down 'government agent' for occupation. Paid cash deposit. Pays rent in cash, according to the landlord. Hasn't missed a due date."

Jennifer paused. "My, the beaststalker police sure have been busy. You suppose they have a file on me, too?"

"Count on it."

"Hope they have a photo of me on a good hair day. Hang on, I haven't seen him for a few seconds. I think he went into another room."

"Or maybe he left altogether?"

Their question was answered less than a minute later, when Rune Whisper came out the ground floor exit that faced the woods. He adjusted his badly fitting suit jacket, scratched the back of his fringe of hair, and took a look around.

"Get down!" Jennifer whispered. She flexed her skin and assumed the shape and texture of a dying birch tree. Out of the corner of her eye, she saw Skip and her father already low on the ground.

Rune did not appear to see anything unusual, and soon he was walking briskly away from them, around the building and onto the sidewalk that ran alongside the parkway. Without a word, all four of them slowly broke cover and began to trail him.

"Do you think we have any chance?" Jennifer asked in a low whisper. "To help Evangelos, I mean. Instead of killing him."

Never taking her eyes off of the green suit in the distance, Elizabeth wrinkled her nose slightly. "I'm a doctor, honey. I always believe there's hope, for anyone, until the very end."

"Even Skip?" Jennifer winked at her mother's annoyed expression.

"Hmmph. Yes, maybe even him."

Rune Whisper did not go anywhere particularly damning, Jennifer thought sourly while soaking in a bath that evening. The hot water seeped into her skin, but could not remove the cold, clammy sensation that had settled into her bones after several hours of furtive scouting in the cold.

Of course, it had begun to rain again halfway through their hunt. That made it particularly hard to track a man like Rune Whisper, who appeared to be in a constant state of furtiveness.

But what was he hiding? They learned nothing from his first and only stop: the hospital. He disappeared inside, and none of them could risk going in for fear they would miss him leaving. Sure enough, several minutes later Skip saw him slide out an exit not far from the new wing Jonathan had designed, which was still under construction.

From there it had looked like he was setting out for the east end of town, toward Winoka High School—but at an inopportune moment, Skip had a coughing fit brought on by an overly enthusiastic sniff in the rain. Despite the boy's heroic efforts to squelch the sound, Rune's head perked up. The Scaleses and Skip tried to flatten themselves in the ditch by the parkway, with Jennifer's camouflaged wings spread as wide as possible over them all, but they were pretty sure the hunt was over.

After that, Rune couldn't seem to settle on a destination. With his pursuers trying to allow as much distance as possible, he had slowly worked his way back around to the south and the Oak Valley apartment complex.

From there, Jennifer knew the only place to go was the bathtub.

She let out a long sigh, wiggled her human toes, and closed her eyes, trying not to think of the obvious. Her mind would not oblige. *He's scoping out the hospital. Where Mom works. Looking for ambush spots.*

How would a beaststalker like her mother deal with something like Evangelos? She recalled the night Grandpa Crawford had died, and the shriek the thing gave when it seemed to realize what she was. She had wounded it, and survived. Wouldn't her mother be an even tougher match?

Eyes still closed, she pushed some suds up over her throat, face, and hair. The warm water assured her. *Mom will be fine. She's not afraid. She'll take care of this thing. Then he won't be around to come after you. Or Dad.*

Lost in thought, she didn't hear the sound of knocking in the distance. She spent another minute just floating a bit in the water, dreaming of a time when it would be over and they could go back to being a normal family. Or as normal as things could possibly get, given who they were.

How normal could things ever be, here in Winoka—or Pinegrove, since that was its original name? What did normal even mean, anymore? There was so much hurt in the past. So many things no one wanted to forgive. Beaststalkers driving out weredragons, weredragons lashing back, werachnids watching from the shadows—everyone seemed to hate everyone else. Evangelos just seemed like the most ferocious criminal—and victim, if she thought about it.

Don't think about him that way! He's not a victim!

With that thought her eyes popped open, and she let out a small gasp. Her father was sitting on the edge of the tub.

Her first impulse was to curl up, freak out, and yell at him to get out. But she saw the look in his gray eyes as he watched her lie there. He was focused only on her face, as if he was looking for something hidden there. There was worry in his own features, and a great deal of uncertainty. He appeared older, and she thought of Grandpa Crawford again. He had already lost his father. What would happen to his wife and daughter?

She gently raised an arm and pushed extra suds over her chest. "What," she said as calmly as she could manage.

"I knocked," he said gently. "You didn't answer, and the door was partway open. Lying there like that, you looked . . . well, it took a second before I was sure you were all right."

"I'm okay." Her voice sounded very small.

He laughed and stood up. "Sorry, ace. Didn't mean to creep you out. I'll leave."

He stepped toward the door, then turned halfway. "It's just . . ."

"What?" She slowly rinsed out her hair.

"I've been a good father, haven't I?"

The crack in his voice made her tremble a bit. Since when did he seek her approval?

"Geez, Dad. That's a dumb question. You're great." Feeling awkward, she tried a joke. "I mean, you could stand to ease up on curfew, but . . ."

He tossed a faint smile for the effort back in her direction, and then stared into the bathroom mirror. "Until a few weeks ago, I hadn't thought much of Evangelos, I'll admit. But I never did completely forget him. A parent just can't forget a child. Even though I never saw him . . . I'd wake up some nights, when it was quiet and dark, and wonder what he went through—what he felt—before he died."

The weight of his words hit her hard. *He feels guilty,* she told herself. *He thinks he's a bad father.* And he was asking her if it was true. This was too much responsibility, she told herself. She couldn't comfort her father. Who could?

But she tried. "Dad. There was nothing you could do. You were in America when it happened. They were in Australia. The Pacific Ocean . . . it's huge! By the time you got there, he was even farther away. Not even his mother could find him! How could you?"

He sniffed, swiped a tissue from the bathroom counter, and wiped his nose with it. "Well, turns out I don't have to, eh? He found me."

Turning back to the door, he couldn't hide the fear in his voice.

"And you."

She felt the same fear for a moment, but then something else rose. Courage, she thought it was. And pride. Neither of them was alone.

"And Mom."

His tone brightened. "And your mom."

Sensing his mood change, she chose her words carefully. "Dad, I know you feel bad for Evangelos. And you should. Because if he tries to mess with Mom, he's going to have a really bad day."

"So how'd it go with my dad?"

"Hmm?"

Jennifer bent down a bit, trying to insert herself between Skip's gaze and the floor. "Your visit to the hospital? This morning? It's Thursday."

He shrugged. She pressed.

"He just dropped you off here at school? Right over there?" Pointing out the glass doors and into the parking lot,

Jennifer felt a twinge of irritation. She had to come to school on time, while Skip got to take a field trip at the hospital's expansion site, rooting around stacked two-by-fours and foundation elements while her father pointed out various architectural features yet to be built. Sure it was no amusement park, but at least it wasn't the same old classrooms.

"It was cool," he allowed, still distant. "Never thought there was much use for trigonometry, but whaddya know: There are people out there who really have to use stuff like *sine* and *cosine*. Poor saps."

"But did you *see* anything?" She waved her arms in exasperation, causing Susan, who was at her side, to giggle. "Did Rune Whisper come back?"

He breathed out and seemed to relax. "Naw. Didn't see him. Just a couple of the construction workers your dad's gotten to know. One of 'em—Angie or somethin'—"

"Angus?" she suggested, remembering the man from the beaststalker trial with the Scottish accent and the shrouded wife. "Angus Cheran?"

"Yeah. He's new in town, right? Your dad made sure I met him. I guess he's trying to introduce the guy around. Though I don't see how meeting me would help."

Skip was probably right, Jennifer thought. After the embarrassment of the Cherons during the beaststalker trial, her dad would take extra steps to make sure they didn't feel unwelcome.

"Your mom also showed up, just before lunch. Wow, she doesn't care for me one bit."

"She thinks you're an ass," Jennifer offered helpfully.

His nose wrinkled. "Great."

"She's right," Susan pitched in, barely avoiding Skip's elbow. "Oooh, everyone shut up now, Gerry's coming."

"Gerry? But I thought you didn't like—"

Now *she* got the elbow in the ribs. "Hey, Gerry! Jennifer and I didn't see you in geometry class today."

The boy with the angelic face floated down the hall and came to a full stop in front of them. He looked slightly worried and glanced nervously at Jennifer and Skip.

He wants us to go away, Jennifer thought. *Fat chance.*

"H-hey, Susan." His high-pitched voice came out in fits and starts. "I w-wanted to talk to y-you. I h-haven't seen you much since the d-dance."

"You mean the dance where you barely talked to my friend, and ignored her, and then just let her leave without even offering a good-night kiss?"

"Jennifer!"

"Hmmph. Sorry. Carry on."

"I was wondering if we could . . . talk later. After school, in the library?"

Skip gave a snort. "Yeah, talk. Good one, Gerry. I'll have to remember that."

Susan stepped in front of Gerry and faced them both with teeth clenched. "All right. I know you two are used to it being *all about you,* but if you could both shut up and give the rest of the world a chance to spin, we'd like to enjoy the ride, too. Okay?"

"Geez, Susan, if you're going to have a fit about—"

"Okay." Jennifer pushed Skip back, her ears turning red. "Sorry, Susan. We're going."

A few steps away, she punched him. "Did you have to be so crass?"

He chuckled, rubbing his shoulder. "I don't know Gerry too well. He's not exactly chatty. But I can tell you, *talk* doesn't mean *talk*."

"Susan's a big girl. She can handle herself. Even if the dance ended badly for them, it's her choice if she wants to see him again."

"Hey, speaking of dances ending badly . . ." He stopped and pulled her next to a row of lockers, his face serious.

"Yeah?"

"Well . . . you just told Gerry off for not giving Susan a kiss at the end. I just realized I left you out in the cold, too. I'm almost a week late now, but . . ."

Before she could respond, his lips were on hers, a bit dry but soft, and his fingers were just behind her neck. She smelled something good—cologne maybe, or just the scent he always had, just more of it.

They were like that for a few seconds, and then they weren't. His hazel eyes stayed close to hers, though.

"So, am I your boyfriend yet?"

Her voice was a whisper. "Oh yeah, you bet."

"Good. Come over for dinner with my aunt next week."

"Give me another kiss first."

A deal's a deal, she thought midway through. Dinner at Aunt Tavia's it was.

CHAPTER 12

Evangelos and the Beaststalker

"Mashed potatoes, dear?"

Jennifer eyed the bowl of potatoes carefully. There were specks trapped in the white, creamy swirls—presumably bits of potato skin, but she couldn't help thinking of dragonflies or some other "catch of the day" from the nearest web. She looked over at Skip, who was watching her anxiously. It had actually been two weeks since she made her promise to Skip—first her family had been hunting down leads on Evangelos (to no avail), and then Mr. Slider had scheduled a horrific test (which she aced after intense studying), and then . . .

Then he reminded her the crescent moon was coming.

Be polite, she reminded herself as she turned back to his aunt.

"Um, sure. Thanks."

Dinner was actually quite good. Tavia Saltin had been a whirl of activity in the wonderfully scented kitchen, preparing two or three different things at once while chatting cheerily and endlessly with the two of them. Even though Jennifer did not trust this woman one bit, there was something compelling in Tavia's rapid questions and friendly tone. She was soon surprised to find herself talking openly about her own dragon nature, her father, and even Evangelos.

"So no idea who Evangelos is?" Tavia arched her eyebrows as she plopped a spoonful of mashed potatoes on her nephew's plate. The sound echoed through the spartan dining room. Gentle strains of familiar Mozart concertos drifted in from an unseen living room.

Jennifer looked back and forth between Tavia and Skip, but saw nothing sinister in how they were acting. Tavia seemed genuinely curious, and Skip looked like . . . well, like a nervous boyfriend, she thought, smiling to herself.

"We've got some leads," she answered. "Rune Whisper still looks promising—he's the guy Skip helped us follow a while ago."

"Ah, yes, Mr. Whisper." Tavia's eyes widened a bit. "They say he's a government agent of some sort. Pepper on your potatoes, dear?"

How did she know that? It had taken her parents a week to find that out. "No, thanks. Yeah, my dad checked in with some contacts he knows around state and federal government, but no agency seems to have a record of him."

Her hostess chewed on a turkey drumstick thoughtfully. "Perhaps I could check in with some contacts of my own."

It sounded vaguely threatening. "Th-thank you. Um, of

course it might not be him. We have no proof of him doing anything, besides creeping around. Mom says—"

"And how *is* your mom, dear?" Here Tavia's smile extended almost literally from ear to ear. Jennifer waited breathlessly for the entire head to split open and reveal the mandibles she knew were inside that bony head.

They were in Skip, too, weren't they? Somewhere. The thought was not new to Jennifer, but it startled her to think of it again at this moment.

"Mom's good." Tavia and Skip kept staring at her, so she offered a little more. "I guess since last spring she's been finding it a little hard to live with two dragons." Right away, she winced. Last spring was when this woman's brother died.

Her hostess didn't appear to notice. "Having Evangelos nearby can't make her any happier, poor thing." She spun the turkey leg completely around, consuming it in record time.

"We're all a little nervous about that, yeah. Especially my dad. I'm thinking we should probably confront Rune Whisper soon."

"I'm not sure I'd do that," Skip interrupted politely.

"Huh?"

"I'm starting to think maybe Rune's not the guy."

"Why not?"

"Yes, dear, why not?" Tavia's echo came through another creepy smile. She turned to Jennifer as she reached across and patted Skip's arm. "He explained it so wonderfully to me earlier. Such a bright boy! His parents would be proud."

Skip's ears flushed a bit. "It's possible Rune may be looking for Evangelos, just like we are. I mean, if he's a government agent of some sort, like his paperwork says."

"A government agency interested in Evangelos? What, like some military thing?"

"Maybe. My point is, Rune may actually be someone who can help us out."

"Okay. But if Evangelos is not Rune, who else could he be?"

For a while, it didn't seem like he wanted to answer. Finally, he blurted out, "Anyone, I guess. Gerry Stowe."

"Gerry?" Jennifer couldn't hold back the laugh. She tried to imagine that angel-faced boy as a cold killer, and just couldn't. "Oh, come on, Skip. You're just saying that because all the girls at school think he's gorgeous—er, I mean, everyone but *me*, of course!" The correction was a bit late; Tavia was looking at her with something that might have been alarm.

Skip gave a forgiving smile. "He's not the first good-looking guy I've seen, Jennifer. I know how girls can be. I'm just pointing out the facts: He's new, he doesn't say much, and he has a reason to be close to you."

Jennifer bristled at the "how girls can be" remark, but kept her tone civil. "But he has a grandfather! How can he . . ."

She stopped at the look on his face. "Do you think he killed the real Gerry Stowe?"

His expression mirrored her fears. "His grandfather's almost blind," he pointed out. "Kinda hard for him to follow changes in Gerry's body or manners. If the kid used to have a slightly bigger nose, who's to know? And there's something else. The Stowes' house? It's between the school and the hospital."

"What does that mean?"

"Well, when we were following Rune yesterday, he looked like he was heading to the school. But what if he was doing research on Evangelos at the hospital—checking doctor visits or something—and then was going from there to the Stowes' house instead?"

"I don't know . . ." It wasn't just that she didn't know, Jennifer admitted to herself, it was the possibility that Susan might be trying to date a monster like Evangelos.

"Of course, it's just one possibility, dear!" Tavia had regained her sunny composure and was spearing pea pods on her dinner plate. "I'll admit I don't follow Skip's school activities too much, but—"

The doorbell interrupted her. She gave a surprised whoop and launched herself out of her chair, bounding out of the room to see who it was. Her voice lost none of its enthusiasm (nor volume, Jennifer noted dryly) as she disappeared down the hallway.

"Why, Mr. Slider! What an unexpected treat! Come in, please! Here, I'll help you get up that little step . . ."

Skip and Jennifer exchanged startled glances. What was Edmund Slider doing here?

After a few moments, Tavia poked her maniacal smile back into the kitchen. "Skip, dear, you wouldn't mind finishing dinner with our guest, would you? And clean up the dishes? Mr. Slider and I have some business to attend to in the living room. There's a dear."

From that point on, Tavia lowered her voice a great deal, and Jennifer could not make out anything of her distant conversation with their geometry teacher. The two teenagers finished their meal, and she helped Skip clear off the table.

"So you're sure it's Gerry?" Time had worn off the initial shock at the idea.

Skip took a gravy boat from her and rinsed it out in the sink. "I'm not *sure* it's anyone, just yet. I'm just trying to stay open to all possibilities." He jerked his head toward the living room. "In independent study, Mr. Slider talks a lot about logic. He says it's important not just to know things, but also—"

"—to know what you don't know," Jennifer finished for him thoughtfully. "Yes, he said the same thing in geometry class."

"We don't know how old Evangelos is. We don't know where else he's been since he came into this world, or how well he can disguise himself, or what languages he can speak."

He leaned in close and breathed frightening words on her neck. "Jennifer, we don't even know if he's killed someone we know and replaced them!"

She shivered. Suddenly, Aunt Tavia's laugh came, shrill and hard, from the living room. The sound made her jump and she looked at Skip, alarmed.

He gave her a grim look. "Come on. Let's load these dishes in the washer."

It was the next morning, just before Jennifer walked through the front door of Winoka High, when she noticed the birds.

They were only specks, circling high above. But she recognized them instantly as birds of prey. Not the golden eagles her mother could call, but something smaller. Hawks, she guessed. Hawks were not uncommon across Minnesota; many of them patrolled the ditches alongside highways for scurrying rodents.

But she was fairly sure hawks were lone hunters. In any case, they didn't normally move in formations of a dozen or more.

Susan's voice came up behind her. "Hey, Jennifer, watcha lookin' at?" A few seconds went by. "Huh. You checkin' out those birds?"

"Yeah."

"Yeah, they're pretty cool. So, um. I've got to talk to you. About Gerry."

It turned out, as Susan told Jennifer, that Gerry did, in fact, want to talk on that day a couple of weeks ago, and several times since. More than talk: He had lots of questions.

"Really? What did he want to know about you?" Jennifer adjusted her backpack and grinned, but Susan didn't return the smile.

"Actually, he didn't want to know much about me. He asked about you."

"Oh?" Jennifer slowed down. "Oh. Oh, Susan, I'm sorry. You know I—"

Susan held a hand up. She was trying to smile, but she was wet around the eyes. "I know. I know, Jennifer. It's like I told you: You're all anyone can talk about!"

Jennifer reached out for the hand, and Susan let her take it with a sniffle. "He's a jerk for using you. I'll crush him if he asks me out. I promise."

"Thanks. No, he's not a jerk. He's just a boy. He doesn't know any better. Like I said before: Boys are sad."

"What kind of stuff did he ask?" Jennifer wasn't sure how to phrase this. "I mean, was it creepy at all?"

Her friend stifled a laugh. "No, not too creepy. He's not

much of a talker, but he's been working you into just about every conversation we've had for weeks. He's asked how long we've been friends, and did I think you and Skip were serious, and . . . um, he's asked if you were a dragon."

Jennifer felt a chill. "A dragon?"

"Well, yeah. I mean, he saw you at the Halloween dance, remember?"

Jennifer relaxed a little, but there was a moment of hesitation.

"Jennifer, I talked to my dad after I found out about you being a dragon. He told me about how my family came here from Duluth, when I was a baby. We moved to get away from . . . well, from . . ."

"People like me."

"Yeah. Um, you remember my mom?"

"Sure." Susan's mother had died of cancer when they were both six years old.

"Well, Mom was pretty superstitious. When I was only six months old, my mother had me in a stroller for a walk when something began to stalk her. It was enormous, with lots of legs, and my mother was convinced it was a giant spider. She told my father. I don't think he believed her, but she was so hysterical, we moved out of Duluth."

"And they chose Winoka, because of the beaststalkers."

"Yeah, beaststalkers. That's what they call themselves, right? They offer protection to families like ours. People who are afraid." Susan wiped some stray brown curls from her face. "Mom didn't say much about dragons, but she talked about spiders all the time. I was terrified of them. Geez, when I think of how much insecticide I would blast the poor things with when I found them. I was afraid they'd grow to the size of a couch and swallow me whole.

"When Mom got sick . . . she told me it was a spider's curse. Dad didn't believe her, of course. But then we heard rumors of a town named Eveningstar. Nobody would talk openly about it, but there were stories of spiders, and fire."

Jennifer couldn't suppress a small shudder. It was Otto Saltin, Skip's werachnid father, who had led the sorcerous charge that destroyed her original hometown, when she was a small child. Her family had been one of the few weredragon families to escape.

"After Mom died, I kinda forgot about giant spiders and beaststalkers—though normal spiders still creep me out. I never saw or heard much of anything magical again . . . until you told me about yourself. I guess that means there are giant spiders too, huh?"

Her deep blue eyes fixed on Jennifer's. "When I didn't go with you that day, it wasn't because I was scared of Eddie or the beaststalkers you told me about. Jennifer, it was because I was scared of *you*."

"Are you still scared of me?"

"No." The answer came quickly enough, and Jennifer breathed a sigh of relief. "But Jennifer, I'm afraid *for* you! I was talking to Eddie a few weeks ago . . ."

"I know. The rite of passage. I'm sorry, I eavesdropped on you guys." She took Susan's hand. "You're an awesome friend."

Susan blushed a bit at that, but still looked worried. "So do you know what this rite of passage is?"

"From what I know, every young beaststalker has to kill a beast of some sort."

"Jennifer, this town is horrible for you guys! Beaststalkers are everywhere!"

Jennifer shrugged. "So what did you tell Gerry?"

"Well, there wasn't much point in denying you're a weredragon, was there? But he didn't seem that surprised. I got him off the topic anyway."

"Thanks." Not for the first time, Jennifer's conscience pricked her for not owning up to all of her secrets. Susan had a right to know about Jennifer's other half. And maybe she could help figure out Evangelos, as well. Sharing secrets and helping out—wasn't that what friends were for?

Later in geometry class, Jennifer reflected on her conversation with Susan. *Tonight,* she decided. *I'm telling my parents tonight that I'm letting Susan in on everything. Then I'll tell her tomorrow.* Her resolve made her feel marginally better.

At the same time, having Gerry Stowe asking questions about her was disturbing—and not just because she had no romantic interest in him. Sure, he was cute—but Skip had made some good points, and the boy could be anything.

She looked around the overheated room, feeling cold. *Any* of these guys could be anything! Gerry Stowe. Bob Jarkmand. Whoever kept sending her love notes through the ever-surly Kay Harrison behind her. (She held another one, still unsigned, crumpled in her hand.) Speaking of Kay Harrison, could Evangelos disguise himself as a girl? Or maybe even as Mr.—

"—Scales?"

Her head jerked up at the name. "Huh?"

From his wheelchair in front of the blackboard, Mr. Slider

peered over the heads of the students in front of her. "I say, how would you solve this problem, Ms. Scales?" He pointed up with a piece of chalk.

Panicked at the mess of lines, angles, and shapes she saw there, she stalled for time. "Er, I'd use logic."

Mr. Slider's head didn't move an inch, but his lips did tighten. "No doubt. And?"

Those few seconds were precious and helpful, but not quite enough. Her eyes flew over the blackboard while her mouth stalled for more time. "Er, well . . . this looks a bit like the proof from last week . . ."

"There are similarities." From his tone, she couldn't tell if he was amused, encouraging, suspicious, impatient, or a combination of all four.

That was all the time she needed—her brain had arrived to the rescue. "Okay, so we use the given statements to establish that segment BD is a median of triangle ABC. Then, if the median of a triangle bisects the side into two congruent segments . . ."

Her mouth and brain now working at the same speed, Jennifer had a random, spare thought.

Why can't my real-life problems be as easy as my math problems?

After school, her mother insisted on training in the backyard. "You need to learn this skill" was the typically short and simple explanation.

Jennifer looked dubiously at the makeshift target—an old plastic sled that hung from a nail in a wooden porch support pillar, at about chest height. She remembered laughing and sliding down the hill behind the elementary school on that thing, with only one mitten on. Now, it was her mortal enemy. "I have to hit that?"

"Yes."

She turned to the beautiful, and now suddenly quite heavy, daggers she held in her hands. "With these?"

"Yes."

She looked around the yard. They were at least thirty feet from the porch stairs. "From here?"

"Yes."

"Um, don't you have a geometric proof or something else I could do?"

"Start with your stance. Whichever hand you're throwing with, that foot starts behind. Keep your heels on a line, toes pointing out a bit from each other, and your knees . . ."

Jennifer never realized how many body parts it took to throw a single knife. Between balancing her weight on one foot or another, measuring the swing by her head, and keeping her shoulders firm, she almost forgot there were arms and hands involved.

The first throw sent a dagger crashing through the basement glass door, handle first.

"Keep your arms straight to start. Point them at the target."

The second knife clattered against the porch railing, six feet above the sled.

"Wait to release until your throwing arm is pointing exactly at the sled."

After retrieving the daggers, they tried again. The third throw hit the sled, but bounced off.

"Don't stop your throw after you release."

The fourth throw stuck dead center, piercing the plastic sled and pinning it to the pillar.

"Not bad at all! Now do that ten times in a row."

A few minutes later, her mother changed the distance. "You won't always be exactly this far from the target," she explained. "In general, you can expect the knife to make a full rotation every seven feet. So depending how far away you are, there might be times when you have to start the throw holding the blade, instead of the handle. Here you go. Try it from here."

Just as Jennifer released the blade, a scream pierced the air. It sounded, Jennifer guessed as she watched her throw go two feet wide and into the vinyl siding under the porch, like it came from the street.

Both she and her mother raced up the hill, Jennifer plucking her daggers out of the side of the house on the way. As they came within view of the street, Jennifer heard a second scream . . . and her heart stopped.

Susan was on her back in the middle of the street, scrambling on all fours like a crab, best as she could toward her house. Her face was flush with terror, but she appeared otherwise unhurt.

Hovering over her was the dark, twisted shape. Jennifer recognized him immediately.

Even in broad daylight, the sight of him was terrifying. The sun's rays could not penetrate the corona of gloom that spilled from his unseen head and partially obscured his body and wings.

A mass of dark clicks, slithers, and hisses, Evangelos advanced on the terrified Susan. His tail and legs twitched in anticipation. Breathless with dread, Jennifer recognized the movement. Her gecko Geddy twitched his tail like that—right before he pounced on prey.

Susan closed her eyes and fainted.

"Susan!"

Before the word even left Jennifer's mouth, the beast swung around and forgot Susan completely. And then the shadow was very still.

Evangelos was facing them both, mother and daughter, straight on, about twice as far away as the sled had been from Jennifer in the backyard. One of the dark hind legs scraped against the pavement.

. . . no love . . .

She hissed with the effort to chase the words out of her mind, but they repeated in a relentless pattern.

. . . no love . . . no love . . . no love . . . no love . . .

"Enough!" Her mother's voice rang clear across the street. Passing in front of Jennifer, she held up her sheathed sword with both hands. "You don't need to fight!"

. . . no love . . . no love . . . no love . . . no love . . .

"Mom!" Jennifer shrieked. "He'll kill you!"

Elizabeth ignored her and kept the sword held harmlessly

high. "We know why you're here! We know you're in pain! Let us help you!"

. . . no love . . . no love . . . no love . . . no love . . .

"Mom, please!" Her throat swollen in desperation, Jennifer had a sudden flashback: her mother, in this very spot in the yard last spring, begging her daughter not to go any farther toward danger. Desperate and afraid for the life of someone she loved.

"There's still hope!"

Miraculously, the voice stopped.

Jennifer took a deep breath. *Hope.* Was her mother right? The shadow shifted and drew back a bit.

. . . hope? . . .

"Yes, hope!" Her mother was flush with excitement. Slowly, she laid her sword at her feet. "We don't need to fight!"

Jennifer began to exhale.

And then Wendy Blacktooth knocked her over from behind, charging at the shadow before her, holding the Blacktooth blade high and unsheathed. The edges of her blue-and-white checkered apron flapped behind her legs like a strange warrior's cloak.

Her voice was high and clear. *"Ready yourself, beast . . . or ready your soul!"*

"NO!" From the ground, Jennifer wasn't sure if it was her or her mother who shouted it louder.

The shadow of Evangelos darkened, reared up, and turned toward the new threat. Like a sonic boom, the telepathic voice sucked away the surrounding air, knocking them all down and leaving them gasping for breath.

ENEMY!

Wendy Blacktooth was still on the ground, scrambling for her sword, when the missile came.

Since the head was invisible, there was no warning beyond a dry popping sound. Then, what looked like a basketball wreathed in a dark green halo spat out of the darkness and splashed over the fallen soldier.

Jennifer had never heard anyone scream like she heard Wendy Blacktooth scream. It was the wail of someone consumed by pain and beyond all help. Her matronly clothes curled and fell to shreds, exposing her back and side to whatever had eaten through. Within seconds, they could smell the burning flesh and hair.

Now Evangelos pronounced a new word.

PREY.

"Mom!"

Jennifer's heart broke at the sound of the new voice. Eddie was running wildly into the street, unarmed, seemingly oblivious to the shadow that extended over them both. With tears running down his face, the boy slid onto his knees before his mother and tried to pull her up off the pavement.

Both Jennifer and Elizabeth moved forward to help . . . but then they stopped at the sight before them.

Evangelos had risen as if to strike again, but the finishing blow did not come. The shadow hung over the mother and child before him, hesitating.

"Mom, come on!" Eddie's frantic voice was the only sound on the street. He tugged at the limp body—*Was it a corpse already?* Jennifer wondered grimly—and turned his head toward the two of them. "Jennifer! Dr. Georges-Scales! Please help me!"

Elizabeth held Jennifer back by the shoulder, gaze fixed on Evangelos. "We are helping, Eddie." She lowered her sword to the ground, and motioned for Jennifer to do the same with her blades. "We're helping as best we can. But Evangelos may charge if Jennifer or I move. Can you get your mother over to me?"

Eddie turned toward his own house. "Dad, help me get her over there!"

The answer came out loud and clear from the yard behind them. "The sword, Eddie! The Blacktooth blade!" Jennifer turned enough to see Hank Blacktooth standing on the edge of his yard, looking past them all at the dully glowing object in the street.

"Dad, she's going to die!" Eddie was scrambling madly for the near side of the street, dragging his mother's body as best he could. The shadow of Evangelos seemed torn between watching his struggle and considering the show of peace Elizabeth and Jennifer were offering a few feet away.

"The blade, son!" Hank's face was an angry mix of impatience and fear. "It's right there!"

Seeing Eddie struggle to get his mother's body up onto the curb, Elizabeth chanced a few quick steps forward to help ease his burden onto their own yard. Since Evangelos still wasn't moving, Jennifer joined them right away. The smell was fearfully strong, but she was less sure now that she could see the woman's burnt, trembling limbs that Wendy Blacktooth was truly dead.

"Hold her still!" Elizabeth quickly checked the pulse—left arm, Jennifer noticed, since the right was scorched. Then she raised her voice in the direction of Hank Blacktooth. *"Call nine-one-one!"*

He gave her an impatient look, still plainly unable to move his feet. "The sword!"

"Call nine-one-one!"

"I'll do it, Mom!" Jennifer stood up and made for their front door. Halfway there, the door opened and her father emerged, damp towel around his waist and cell phone in hand.

"I'm calling!" Jonathan was shouting, not even looking up to see why his wife had yelled for help from the front yard. "What's—"

He looked up at the same time Evangelos turned toward him.

FATHER?!

Jennifer's spine tingled. "Oh, *shit*."

"Get him inside!"

Jennifer did exactly what her mother ordered, thrusting her father—towel, phone, and all—back through the door and pulling it shut before he could say another word. She turned around on the doorstep in time to see Evangelos preparing to run through her.

"Hey! No! Over here! *Over here!*" Elizabeth jumped up from Wendy's side and threw her hands into the air. "Not them! Me!"

The shadow hesitated again, confused. Seized with a new idea, Jennifer gritted her teeth and darted away from both house and mother. "No, over here! Not her! Me!"

"Jennifer! Don't you dare! Hey, you! I said *over here!*"

"Take care of Eddie's mom! *Keep coming over here!*"

"Jennifer Caroline Scales, you stop this instant!"

The shadow rocked back and forth between the two women, front door forgotten. Finally, it rested on Jennifer alone.

She looked at her mother. "I love you!"

Then she turned and ran like hell.

The sudden flap of wings, the growl in the back of the shadow's throat, the scrape of claws as they left the pavement—all these sounds suggested success. Success, of course, being relative in situations like this.

Don't look back, don't look back, she told herself. She resisted for about half a minute, but then she couldn't help it—she needed to be sure Evangelos was following.

She turned and looked down the street.

Evangelos wasn't following her.

In fact, Evangelos wasn't there at all.

INTERLUDE

Confusion

Why didn't you kill them?

Evangelos huddled under the oaks and maples deep behind the Oak Valley apartment complex. This encounter had been a surprise, a hunt, a success, and a disaster, all rolled into one.

Meeting up with Susan Elmsmith on the street outside the Scales house had been unexpected. Her screams had been unnecessary: Evangelos had no desire to kill her. But that neighbor beaststalker—the one who burned so delightfully well. Monster killers, indeed! If that's all it took to bring down a beaststalker, Evangelos wasn't so sure why they had such a horrific reputation.

Was there a twinge of regret for the woman? Very well, there was regret. Evangelos hadn't wanted to involve other *people in what was essentially a family matter. In fact, the woman's interference would greatly complicate things. The Blacktooths—that was their name, right?—yes. The Blacktooths would want revenge now.*

Her son, Eddie. So brave. So concerned with his mother.

That was what had made Evangelos pause, instead of dealing the death blow. And then Father's wife and their daughter had shown the same concern for each other. All of them struggling to save the other's life. Was such a love between parent and child possible?

Was that what Dianna Wilson had felt?

Or Jonathan Scales?

There is no love!

But there was a memory there, back in Australia. One of the very first from this world. Before the horror and grief at what had happened. Before the fear of a premature delivery.

She had felt love. For her husband, and for their child. It was there, wasn't it? Was that what made the boy on the street do what he did?

Evangelos had dismissed the memory at first, out by the desert surrounding the underground town of Coober Pedy. Perhaps that had been a mistake.

No mistake. What the boy felt doesn't exist for you. Father doesn't feel that.

But was there no chance? None at all? Was there no hope? Evangelos growled at the unbidden thought.

A gentle rain began to fall—a phenomenon unique to this world. But in fact, the pattering of the raindrops made it easier to think, trace, and remember. Still clear were the memories left here in these woods by the Scales family days ago, when they hid and followed Rune Whisper.

There is always hope, *the woman had said. She was a doctor.* For everyone. Until the very end.

Doctors, like rain, were unique to this world. Evangelos struggled with this woman in particular, and the memories she had, and the things she said.

The very end? When was that, exactly? How long would the killing continue? When would the end come?

She used to be a killer, too.

But then she stopped. When will this stop?

When Jonathan Scales has paid the price. You should have killed her. And the daughter. And the neighbors. All of them. Why did you show mercy?

Mercy. Doctors. Rain. So many new things in this world. Since arriving in Coober Pedy, so much had happened, so many memories lingered, and so many voices had emerged that Evangelos was not sure what to do with it all.

A harsh conviction rose out of the uncertainty.

You must go back and finish the job.

But deep inside, there was resistance. The idea of going back was not appealing. It had little to do with danger— plainly beaststalkers were not invincible.

Cruelty. Yes, that was it: This was all becoming too cruel, to hunt down family and kill them. It was too cruel to ambush an old man in his cabin; it was too cruel to kill father's friend, miles away, who had nothing to do with this. Nothing at all . . .

Too cruel!

Evangelos almost laughed at the thought, and spat instead. The leaves beneath him hissed and smoldered.

Too cruel! Like the world I grew up in?

There was no immediate reply within. Evangelos pressed the matter.

Go back and finish the job.

There was fatigue, defiance, desperation in there. No easy answers. Go back? Not now. It was too much.

No. Now.

The rain drove down harder, and the drops off the branches above struck black skin and sizzled.

Go back. Finish it. Now.

CHAPTER 13

Sanctuary

"He flew away," Elizabeth told her daughter, plainly furious at her as the three Scales sat around the kitchen table. Jonathan was trying to cool them down with iced tea, but it had no apparent effect on his wife. "I don't know why he didn't chase you down. Quite frankly, I find the idea of beating some sense into you quite appealing right now."

"Wendy Blacktooth needed you!" Jennifer protested. "And it worked, didn't it?"

Her mother made an indescribable sound—something teetering between disgust, relief, and surrender. Fortunately, she then changed the subject to Wendy's injuries.

The medics had arrived for Wendy Blacktooth almost immediately after Jennifer returned from reviving Susan and taking her home. Wendy had been unconscious but alive, her prospects for survival decent. Eddie and Hank had gone with her in the ambulance—after Hank retrieved his precious Blacktooth blade, of course.

"I'd like to cram that family heirloom of theirs right up his butt," her mother reported in clipped tones when Jennifer asked about it. She turned on her husband. "If you ever put a stinking piece of metal above my own welfare, Jonathan Daniel Scales, I will skin you, wings and all!"

"Noted," her prey responded dryly. He put the iced tea back in the refrigerator. "Jennifer, how was Susan? Did she say anything when you walked her home?"

"Not much." In fact, Susan had said nothing at all after her ordeal, not even good-bye at the door. Jennifer tried to believe that allowing the block-long escort was at least a hopeful signal, but the blank look on Susan's face had been less encouraging.

I should have told her everything long ago.

"You should call Skip. If Evangelos was attacking Susan, Skip may be next."

As if on cue, there was a knock at the door and Skip poked his head in.

He hadn't heard anything about the attack, but after Jennifer and her parents filled him in, he shook his head sadly.

"That increases the chances that Rune Whisper is Evangelos."

"What do you mean?" Jonathan asked.

"Well, I decided to follow Rune again today, and—"

"You *what*?" Jennifer couldn't tell if Elizabeth's harsh tone meant she was still upset at Jennifer or newly irritated at Skip. "Without us?"

"Yeah." Skip stuck his chin out a bit as he plopped his iced tea down. "Without you. I'm a big boy, Mrs. Georges-Scales."

"That's *Doctor* Georges-Scales, and you're not as big as . . ."

"What did you find out?" asked Jennifer hurriedly. "Where did Rune go?"

The boy gritted his teeth, but turned. "Well, that's just it—Rune wasn't there."

Jennifer mulled that over. "Well, that makes sense if Rune is Evangelos. Because he was here with us, instead of somewhere else with you."

"That's possible," Skip admitted. "But then again, it's still possible he's just on the trail of the real Evangelos. So I went to the places Rune went last time, and looked around. Checked employment records, watched folks, that sort of thing . . ."

"You checked the employment records at the hospital?" Jennifer saw her mother's face turn from irritation to alarm. "That's illegal."

Skip looked at her with a small smile. "It's not the first time I've broken the law, *Mrs.* Georges-Scales."

Why is he provoking her? Jennifer wondered, holding her mother's hand and squeezing. The answer came right away: *Because he likes it. He likes bucking authority. He's liked it since the day you met him. That's what gave him the courage to stand between you and his own father.*

Jonathan intervened smoothly. "Skip, did you learn anything new?"

"Well, the most recent employee at the hospital is, get this, Martin Stowe. Custodial work. I guess he can still do that much, even with his bad eyesight. And I also saw Angus Cheron—"

"Yes, wonderful research," Elizabeth interrupted, sarcastically. "People who are new in town are apparently the most recent hires at local employers. A true investigative breakthrough. And if you saw them, we'll grant you they couldn't be Evangelos. But as my husband asked you, do you have anything *new*?"

Skip pushed his chair back. "You know, I'm not your trained monkey! I don't have to tell you anything!"

Jonathan rose enough to rest a reassuring hand on Skip's shoulder. "We're glad you're here. Aren't we, honey?" This got a noncommittal grunt. "And we're all working for the same goal."

"I'm not so sure of that," Skip snapped. "After all, if he's trying to kill you, you're probably trying to kill *him*. Are you sure you guys are completely blameless, here?"

"What are you suggesting?" Jennifer snapped. "That we're murderers like him?"

He bit his lip as he looked at her. "Well, people do have a habit of dying around you . . ."

Jennifer felt like he had taken a hot poker to her lungs. She opened her mouth and found no words to say.

Even though she saw his face change at the sight of hers, she didn't want to give him a chance to apologize. She kicked her chair away, ran out of the kitchen, and made sure she slammed the door to her bedroom so everyone downstairs could hear it. She set about her charcoal sketches immediately.

Ten minutes later, her father knocked on the door.

"Is he gone?"

The door cracked open. "No. He says to tell you he's sorry. He didn't mean to remind you of Grandpa Crawford like that." There was a pause. "He sounded pretty sincere."

"Why isn't *he* up here?"

Another pause as he reviewed her artwork. "I didn't want you to kill him."

This got the corner of her mouth twitching. "Huh. No, I'd be satisfied if he just left."

"He's not leaving. We are."

"Why?"

"Crescent moon's coming. Seems like a good time to get out of here. I'd been thinking of doing this anyway, but after today I'm sure."

"What?"

"We're going to go to Crescent Valley," he announced briskly. "You and me. Plainly, there are too many beaststalkers who are likely to ignore the mayor, like the Blacktooths did. That makes things doubly dangerous for us. We need time to think, in a safe place. And I'm going to ask the Blaze for permission to bring your mother with us. Skip, too, since Evangelos may be attacking your friends."

Who cares about Skip, she thought bitterly. *Okay, I do.* Her thoughts turned briefly to Susan, but she realized what her parents had probably already figured out: Here in Winoka Susan had more certainty of beaststalker protection than Skip did.

"And Skip's staying here with Mom while we go?"

He nodded, with the faintest of smiles. "Your mother insisted. For his protection, until we return. He looks pretty miserable about the idea, but he feels so bad about what he just said to you, he couldn't refuse."

She let a small, satisfied smile escape. "Let's go."

* * *

Despite her nervousness about what they were here to do, Jennifer found herself relaxing again the next morning when she broke the surface of the dark lake near Crescent Valley. Geddy the gecko was on her nose horn, braving the underwater voyage with unnatural aplomb. His head perked up at the sound of fire hornets in the distance, and he turned just in time to see the belt of fire surround the eternal crescent moon.

Looking at his expressionless, reptilian face, Jennifer couldn't help but wonder if he knew more about the venerables and what else was up there than she did.

"I sent word ahead of us," Jonathan told her as they broke free from the water's surface and spread their wings against the starlit sky. "The Blaze should be assembled by the time we arrive."

This much was true. Even from miles away, Jennifer could spot five or six large silhouettes floating just below the tip of the crescent moon. Like dark albatrosses, they simply let the gentle wind carry them where it would. Upon Jennifer and her father's approach, however, they began to turn over and dump the wind from their wings, descending in rapid circles to a point she quickly recognized: the dragons' amphitheater.

It was full, as it had been last time. Jennifer spotted Winona Brandfire without much trouble, and was surprised to see Catherine sitting right next to her grandmother. A few rows away, the prickly dasher Xavier Longtail sat restlessly on his haunches. He watched Jennifer as she eased herself to the ground next to her father.

Winona Brandfire wasted no time; Jennifer didn't even get a chance to sit down. "Jonathan Scales. You have summoned this Blaze." Her tone was sharp and inquisitive enough for Jennifer to hear the implied question: *Why?*

"I have, Eldest. Thank you. I am here to make a simple request: My wife requires sanctuary from clear danger. I need approval for her entry to this refuge, so that she can remain safe while we reconsider our strategy for hunting Evangelos."

He had not even finished speaking before several weredragons began mumbling and growling. Xavier was the loudest among them. Jennifer couldn't hear every word he said, but "preposterous" and "never" were easy to catch.

Winona held up a wing claw for silence. As she had before, Jennifer spotted a small, mysterious gleam on one scaly finger. "Elder Scales, you know our law. Not even weredragons before their fiftieth morph are allowed to know where this refuge is, much less come here." Jennifer caught the sideways glance to her granddaughter. "Why should we allow a beaststalker?"

"Because she's my wife, and I love her."

Jennifer, along with the rest of the dragons assembled, waited a few moments for more. But Jonathan offered nothing else.

Xavier rose and flicked his indigo tail irritably. His voice was loud, but the anger appeared just under control. "We are not responsible for your life decisions, *Elder* Scales. Had you married a weredragon, even one who hadn't reached her fiftieth morph, your request might be reasonable. But you cannot seriously expect us to allow one of our most dangerous enemies into our last and most sacred refuge!"

"I do," Jonathan replied calmly. "And she is not your enemy, Xavier Longtail. No matter how many times you say it, it will never be true."

"And no matter how many times you argue it, I will never believe you," the dasher snapped. "Do I need to remind everyone that Elizabeth Georges-Scales is descended from Saint George of England, the most bloodthirsty enemy our kind has ever known? That her grandparents and parents were among those who assaulted Pinegrove, drove out our kind, and settled there as if the land had been theirs all along? That *she herself* is responsible for the *murder of three dragons*, all of whom have family here tonight?"

"Only one of those was her choice!" Jonathan barked. He did not look at Jennifer, who was plainly wondering how much Xavier said was true. She had never heard her mother speak of killing dragons. *More secrets?* With great effort, she quelled the feelings of dismay and irritation and tried to focus on what her father was saying.

"Beaststalkers do not corner the market on unprovoked attacks. What Elizabeth did in her own defense, any of us would do."

"I doubt she shed a tear when my brother died at her hand," Xavier hissed back.

Jennifer's eyes widened. *Aha! There it is.*

Jonathan sighed. "I am now, as I have always been, sorry for your loss. And I will not defend the beaststalker's bloody rite of passage, which has caused our people pain for thousands of years. But from the day Elizabeth slew your brother, you and she have each had a choice to make. Since that day, she has never raised her sword with the desire to kill a dragon. Since that day, she has sworn an oath to do no harm—and has healed thousands of people, including hundreds of our friends and kin. Since that day, she has raised a weredragon as a child, and would sooner die herself than see the Ancient Furnace come to harm.

"Since that day, Xavier Longtail, what choices have you made? How many beaststalkers have you attacked and killed? How many have you healed or saved? How many have you even gotten to know?"

In the wake of these questions, a loud ripple of approval and acceptance rushed through the gathering. But Xavier was unmoved.

"I do not need to get to know them, Elder Scales. There is no point to knowing them. They are separate. They are the enemy."

"There is a point if we are to learn to live with them peacefully, someday."

The dasher's elaborate tail struck the ground with enough force to jolt the entire amphitheater. "No! We will *not* live with them peacefully! Not today! Not tomorrow! Not ever! That is our law."

Winona Brandfire's strong voice interrupted the two dragons. "Where is such a law written?"

Smoke curled around Xavier's crusted yellow eyes; he never took them off Jonathan. "It is written on my brother's grave."

Dasher and creeper stared at each other for long enough to make Jennifer fairly certain one would go for the other's throat. But her father suddenly broke eye contact and turned to the rest of the Blaze, Winona Brandfire in particular. "You all knew my father, the Venerable Crawford Thomas Scales." A murmur swept through the gathering. She guessed her father used the title "venerable" purposefully. Whatever it meant, it drew respect here.

"He taught me something long ago. Whenever I'd get worked up about something bad that had just happened, he'd sit me down, work a wing over my back, and tell me: 'Jonathan, if dragons were meant to fly backwards, they'd have eyes in their tails.' He insisted this was a common saying among dragons, though I've never really heard anyone else say it."

This provoked some chuckles. Jennifer sensed the mood shifting toward her father, and felt a surge of confidence. *If they say yes to Mom, they'll also say yes to Skip!*

Jonathan continued after a short pause. "Of course, what he meant was, we're built to look forward and move forward. We cannot stay fixed on the past. We must look for opportunities to reach out to those who can help us heal. My wife is a healer. And she needs our help. I hope we can look forward far enough to help her."

"Forward, not backward," a creeper Jennifer didn't know spoke up. "Something to try for once!"

Yes! They're going to agree!

"And then," Xavier puffed sardonically, "we should try turning our back on other traditions, such as honor, nobility, and—"

Blah-blah. Hate, hate, hate. Whatever— Hey, where's Geddy?

The small gecko was no longer near Jennifer; she'd been so caught up in what was going on she hadn't noticed him slip away. She tried to look around subtly without looking frantic. *Argh! Of all the times to lose track of him! Geddy!*

"—loyalty to family and friends! Or . . . eh?" Xavier's rant stopped suddenly as he looked down to see something on a scaly toe. "I only bring these up— Huh." The dragon seemed totally distracted from his tirade, and Jennifer had a horrible thought.

Don't squash him!

Xavier reached down and held Geddy up in one enormous clawed hand. His expression was sincere and thoughtful. "Did someone lose a friend?"

"It's—uh—it's mine, Elder Longtail." Jennifer darted forward and practically snatched Geddy out of the elder's claws.

"That gecko's yours, eh?" He curled his lips and wrinkled his wings, but his tone showed measured respect.

"Yes," she said, thumbing the scaly skull of her pet.

A short silence greeted the admission.

"You were saying, Elder?" Winona prompted gently.

"Yes. Thank you, Eldest. I've . . ." He trailed off and stared at the gecko again, and the girl who held it. "I believe I've made my point. I urge unity in this matter."

"I've met Dr. Georges-Scales," said the creeper who had spoken earlier. "I was in a car accident not far from Winona. Hers was the closest hospital. I could've sworn she saw right through me—knew exactly what I was, though I hadn't a clue who she was at the time. But she fixed me up right."

"I know Jonathan Scales," offered Ned, the ripened trampler. Jennifer smiled at him as he stood up straight. "Good man. Good choices. I trust him. I say we let 'er in."

There were more voices, more testimonials. Alex Rosespan, still loyal to Jennifer after tutoring her last year. Joseph Skinner, who had taken a break from watching over the farm to come weigh in—favorably, she was relieved to hear.

"Are there no other dissenting opinions?" Winona asked after a time. "Has the Blaze come to a decision?"

Xavier sighed. "We will regret this day."

"We may," Jonathan replied softly. "But I doubt it."

"We are decided, then," Winona announced. "Dr. Elizabeth Georges-Scales may immediately find refuge here in Crescent Valley, for a period of two weeks. She must be accompanied by her husband at all times. After two weeks, we will reconvene to determine if further time is warranted."

"Thank you!" Jennifer couldn't help the outburst; she was jumping up and down. "Thank you, thank you, thank you!"

"And . . ." Jonathan took a deep breath. "We must make one more request, if you are willing."

Piece of pie, Jennifer thought in an optimistic thrill. *Mom's a grown-up warrior, but Skip's just a kid. We're trying to protect a minor! He's a shoo-in.*

The wind was whistling past them pretty loudly, but Jennifer could still make out the profanity Jonathan unleashed once they were a safe distance away.

"I guess we pushed our luck," she comforted him, feeling rotten herself. "And hey, they *did* let Mom in! You know, conditionally."

"Hmmph."

"It's the best we can do for now." She had an odd thought: Who was the child here? And who was the grown-up? Had he really thought they'd get a 'yes' to both? Had *she* really thought that?

"Maybe we can sneak him in later."

She nearly fell out of the air. "Sneak him in?! How's that going to work?"

"No idea. We'll figure out what to do once we're all together. Skip can decide for himself what he'd like to do, at least."

"I guess. So we go home now?"

"I'm just seeing you to the lake. I'll stay here and make arrangements for comfortable living quarters. Your mother doesn't have a dragon's hide, and our nests and caves are unlikely to appeal to her without additional furnishings." He winked. "Tell your mother to pack a waterproof bag. And have Skip make a decision. I'll come through and meet you at the cabin in a few hours."

"Okay. See you soon! Watch Geddy while I'm gone?" She plucked the lizard off her nose horn and tossed him lightly over to her father. The stunned lizard landed on the other dragon's back.

Jonathan spared a glance at the pet before it crawled up the back of his neck and settled behind his purple crest. "I told you this gecko was special. Did you see how he calmed Xavier down?"

"That *was* weird," Jennifer agreed. "Longtail's got a thing for geckos, does he?"

He shrugged. "Whatever it was, it helped us get your mother here. She'll be thrilled to hear she owes her sanctuary to a small lizard."

They laughed together, and then he veered off with a quick good-bye, and she was through the lake again.

Mom's coming through!

It was almost enough to ease her anxiety about Skip.

* * *

The euphoria Jennifer had felt about the weredragons' decision vanished as soon as she approached the house. Phoebe the dog was cringing in the far corner of the yard, and the green front door was off of its hinges.

She immediately felt the freezing sensation of danger as she broke out of dragon shape and entered the house. The living room was in tatters—furniture ripped and overturned, wallpaper scraped off as if by knives, and the walls themselves gauged and dented.

"Mom?" There was no answer.

"Skip?" More silence.

There's another explanation, she insisted to herself. *There's another explanation.* But, of course, there couldn't be. What else could possibly have happened here?

Everything she could see was broken. Everything. Coffee tables, end tables, the dining room table . . . the china hutch, all the china *in* the hutch. The vases, even the small bowl of alabaster eggs her mother kept on the key table in the hallway. Shattered. Shambles. She could hear Phoebe crying in the backyard.

To the side, she caught a glint of moonlight on steel in the kitchen. Pushing debris out of her way, she stepped up and made out the straight shape of her mother's sword, plunged several inches into the tile.

A few feet to the right, in front of the steel refrigerator's smashed door, Jennifer saw a collapsed shape and screamed. For a moment she felt her sanity tipping like a sailboat on an angry ocean. *I'm going crazy and none of this will matter soon.*

Elizabeth Georges-Scales lay on her back. There were new white strands among her blonde hairs, and new wrinkles around her wide open jade eyes. She stared at the ceiling, whispering so softly Jennifer was certain all that was left of her mother was a ghost.

"No love. No love. No love . . ."

There was no sign of Skip at all.

CHAPTER 14

No Love

"She's lucky," Jennifer dimly recalled a nondescript doctor telling her some hours later. Dr. Freeborn, or Treehorn, or some such. "Very lucky."

Is that what they call a coma nowadays? Jennifer wondered silently as she stared at the still, prone form of her mother upon a bed nestled within machines and tubes. *Lucky.*

Elizabeth Georges-Scalso was now asleep—not that she had been exactly awake before. The doctor went on to guess at how long it might be before she opened her eyes again, or talked, or made some sardonic comment, or cooked badly, or snapped angrily, or did any of the things that drove her daughter nuts. The answer, it turned out, was anywhere from the next minute to never.

She stopped listening to the doctor at that point—clearly she would learn nothing helpful from the man—and thought about her father. She had left a desperate phone message at the cabin. With luck, her father or Joseph would arrive there soon. Just in case, she had sent a black mamba cooled tentatively (and none too happily, for mount or rider) on the back of a snake eagle. How these emissaries would make it to the farm or through the lake without drowning, or how they would communicate the exact nature of the emergency, or how her father would appear in any event under a crescent moon here at the hospital, she had no idea. She just had to hope.

The doctor's voice droned on. The fluorescent lights above made him look sickly and pale. Jennifer felt sweat trickle down her own cheeks, following the tracks of tears. Was she about to faint? That would be all right, wouldn't it? The doctor would understand . . .

She had no more time to wonder before she collapsed.

What must have been a while later, she woke up with a breathing tube attached to her face and an intravenous solution dripping into her arm. The staff had thoughtfully set her up in the same room with her comatose mother.

She began sobbing again—how many times had she cried, since Evangelos returned? Thinking of her father, she tore the machinery off of her own body, swung her legs off the bed, and sat up.

Not like this. I won't let him come back and find us both like this.

A breeze ran up her bare back, and she realized she was in a hospital gown. She was still scanning the room for her clothes when there was a knock at the door. The person who poked her head inside was unexpected, and unwanted.

"What do you want?" Jennifer sniffed as stiffly as she could at Mayor Glorianna Seabright, while adjusting her gown and standing up. There was one good thing about the woman being here: It put crying out of Jennifer's mind.

The mayor's long, white locks framed a grave and cautious expression. "Ms. Scales. I was visiting Wendy Blacktooth down the hall, and I heard . . ." Her oddly pale gaze came to rest upon Elizabeth's body. "I came to pay my respects."

"Pay respects!" Jennifer couldn't help the spittle that flew out of her mouth. "Cripes! She's not dead!"

Mayor Seabright flinched. "That's not what I meant. I meant—"

"Visiting hours are over."

The patronizing sigh that followed rankled Jennifer. "Dr. Georges-Scales was popular here at the hospital, and throughout town. I'm sure many others—"

"Was!" She came at the door so fast, the mayor very nearly closed it between them. "*Was?!* Are you serious?!"

With their noses inches apart, Jennifer let the shape of her face change just enough for the blue scales to surface over her human features, and the reptile to peek out from behind her gray eyes.

Her voice was only a whisper. "When my mom wakes up, she and I are going to march right into city hall and kick the ass of every crazy loon on that council of yours. And then my dad and I are going to burn that building down, sick ceiling artwork and all! *You wait.*"

She willed herself calm, flexed her features fully back to human, and stood up straight. "Now go back and tell your friends I don't want them swinging by to pay respects or anything else!"

"Ms. Scales, please. I regret—" But the mayor was already backing out the door, which made it all the easier for Jennifer to slam it in her face.

A few seconds later, the door opened again. Jennifer turned to shove it closed when the elderly features of Martin Stowe appeared. He was wearing a custodian's jumper and had his hospital employee badge on his belt. The failing eyes were wide as he set his mop against the doorframe and tried to take in the comatose shape on the bed.

"Gerry told me your mom was hurt."

She eased away from the door, still wary. "Yes, Mr. Stowe. Come on in."

"I've been on shift," the man explained. "I didn't believe Gerry right away, but the nurses told me he was right. What do the docs say?"

"Not much." She supposed it was unfair, but she was still not entirely convinced about the man's grandson.

He nodded slowly, staring at objects in the room but not, Jennifer guessed, truly seeing them. She still felt compelled to adjust her hospital gown.

"Gerry tells me you kids have been awfully good to him at school. You and Susan, especially. I wish there was something I could do."

Jennifer didn't quite know what to say to that. Of course Susan talked with Gerry, but she had never thought of herself as Gerry's "friend." For a new kid with no parents, though, who knew how much good an occasional smile from a random girl at school would do?

He wringed his hands. "The docs really have nothing to say?"

Jennifer shook her head. "Nothing helpful."

"I can't see her too well, but from what I can tell, she seems restful," Martin almost whispered. He took a tentative step forward, but could not summon the courage to get closer than the foot of Elizabeth's bed. He turned to Jennifer and gave a wan smile. "You'll tell her I was here?"

"Sure."

"Are you . . . uh . . . feeling all right yourself?"

"Sure. I'm fine." She just wanted him to leave now. "Thanks for coming by."

The custodian nodded and backed out of the room. "I'll tell those nurses to keep an extra eye or two on you both." He waved a hand in front of his weakening eyes, grinning wryly. "For me."

Jennifer nodded gratefully and gently closed the door. Five seconds later, there was another knock on it. *Who now?*

It was Susan, in tears. Seeing her like that made Jennifer start to cry again.

"Oh, Jennifer!" She rushed in with a hug. "I got your message and came as soon as I could. Is your mom okay?" Without waiting for an answer, she looked past her friend's shoulder at the patient's bed. "Oh . . . she looks so peaceful . . ."

"Don't say that," Jennifer snapped, immediately feeling bad. She softened her tone. "I mean, that's what they say about dead people."

"I'm sorry. Hey, it's okay." Susan tightened her embrace. "I understand."

Of course she does, Jennifer realized, remembering Susan's own mother.

Susan backed up a step and dabbed her cheeks with a sleeve. "What—was it—"

"Yeah, it was the thing you saw yesterday. Which I'm so sorry about! It wasn't after you, it was after . . . Listen, Susan, I can't keep any more secrets from you. You're my best friend and it's too much."

Susan nodded, found a chair, and sat down. "Okay. Go."

"Okay, first thing. Remember that day last spring I told you I was a dragon and so was my father? Well, I learned something else about myself. Later on. It has to do with my mother."

"Well, she must be a dragon, too, right?" Susan's look of complete innocence and trust broke Jennifer's heart.

"Um, no. It doesn't always work out that way. It turns out . . . well, she's a beaststalker. So *I'm* part beaststalker, too."

Susan's expression was unreadable.

Jennifer had to say something. "Um, anyway, I just thought you should know that. I haven't told Skip yet, because my mom killed his dad. But I'm going to tell him soon, I swear."

More staring. The sounds of the hospital rolled over them—hustling nurses, patients muttering to visitors, voices calling through the speaker system.

"Also, um, funny thing, Skip and I share a half brother. Kind of a half-dragon, half-spider thing. That's, um, that's what you saw in the street. You know, uh, earlier today. Which I'm really sorry about. Again."

Susan's mouth gaped open.

"Yeah. Um, one last thing. This half brother's from a completely different dimension. He's already killed my grandfather, and he wants to kill everyone close to my dad. Including me. And that's it. That's everything. Just wanted, you know, to keep you up to speed on things."

Somewhere in the distance, someone called for Dr. Evanston, whoever he or she was, to get to surgery immediately. Susan didn't budge. Her expression was one of tear-streaked awe.

She can't handle it, Jennifer was certain. *She's going to bolt, just like she did when she found out I was a dragon. But I will not judge her, I will not blame her, no matter how much I need her to stay. She never signed up for this.*

Suddenly her friend's features firmed up, and the tears were gone. Susan Elmsmith stood up, took her best friend's hand, and kissed her on an astonished cheek.

"Okay, Jennifer. So I'm here to help. What do you need?"

Susan agreeing to keep watch over Elizabeth made it easier for Jennifer to leave the hospital, but going back home to the awful mess was still difficult. She had just begun surveying the wreckage inside the house when she heard someone approach the front doorway. Phoebe—who had stuck close to the house even with the door kicked open—barked at the noise and ran out of the destroyed dining room. Jennifer followed closely, weapons in hand and adrenaline surging as she saw the winged shadow approach before the hovering afternoon sun. *This is it. He's back for me. Come on, you. Let's go. I cannot wait to bury you.*

"Jennifer!"

"Dad!" He was still in dragon form. Phoebe was whining

around his hind legs. Jennifer raced through the door and hugged him.

"I got the message from Joseph. Where is she?"

"At the hospital now. The doctors say . . ." She trailed off, unwilling to continue. Somehow, telling him would make it more real—even more real than watching her mother asleep.

"She's still alive?" His gray eyes shone a bit. "She's not dead?"

Jennifer shook her head, sniffling, and told him about the coma.

He folded her in his wings tightly.

After a while, he let go. "I should go to see her. If she's alone when she wakes up . . ."

"Susan's watching her. She's got my cell phone number, and a cell of her own." Jennifer patted the device on her skirt belt. "I thought I should come back here and figure out what I could."

"Good instincts, ace." He looked over his shape ruefully. "Okay, I suppose we could take a look around first."

They picked through bits of plaster, fabric, and wood, looking for clues that would tell them the story of the fight that took place here. Phoebe settled down in the front doorway, content to see part of her pack home, and stood watch.

Stepping carefully through the living room, Jennifer spotted a small marble ornament on the floor—the dragon carving Susan had given her for her fifteenth birthday. Her parents had let her put it on a fancy end table, which was now in splinters across the room. She picked up the miniature dragon and cradled it in her hands for a moment, before gently placing it on the windowsill. Then she continued her investigation.

In her peripheral vision, she caught her father wiping his face several times as they surveyed the wrecked furniture and damaged walls.

"Wow, she really kicked his ass," she offered in the way of comfort.

Jonathan sniffed quickly and looked up with red eyes. "What makes you say that, ace?"

"Well, look at these marks on the table." They were in the dining room, and she pushed aside some hanging fragments of wallpaper as she pointed. "These look like thrust marks from Mom's sword. They're covered in blood—and Mom didn't have any major wounds when I found her. Not even any minor ones—scratches at worst. She must have slashed him at least five, maybe six times, in this room alone. And with all these claw marks, it looks like he was struggling to get away. He left the dining room and went into the kitchen —see the direction of the blood stains?—and I can't imagine he'd be chasing someone who was stabbing him over and over."

A corner of his mouth raised. "She had him running away from her, at one point."

"I can't figure out what happened here, though." Jennifer examined the remains of the kitchen table and chairs. "She had him backed into a corner. See where the paintings got knocked off? By wings, or legs, up against the wall. But then she got her sword stuck here in the floor, which seems too far away from her target. And I found her . . . I, uh, found her over there." She pointed vaguely this time; it felt almost like bad luck to get too specific.

"I know what happened." Jonathan sighed. "She reached out to him."

"What do you mean?"

"She drove her sword point down to show Evangelos she was done fighting. She showed him mercy."

"And in return, he attacked her." Jennifer felt the back of her neck get warm. "When she didn't even have her sword."

"Yes. A cowardly act. But then he did something extraordinary, Jennifer."

"What's that?" Now it was her turn to wipe her eyes.

"He left her alive."

She cleared her throat and scanned the kitchen. "I haven't seen much sign of Skip."

Rubbing her shoulder for comfort, he silently agreed to the shift in investigation. "The door to the basement stairs is still open," he pointed out after a few seconds of investigation. "But it doesn't look like there was much fighting over there."

"We usually keep it closed, don't we?" Biting her lip in fear for what she may find, Jennifer jogged down the hallway and peered down the stairs. "Skip! Are you down there?"

There was no answer. The wood paneling and carpeting were intact, and it was clear Evangelos had not entered this part of the house.

As her father folded his wings and squeezed behind her, she crept down the stairs. Only the hum of the furnace was audible. The stairs turned a corner at the landing, and Jennifer held her breath as she peeked past.

The basement was empty, save for the cardboard boxes where they kept seasonal decorations, and a few spare clean clothes piled up by the washer and dryer next to the furnace.

Her father immediately moved past. "Back here." He led her past the furnace and motioned toward some carpet remnants that had been pushed from their normal position. On the floor where they used to be was something Jennifer had never seen before—a metal trap door in the cement floor. *The tunnel*, Jennifer remembered from her conversations with her grandfather and mother.

It was open. Jonathan approached it and flicked a wing claw against the sharp corner of the metal square.

"Skip hurt himself squeezing through." He drew the claw back and showed Jennifer the thickening blood he had scraped off. "Not seriously, I don't think. In any case, I doubt we'll find him anywhere near here. Not the way he is now, anyway."

Jennifer looked closer at the blood. Trapped in the substance was a dark hair—not thin and wispy like the sort she could run her fingers through on Skip's scalp, but unnaturally thick.

She had seen that sort of tactile hair before—on the spindly legs of Otto Saltin. Now his son had them, on whatever shape he took under the crescent moon.

"His first change," she whispered.

"Ms. Saltin, I just want to talk to him for a sec. Please?"

The voice on the other end of the line somehow managed to be both friendly and terse. "Goodness, Jennifer, I don't think so. He's really not inclined to come to the phone right now."

Jennifer imagined a large bulbous form, a female version of Otto, hovering over the phone in the dark with the shades drawn, plying the buttons with a spare tarsus. Perhaps in a corner of the same room, another bulbous shape would be cowering in fear of what had just happened. *Is he as scared as I was my first time?*

"Can you tell me at least, is he all right?"

"Oh, how sweet of you to ask." *Was that sincerity or irony?* "He's fine, dear. In fact, I don't think he's ever been stronger."

"Will you tell him I called?"

Tavia made a sound—it might have been clearing whatever throat she had under a crescent moon, or a clicking of mandibles, or something completely different. "He knows you've called, dear. He knows *everything* now."

Jennifer's blood chilled as the line went dead.

Her father put a comforting wing around her shoulder. "I think we've done all we can for him today, ace. It's time I went to see your mother."

With careful use of Jonathan's camouflage, they maneuvered through the hospital hallways and made it to Elizabeth's room. Susan looked relieved to see Jennifer, but started in surprise when Jonathan appeared behind her.

"Oh, I didn't see— Mr. Scales, that's you, right?"

His reptilian head bowed slightly. "Susan."

She turned to the patient. "She's not—she hasn't—um, there's been no change."

Jennifer watched him creep toward her mother's bed, as though he were afraid to wake his wife. His wing gently skimmed the bed sheets, brushed Elizabeth's face, and smoothed out the whitened locks on the pillow. Leaning down, he whispered something to her. Elizabeth did not move.

Finally, he lifted his head. "Susan, I can't tell you what it means to me that you stayed here with her."

"Of course." She blushed. "I could stay longer, if you need to—"

"That's very kind," he interrupted. "But I can't ask any more of you. I'm sure your father will be wondering where you are."

"Oh, it's okay. He's on a work trip anyway. I've, er, been driving the car kinda illegally." Her face got even redder. "But it's for schoolwork tonight! I'm going to the mall with Mr. Slider."

"Mr. Slider?" Jennifer wrinkled her nose. "What does he have to do with anything?"

"He decided on a field trip tonight with our geometry class. At the Mall of America. He says there are lots of geometric puzzles we can create and solve there. Not to mention fabulous shopping."

"Huh. Well, yeah, Susan, you should go. Dad and I will stay with Mom for the night."

"Actually," Jonathan cut in, "you both should go."

Jennifer felt the blood drain from her face. "Dad, I'm not leaving Mom! I'm not leaving you!"

"Ace, I'm not going to say you *have* to go—"

"Good!"

"But I'm asking. Please."

"Why?" She looked around, confused. "What if Evangelos comes back?"

"Exactly. Jennifer, we don't know what his next move will be. He could come for you . . . or he could come back here to finish the job with your mother. If you stay here, he'll definitely show up here, and all three of us are in danger. If you go, he'll probably leave you alone, especially in a crowded place like a mall."

"But that just means he'll come here!"

"Yes." His expression did not waver. "And I'll be waiting for him."

"You can't face him alone! I should stay here to help!"

"Jennifer." He advanced, but she backed away so he couldn't touch her. "If we're all together, we could all die. If he comes here and finishes the job, and you're somewhere else . . . maybe he'll leave you alone. Maybe he'll decide I'm enough, finally. He showed your mother mercy. He might show you some, too."

Panic welled up in Jennifer's throat. "You're sending me away. Just like you did the night Grandpa died!"

He closed his eyes. "I'm sorry, ace. I'm out of options."

Susan tried to take Jennifer's hand, but Jennifer shook her friend off. "Dad. Come on. How will you fight him if he comes?"

"Maybe I won't have to," he said softly, looking at his wife. "Maybe her being here will help. Just seeing her, maybe Evangelos will remember some mercy. Maybe she'll protect me, one more time."

"And if she doesn't?" The words almost didn't come out.

He stepped forward quickly enough to swing one wing behind her and grab her by the back of the neck. His head close, he whispered in her ear, "It may come to that. But I am not completely helpless, Jennifer. I am an elder."

His scaly back straightened, and his silver eyes gleamed with pride. Jennifer saw some of the strength and resolve that

Evangelos had inherited. Perhaps her father was not so foolish after all.

He leaned in close. "If the worst happens, make for Crescent Valley. Winona Brandfire will know what to do."

"*I* won't." She wrenched herself out of his embrace and stared at the clean linoleum floor. "*I* won't know what to do."

"Don't sell yourself short."

He let her go and turned back to the bed where Elizabeth lay. "You've heard my wish, ace. Like I said, I can't make you do it. But I hope you will."

Her lips trembled as she tried to look up again. He didn't say any more, but set about smoothing his wife's hair with a wing claw.

"Okay, Dad. For a few hours, we'll try your plan. But I'm coming back tonight to talk about this some more."

His reptilian head gave a slight nod.

Susan took her hand successfully this time. "Come on, Jennifer. We'll do this, and we'll come right back."

They took a few steps toward the door before Jennifer stopped. "Dad."

"Yes."

"Mayor Seabright said Mrs. Blacktooth is right down the hall. Eddie or his dad may be around. You might . . . if Evangelos comes, I mean . . . you might ask them for help."

"Good idea, ace. Keep your eyes open out there."

"I love you, Dad."

"I love you, too, Jennifer Caroline."

She squeezed Susan's hand, and they left together.

* * *

Leaving Winoka, Jennifer gazed out the passenger seat window at the early sunset—a dazzling array of orange and pink clouds suspended in a violet sky. Movement against the easterly clouds caught her attention, and she turned slightly to view the darker, wispy shapes beneath them. There were hundreds, perhaps thousands, of birds in the sky. Jennifer recognized their shapes immediately, but Susan gawked at them for a while.

"Wow, a lot of geese up there today."

"They're not geese. They're birds of prey. Eagles, hawks, falcons—probably owls, too." Jennifer rubbed her temples and thought of her mother, and the pygmy owls they had argued over two short months ago.

"That's impossible! There are too many."

"Not for this town. The beaststalkers use them."

"For what?"

She shrugged. "Hunting Evangelos, I expect." *Maybe they'll do me and Dad a favor and kill the thug now,* she thought to herself. The thought gave her a sort of nasty pleasure, which she no longer tried to suppress. It also gave her a more wholesome feeling of relief—her mom and dad really might be safe.

Susan squinted at the birds. "I bet Eddie and his dad have a bird up there, somewhere." She sighed. "I so want to get out of this town."

Jennifer wrinkled her nose. "Badly enough to break the traffic laws, I can see. I didn't realize you were driving around alone with your learner's permit!"

Her friend blushed. "I can't help it if my dad isn't in town, and I need a vehicle for emergencies. Like getting to school. And the mall tonight," she added defensively.

"Yes, the mall. A true emergency. Even the most heartless police officer will understand."

That got them smiling, and then Susan turned on the radio.

"Ugh! That song again!"

It was the same tune they had heard in Jennifer's room on her birthday—the one they had both loved over the summer, but gotten tired of so long ago.

Jennifer stopped Susan's hand from switching the station. "Just leave it here, will you?"

"Hmmph. Yeah, okay, I guess. Didn't you get sick of it, too?"

"I did."

Jennifer closed her eyes, leaned against the window, and dreamt of an early birthday party at her grandfather's cabin, when she was an only child surrounded by family.

An airplane screamed not far overhead as Susan fussed about which level of the parking ramp would be the best option. California level? Or the Texas level? Or perhaps on the other side of the enormous Mall of America, where states like Maine and Pennsylvania were stacked upon each other?

"God, I hate highways," Susan muttered, taking the mall exit that headed for the western states parking ramp. "I can't believe all the cars on it."

"Oh, well, you know," Jennifer replied vaguely. "Traffic." She eyed Macy's as they passed and wondered for the hundredth time whose dumb idea it was to replace the apostrophe with a star. "Maybe we should check out some three-hundred-dollar raincoats while we're here."

"Well, *I* don't have that much money to throw away," Susan said with a sniff, pulling into Colorado.

"So where's the class meeting?"

"Mr. Slider told us on the west side, second floor, by Tiger Sushi. He said he had a hankering for their spring rolls."

"Huh. He's a weird one."

"Yeah." Susan's face suddenly lit up. "You know, I've seen him outside school a few times. He hangs around with this strange, thin woman—and I found out later it's Skip's aunt! Can you believe it?"

Jennifer thought of Mr. Slider's unexpected visit to Skip and Tavia's house. "Huh. Yeah, I guess so."

"I wonder what *that's* about. Oh, which spot? I haven't practiced parking much. It looks a lot easier when my dad does it."

After some hunting and a few valiant maneuvers, Susan managed to fit the car across two spaces in a remote corner of the yellow level (Hawaii, with pineapple reminder signs), far away from anyone else's vehicle.

"You have a bright future as a valet, Elmsmith."

"Stuff it, Scales."

They were giggling again as their shoes clicked against the parking lot pavement. Jennifer had almost set aside the image of her parents in the hospital when a tall shape advanced toward them from behind a cement pillar. Instinctively, she pushed Susan back and reached under her skirt for a blade.

"Oh, it's you." She relaxed, but then tensed again when she saw how he was dressed. "What?"

Eddie Blacktooth wore a white robe with black accents, not unlike what his father had worn at the beaststalker trial.

His close-cropped brown hair was matted down with sweat, and his face was fixed in determination.

Susan stepped out from behind Jennifer. "You're not in our geometry class," she snapped. "Why are you here? Why are you dressed like that? Are you following us?"

He nodded. "Since the hospital. Sorry about your mom, Jennifer."

"Sorry about yours." *What's he up to?* "So you drove? You're not old enough to have a license."

A smile almost forced itself across his sparrowlike features. "Neither is Susan."

"*My* dad's out of town," Susan said with such righteousness, Jennifer almost believed she hadn't broken the law regardless. "What's your excuse?"

"Well, my dad was okay with this. After all, he sent me here. He thinks Evangelos is following you, so I don't have much time."

His right hand came out from behind his robes and Jennifer instinctively reached for her blades again.

The Blacktooth blade reflected the dying light of the sunset behind him. "My father sent me on my rite of passage," he explained with almost touching formality. "He says I must fulfill my quest or die trying."

Susan's voice wavered. "You must be after Evangelos, too, after what he did to your mother. You're here to help her, right?"

Jennifer smiled grimly. "No, Susan. He's not here to kill my brother. He's here to kill *me*."

CHAPTER 15

Evangelos Exposed

"Susan, you'd better get out of here."

"I'm not going anywhere! You're my friend, and I'm going to help you."

Jennifer straightened up and looked at her. "Susan, Eddie's not himself."

"Try a new one!"

"I mean, he might hurt you. You should go."

"Don't talk about me like I'm not here!" A ruddy hue came to the boy's pale cheeks. "Susan, get out of here. You're a civilian. It's not safe to be with Jennifer. She's dangerous—a monster."

"No, *you're* the monster." Susan spat. "You and your horrible father. You should know better than him. You should *be* better than him."

Eddie's face twisted in anger, but Susan went on more

gently. "Don't you remember, Eddie? You and Jenny and I used to joke about him and your mom all the time. We used to joke about *all* of our parents. They're all crazy, in one way or another. We all swore years ago we'd never let them come between us. But you were especially disgusted with your dad. Since when did you turn your back on us, for him?"

"Since I grew up," Eddie said through gritted teeth, glaring at Jennifer. "Since my best friend in the world lied to me, and my parents started telling me the truth. Since the girl I've loved since first grade betrayed me!"

Jennifer felt herself start to shake. She couldn't take her eyes off of his, even with his sword raised between them. *What did he just say?*

"Wow." Susan turned to Jennifer. "There's a lot of information right there."

"I never lied to you, Eddie." Jennifer sheathed her blades and took a couple of steps toward him. "I was just trying to figure out who I was. I needed time."

His voice trembled. Moisture welled around his eyes. "We *never* kept secrets from each other! Not like you did!"

"Didn't we?" She said it as softly as she could. "Eddie, when exactly did you come to tell me what you and your parents were?"

He looked from Jennifer to Susan to Jennifer. "My parents swore me to secrecy."

"You think mine didn't?"

"They told me even in a town like Winoka, there are always spies."

"And was I one of those spies? Was my mother?"

"You lied to me!" The point of the Blacktooth blade,

which had been drooping steadily for the past few seconds, jerked back up between them.

"Eddie, this is insane!" Susan nervously ran her hand through her dark hair. "*You're pointing a sword at your two best friends*. Stop and think about what you're doing!"

"Thinking," Jennifer said with a thin voice, "appears to be in short supply in the Blacktooth family nowadays."

He didn't reply. Instead, he shook his head and fixed his gaze back on Jennifer. With tight lips and a determined stance, he leaned forward with the blade.

She needed to get her friend out of here. "Susan, go."

"Jennifer—"

"Now, Susan! Drive back to the hospital, get my dad—"

There was no more time to talk. Eddie lunged forward and Jennifer flicked her left dagger out of its sheath just in time to deflect the blow away from her head. As she staggered back in surprise—he had actually tried to stab her!—she heard Susan's footsteps racing back toward the car.

"Eddie, what're you—"

"Ready your weapon!" It was a demand and a plea at the same time.

"Eddie, I'm not going to fight—"

"Ready yourself or ready your soul!" The Blacktooth blade surged forward a second time. Again, her own dagger came up to block it.

Jennifer felt tears rising. She turned briefly at the sound of Susan's car screeching on its way out of the parking garage. No one else was around. "Eddie, please! I can't. Not like this. Not with you. Can't we just—"

"My father told me you'd beg." His words were cold, but

Jennifer saw the single tear draining down his cheek. "He told me you would refuse to fight. He told me you were weak. Just like your mother."

For the third time, he thrust the blade at her.

You shouldn't have talked about my mother like that.

This time, she trapped the blow between dragon's jaws. The point stuck out the other side of her teeth. In a red fury, she clamped down hard on the blade. Eddie pulled back, but the sword did not budge. He pulled again, until she twisted her head and yanked the weapon from his hands. Drawing herself to full height, she let the steam pour from her nostrils and squeezed her jaws until she felt the dark steel bite into her gums. Then she squeezed even tighter, and she felt the sword fail.

KKKRRRRRKKKKK. The splinters of the blade snapped into the roof of her mouth and her forked tongue. She spit the bloody pieces out onto the pavement. Then she let loose with a scream, filling the garage with a primal roar. Her blood—the blood of the Ancient Furnace—was boiling.

"How dare you!" she roared, her original scream still echoing through the parking ramp. "HOW DARE YOU!"

His face full of fear, shock, and dismay, Eddie fell to his knees and bowed his head.

The boil inside was nearly too much. She felt the fire in her throat before she caught a glimpse of his down-turned face: the brown eyes that had once cried for her when she fell off her bike as a little girl, the soft cheeks that had cushioned his smile when he told her about the family's latest trip to Europe, the sharp nose she had punched once when they were seven and got into an argument about comic books.

He was wrong then, and he's wrong now.

The random thought gave her time. With a small hiss, she calmed herself down.

"Eddie."

He did not look up. His voice was toneless. "What."

"Eddie, that hurt."

"Good."

"I know you don't mean that."

Raising his head, he looked at her with overflowing despair. "You don't know that. You don't know me."

"Yes, I do. You're my friend."

"Since when?"

"Since forever."

"No, I'm not. I'm your enemy."

"Eddie, if you were my enemy, you'd be dead by now."

"It doesn't matter." He picked up the hilt of the Blacktooth blade, which now had nothing more than a staunch three-inch fragment jutting out. "My father will kill me when he sees this." The corner of his mouth twitched. "You had to destroy the family heirloom?"

Jennifer couldn't help herself. She chuckled. "You had to try to stab me with it three times?"

His smile turned more genuine. "You and I both know you were never really in danger. You were always the strong one. I was always weak."

"That's not true."

"Yes, it is. I'm sorry, Jennifer."

She morphed back into a girl. "Stand up, Eddie."

"What?"

"Stand up."

"Why?"

"Because you need to brush yourself off and get your dignity back. Because you're more handsome when you stand up straight. Because you're kneeling in my blood and it's gross. Do you need another reason?"

He stood.

Just in time for Skip to knock him back down.

"Skip!" She hadn't seen or heard him coming.

"I told you to stay away from her!"

Skip landed a hail of punches to Eddie's midsection, head, and kidneys before Jennifer could finally pull him off. Her mind was whirling with emotions—relief that Skip seemed alive and well, irritation that he had chosen this worst of all moments to reappear, surprise that he wasn't in spider form under the crescent moon, and concern for Eddie's health since the other boy was limp and not fighting back at all.

"Skip, cut it out! You're hurting him!"

He wriggled out of her grasp and began kicking Eddie's torso. "That's the idea."

"Skip! Eddie's sorry, and I can handle this myself!"

"Yeah, whatever." Skip's eyes sparkled with a mixture of rage and glee. He gave his adversary one last kick to the chin as Jennifer pushed him back. Eddie flipped over, landed on the pavement with a sickening crunch, and did not move.

"Knock it off, you creep! You'll kill him!"

Skip actually smiled. "Creep. That's a good one, Jennifer. Creep. Yeah, I'm a creep. So are you. We creep around in the dark, monsters like you and I, hiding from bullies like this sick bastard." He pointed at Eddie, who was plainly breathing but doing little else. "My father was a bully, Jennifer. I know one when I see one. Do you want to protect a bully? Do you want to see what happens when you do?"

"Skip, hurting him isn't going to make you feel any better. We've got to focus on Evangelos! Eddie says he's around here somewhere."

His reaction took her by surprise. He began to laugh.

The patience drained from her. "Skip. Why are you laughing?"

He wiped his chin. "No reason, I guess. Hey, look! We finally made it to the Mall of America. Just like I promised."

They stood there looking at each other quietly, and then Jennifer's skin began to crawl. She had felt this feeling before with this boy. "Skip, you've been holding back something. You haven't told me the whole truth."

"Well, true," he said with a sneer. "But then, you and your family have been holding back, too, haven't you? I mean, about you and your mom being beaststalkers and all."

"Skip, this is a bad time—"

"This is a *great* time," he corrected her. "Because I've been waiting for weeks for you to own up to it. Honestly, Jennifer, how stupid do you think I am?"

She sighed in exasperation, casting her gaze about for signs of Evangelos. "What, you want a numeric rating?"

"I figured out what you were even before I saw your mom fighting."

"So you were there when she fought him, when . . . she got hurt."

"Of course I was. Did you think I was running away from Evangelos? I was running away from *her*."

Her skin went cold. "Did she try to hurt you? Or did you try to hurt her?"

His angry expression faltered for the briefest of moments. "No, and no. But once I changed I knew I had to leave. Evangelos showed up, which gave me the chance. She had mentioned the tunnel to me as a possible escape route, so I used it."

"You said you'd stay there with her."

"Yes," he agreed. "I said that."

"So you abandoned her. You lied."

He stomped impatiently. "What, hasn't anyone lied to you before, Jennifer?"

"Come to think of it, yes. *You* have."

"Yeah, I lied about my father last year. Just like you, right? Once I knew your mom was a beaststalker, it didn't take much for me to figure out who had saved you and your dad in the sewers while I was unconscious. Of course, that means your mom killed my dad. A truth your family's been trying pretty hard to keep from me."

"We always planned on telling you someday, Skip . . ." Even now, the words sounded hollow in her own ears.

He rolled his eyes. "Spare me."

"We needed to track down Evangelos! He's been attacking my family! Hello, priorities? We needed your help!"

"And you could've had my help, if you had bothered to be honest with me. As it stands, I learned I can't trust you. So now you'll have to learn the truth on your own."

She stared at him. "What do you know about Evangelos that you haven't told us?"

He leaned against the rusted fender of a beat-up station

wagon and ignored her question. "Do you mind if I ask you something?"

Fixing her jaw, she glared at him. "Shoot."

He pointed at the Moon of Falling Leaves necklace she was wearing. "Did I ever mean anything to you or were you always just using me to solve your own stupid little problems?"

She fingered the wooden emblem of the necklace. "I can't believe you asked me that."

"Believe it. And answer it."

"Skip, you're pathetic. If you think our relationship was part of a family conspiracy, you're hopeless. And you'll be your father's son forever. Think what you want—I've got to help Eddie."

She tried to walk past him to get to where Eddie lay, but he sidestepped to block her path.

"Skip, I just spanked one bad boy. Don't make me do it to you, too."

The corners of his mouth curled up. "I'm not a boy anymore, Ms. Ancient Furnace. I heard you calling my aunt. You know I've had my first change."

"Sure, you had your first change. Big deal. Go home and wait for your big-boy underpants to come in the mail."

"And did you happen to notice what phase of the moon it is right now?"

A short glance beyond the cement fixtures of the parking garage reminded Jennifer of the crescent moon slipping through the wintry clouds. "Yeah, you should still be changed. So what, you're like me?"

"Maybe a bit better."

The sigh escaped her before she thought of how it might

sound. "Skip, I don't care. This is so juvenile! Susan's right—boys are so sad! If Evangelos is coming, we should get Eddie someplace safe. Either help me or get out of my way."

Again she tried to get to Eddie, and again he blocked her path. "I'm not sure I want to help you."

She stared at him.

He stared back.

"Skip. Why are you here?"

He shrugged. "I haven't decided. I'm not as cold as you, Jennifer. I'm not ready to kill Evangelos."

"Well, jeez, I don't want to kill him either." Even as she said the words, she wondered if they were true. They ought to be true. *But what about what he did to Mom? And Grandpa?* "He may not leave us with a choice. You've seen what he can do."

"Yes, your family seems to lose a lot of sleep over what Evangelos has done to others. But what about what *your family* has done to *Evangelos?*"

She blinked. He was working himself into a fury again, and for what? "What's your point?"

"I know what it's like to feel abandoned by parents. My mother was kind but distant. All she focused on was learning the rituals she needed to find Evangelos, to re-open the portal. I lost her to that obsession. After she was gone, my father gave me no time to grieve. He was all about his schemes and plans for you, and how I could help him. And then just like that, he was gone, too."

"None of that's your fault."

"I know! My point is that my parents cared about everything except me. I was never first on their list. I wasn't a priority."

"Well, I'm sorry! But what does this have to do with us and Evangelos?"

"It's simple, Jennifer. You're the child Jonathan Scales *wanted* to raise. Weren't you? Just like Evangelos was the child my mother *wanted* to raise. I have to say, as much as I hated this thing my mom was chasing when I was younger, I'm beginning to feel a common bond."

"So, what? You're best buddies now? He's going to party with you, help you with your math homework? Share a laugh or two about how you both screwed my mom over?"

Skip shook his head. A few bulges began to appear at the back of his neck. "No, not buddies. But I'm still a brother. I may be the only person who understands. Both our parents abandoned us. I'm here to help Evangelos."

Jennifer was incredulous. "Help him what? Kill me?"

Somewhere along Skip's spine, ridges were forming. The sound was unmistakable. *So like a weredragon's change, yet so different,* she reminded herself.

"I don't want to hurt you, Jennifer. I like you. A lot. I even thought of you as my girlfriend for a little while. But you shouldn't come between Evangelos and me."

There was something rising behind Skip. It took Jennifer several seconds to realize it was a segmented tail, with a large stinger dangling from its end. She took four quick steps back.

"Wha-what kind of spider *are* you?"

Skip's smile broke into mandibles and several more small eyes emerged around his forehead. "We're not were*spiders*, Jennifer. We're wer*achnids*. Arachnids count for more than just spiders. My genealogy is pretty broad, both on my mother's and father's side. In fact, my aunt Tavia tells me I'm rather special among our people."

Oh, swell.

He was a full-fledged scorpion now, six feet long and five tall, brown as his chocolate hair used to be, with gold ridges down his armored body and tiny greenish eyes. The clicking of his massive foreclaws did not appear to threaten her, but seemed more an exercise of muscles.

"*Pandinus imperator,*" he explained. "Emperor scorpion. My favorite form, so far."

"Favorite? So far?"

The mandibles flicked with a light chuckle. "As I was telling you, I'm a bit unique. Watch this . . ."

Jennifer gasped as he shifted form. His body was still dark brown but now bore the thick hairs of a spider instead of a scorpion's armor, while his mandibles and forelegs were bright red.

"*Habronattus americanus.* This one's good for jumping."

He shifted again. Now the body was more uniformly brown, larger, and softer. It was also considerably more terrifying.

"*Grammostola pulchra.* Brazilian black tarantula. This one's good for just scaring the hell out of people."

"Congratulations," Jennifer squeaked. She took another four steps back. "So, you're not stuck with a single form? I'm, er, so happy for you." *Happy, horrified, same difference.*

"Aunt Tavia tells me the possibilities are endless." The enormous mandibles worked around the careless tone. "She says a werachnid like me comes along once every fifteen hundred years or so . . ."

"Once every fifty generations."

"Yeah. Something like that. I've started quite a stir among my family's friends. Some say I'm an omen. Others say I have our kind's strongest known poison running through my veins."

"Powerful blood, eh? Good thing your father didn't get his hooks into you." Jennifer immediately regretted the jab.

The massive tarantula's position shifted abruptly, all eight legs tensing at once. Several of his eyes fixed on her. "Yeah. I guess so. Anyway, Jennifer, I didn't come tonight to hurt you. I came to talk with Evangelos. Leave now, and let us talk."

"Skip, I get he's your brother. But if Evangelos is coming I can't just walk away! He probably wouldn't let me leave anyway. If you want to talk to him, let's talk to him together. Maybe the two of us should try—"

"There *is* no us!" In a flurry of legs, he advanced upon her and pressed her back into a parked sports utility vehicle. She could smell the stench of poison on him. "Jennifer, we're through! You're a liar and a lousy girlfriend. Go home."

Her jaw tightened. "You know, Skip, you're not turning out to be much of a prize boyfriend yourself." And with that, her daggers were crossed in front of her mouth and she was screaming brilliant light and sound.

He took the assault directly in the face and scrambled back with a shriek. And just like that, he had changed again . . . back into a boy.

Jennifer stopped and sheathed her daggers. Skip's eyes were tearing and he held his hands over his ears, but he was grinning. "Good one, Jennifer. Aunt Tavia warned me about that, but I'd never heard it before. Pretty careless of me."

Far up the ramp behind her, she could hear voices,

footsteps . . . and something familiar she couldn't exactly place. "Skip, let's not fight. Please. I don't care who would win. We'd both lose."

"Jennifer, I—"

"We'll try your plan together! I think you're right to try to reach out to Evangelos, and I want to help you help him. Doesn't it seem smarter to do this together, instead of fighting each other?"

He was looking past her. "Evangelos is here."

Jennifer turned and immediately placed the familiar sound. It was Mr. Slider's wheelchair.

The geometry teacher was with several other people, she noticed. Half of the class was there for the field trip, including Bob Jarkmand and Gerry Stowe. There were also a few chaperones, though Jennifer couldn't see much past Martin Stowe.

Then she saw Rune Whisper behind them all.

There he was, the mysterious figure, still gaunt in his ill-fitting green suit. He didn't really seem like part of the group, walking a bit behind and to the left of everyone else. But he was staring at both Skip and Jennifer.

"It's Rune, isn't it?" She took a step back so that she and Skip were side by side. "We've got to get Mr. Slider and the others out of here!"

Skip chuckled. "Mr. Slider's an interesting guy. During my independent study lessons with him, I figured out the truth about Evangelos."

Jennifer caught her breath and stared at Mr. Slider. She whispered urgently, "*He's* Evangelos?! But how can that be? He—"

"He's not Evangelos," Skip interrupted. "I don't think he even knows who is. But using the logic he taught me, along with a little research of my own, I was able to deduce the truth. It began with following Rune Whisper."

"So it's Rune." This made the most sense to Jennifer anyway. She clenched her teeth as the crowd drew nearer and he along with it.

"I think he was always aware who was following him," Skip continued. "He *must* have known. There was no way we could stay completely hidden from something like him. But he may have wanted us to learn the truth anyway."

By now, Mr. Slider was only a few feet away. As he started to turn past them, he nodded curtly in greeting. Then he noticed Eddie lying not too far away, obviously beaten. And then he noticed the shards of the Blacktooth blade at Jennifer's feet.

"Ms. Scales," he began, "what's going on? We thought we heard a scream just a few—"

But Jennifer never heard the rest of the sentence. Like a dreadful alarm, a horrible thought triggered in her mind. She tried to close her ears but the voice was inside, just like at her grandfather's cabin weeks ago.

No daughter! No daughter! No daughter!

"Skip, he's coming for me!" For all of this boy's intransigence, Jennifer couldn't help clutching his arm. She had known this moment would come for some time, of course, but there was no hiding the panic in her voice. This predator had followed a long, winding, inevitable course to her. Every incident had hit closer and closer, like a series of bullet holes approaching the center of a ripped paper target. All this time, nobody had found a way to stop him—not her grandfather, not her father, not even her mother. Now he was here. For her. *What was she going to do?*

Rune Whisper did not attack. He idled behind the others, never taking his eyes off of her. She dragged Skip back a few steps. Mr. Slider was still talking, but could easily see they weren't paying attention.

"—so should I call the authorities? Ms. Scales? Mr. Wilson? Hello?"

...no daughter...no daughter...no daughter...

"Yes," Jennifer agreed softly without looking at the teacher. "You should call the authorities. And then find Susan. She'll get in touch with my dad. Tell him and my mom I never stopped thinking about them."

"Ms. Scales, I—"

"Mr. Slider." Jennifer saw Skip and the teacher exchange glances. "You should probably get everyone out of here."

The geometry teacher turned his chair back and forth to look at the two of them, and the rest of his students, and the adults. Finally, the chair moved past them. "Class, let's move on. I'm afraid I don't have a phone with me—something about this chair seems to disagree with the reception—so perhaps one of the chaperones would be so kind as to . . . Mr. Stowe? Hello, Mr. Stowe?"

...no daughter...no daughter...no daughter...

What Jennifer saw confused her. Most of the class and adults had moved along with the teacher. Gerry and his grandfather, however, stayed between Jennifer and Rune Whisper. Two more people Jennifer couldn't quite make out were right behind them.

"Rune Whisper went to the Stowes's house a lot," Skip was explaining quietly. "And to the school, and the hospital, and the building site there. I think he was a messenger or scout of sorts, running between the rest of them. But he went to *their* apartment the most, right in the same building as his own at Oak Valley. It was like a headquarters."

With those words he pointed at the last two emerging figures—Mr. Cheron and his wife. Standing tall in a sharp gray suit with a dark T-shirt, Angus kept a muscled arm around Delores. Just like at the beaststalker trial, she was in flowing robes of soft green, with her face hidden behind a thick veil.

Jennifer tore her glance away from Rune long enough to focus on her. What could she make out through that veil? There was something about her . . .

No daughter! No daughter! NO DAUGHTER!

The intensity behind the words shocked her. It wasn't quite anger, she realized. The rage was there, but something deeper fueled it.

It was sorrow.

Yes, that was it. There was so much sadness behind the words, so much misery and wretchedness that Jennifer herself could not help but feel deep grief for this woman.

The words were coming from Delores Cheron! She was the source! This was Evangelos!

. . . no daughter . . . no daughter . . . no daughter . . .

The stench of woe filled the air. Jennifer stumbled back into the cement fixture that overlooked the street four stories below. Gritting her teeth at her foolish assumptions about her sibling, she reached for Skip's hand to help steady herself.

"Skip . . . it's not Rune . . . it's her . . . it's Delores Cheron!"

He squeezed her arm back as he lifted her up. "Yes. And no. It's pretty clear to me now that your father made a mistaken assumption about Evangelos. A big one."

Rune Whisper and the two Stowes closed in around the Cheron couple.

The full truth hit her right before he told her. She gasped.

"Evangelos isn't exactly what you'd call an only child."

"There are *five* of them!"

"Yes, five. And yet one. Best I can tell, my mother had quintuplets. Maybe more, before they died in that other dimension. Werachnids, like most spiders, often have multiple births."

She didn't know what else to say, not one clue. How had this happened? How had she never thought of this possibility? *You have to know what you don't know,* Mr. Slider's voice chided her. *Otherwise, you can't solve the puzzle.*

Skip went on. *He had figured it out,* she thought with a shot of envy. "Lost and on their own in another world, the surviving children must have learned to work together. They hid together, hunted together, even thought and moved together. After a while, Delores must have taken charge, and taught her brothers to *be* together. And when it suited her, the one could become two, or three . . . or five. Apart, each child could learn something unique about the hell they lived in, maybe specialize and learn a particular skill. Together, they formed a whole greater than the sum of its parts."

The people around the Cherons were now incredibly close, Jennifer saw—so close that it was hard to tell where one person ended and another began. In fact, Angus and Delores themselves seemed more like a single entity than a couple. She rubbed her eyes and looked again. Were there still even five people?

No, she didn't think so. And they certainly weren't people anymore.

Each part was a black twist of scales, wings, and legs—clearly miniature versions of what Jennifer had fought in Grandpa Crawford's cabin. As one merged with another, the resulting beast became larger and larger.

The soul—where Delores had stood—was shuddering as Angus added his muscle. Not far away, Jennifer guessed, the elder Stowe was blending his knowledge and wisdom with Gerry Stowe's youth and energy.

"Once she came to our world," Skip mused, "she adapted, just like she did before. She followed trails of memories and learned to mimic people's faces, clothes, even their accents. The people we've seen here tonight probably still exist somewhere else in the world. She just borrowed their images and voices as disguises."

"So Evangelos is all of these people."

"Evangelina, I'm guessing. Yeah, in a way she's all those people—as many at any time as she wants to be. What attacked your grandfather could have been one of them, or two, or all five together. While I was watching Martin and Angus working at the hospital the other day, the other three parts were probably with you, scaring Susan and attacking Eddie's mom. That was Delores's own first real look at her father."

"They've been everywhere," Jennifer whispered. "Gerry's been at school to keep an eye on you and me, his grandfather's been at the hospital to watch mom, Angus has been near my father, and Rune's been running between them all."

"Only Delores has been hidden in the apartment," Skip finished. "She uses her brothers to learn and adapt. But she's the center. She drives them all. She's amazing!"

He could not hide the admiration in his voice, but he kept a protective hold on Jennifer's arm.

The last part, what they had known as Rune Whisper, was different from the others. Barely visible under the bright lights of the parking garage, the new form had no definable shape. Instead, it was the murky suggestion of a child of a dragon and a spider. Surely, this was the part of Evangelos that had learned to hide as prey . . . and then to hunt as a predator.

Just before Rune's shadow passed into the whole and clouded the head and torso, Jennifer caught a glimpse of Evangelina in her full glory. To her amazement, it was like looking into a dark mirror. There were three horns pulling back from a crest, and a nose horn in front of cloudy eyes.

"Sister . . ." The word escaped her without thought.

No!

Jennifer could make out the surprise and horror in the silent reply. Tendrils of darkness covered the head and splayed out over the pavement. The next words were calmer, but still steeped in rage and melancholy.

There is no sister. There is no daughter . . .

"I can hear her, too," Skip said with excitement. He stepped between Jennifer and Evangelina. "You know who we both are, don't you? She's your sister. I'm your brother. We don't want to hurt you. We—"

NO!

Faster than anything Jennifer had ever seen, a dark tail whipped around from behind the cloud and slammed into Skip's head. He crumpled to the ground.

"Skip!" She caught his limp body and dragged him back a few feet. Blood seeped slowly down his neck.

No brother! No sister! No daughter! Just Father. Father will pay!

"Back off!" Jennifer burst out. "Get away from us!"
The shadow advanced as Jennifer kept backing away with Skip.

No brother. No sister.

Jennifer couldn't even describe what she felt. Perhaps it was the same sort of senseless, crazy courage that had consumed her at Grandpa Crawford's cabin. Maybe it was her desire to defend Skip and Eddie. Or maybe it was something deeper. Whatever it was, it commanded that she drop Skip, slip one dagger out, and throw it with all her might into the middle of the dark cloud.

She couldn't see where it landed, but she heard the blade plunge into flesh. The resulting shriek pierced both ears and mind.

A thrill went through her. *Hey, Mom, I got the distance right!*

By the time Evangelina was done screaming, Jennifer had checked Skip for a steady pulse and determined he was indeed all right, if firmly unconscious. She quickly readied her second dagger.

Evangelina did not return the attack. Instead, she reached up with a claw into her dark corona, gasped with pain, tore her foe's blade from wherever it had pierced, and tossed it back. It skimmed across the pavement, skittered through the shards of the Blacktooth blade, and slid to a stop right before Jennifer's feet.

The next thoughts Jennifer heard were far more complex than anything this thing had offered before. There was still overwhelming sorrow and rage, yes. But there was also curiosity, and a grim sort of humor . . . and perhaps doubt?

Like your mother. And yet different.

"Don't you talk about my mother, you *bitch*!"

For a brief moment, she felt a door open—a sort of empathy, she was sure. Evangelina had a mother, too, didn't she? Didn't she understand what having one meant? Was that why she had spared Wendy Blacktooth, and Jennifer's own mother?

Just like that, the door closed. The empathy and the doubt disappeared. Only the wrath and sorrow, and a last vestige of curiosity, remained.

I will enjoy hunting you tonight. What is it you beaststalkers like to say? "Ready yourself, or ready your soul." Sister.

Irony dripped from the last word. Before the thought was even complete, Evangelina had turned and vanished into shadow.

Jennifer was alone.

CHAPTER 16

Sibling Rivalry

Damn these boys anyway! It was not a charitable thought, Jennifer admitted as she pulled Eddie's unconscious body close to Skip's, all the while keeping an eye out for another sign of her sister. But she was dismayed neither had been exactly helpful this evening. *If I survive this, I'm beating them both into body casts.*

She had barely taken a step away from the two of them when the first missile came whooshing down the parking aisle. A viscous, dark green blob spat from the maw of Evangelina exploded ten feet away.

In an instant, Jennifer had changed into dragon form and curled over the boys to protect them. The acid struck her armored wings and trickled away harmlessly.

Why do you protect them?

She felt her sister's curiosity and disdain crawl down her skin with the venom.

I hear your memories. These two boys have given you nothing but grief since you've learned what you are. Since they've learned what you are.

"It's what friends do," Jennifer retorted. "I wouldn't expect you to understand."

She felt the waves of displeasure, even though she still couldn't see her sister.

Friends are a luxury you can afford in this world. I could not, in mine.

"Well, now that you're *here,* have you thought about *trying?*" Jennifer felt self-conscious about her voice echoing through the mall parking lot, but they were alone. "I mean, all we hear from you is 'no friends, no family, no love' . . . have you ever considered you might *get* those things, if you stopped acting like a *psychotic?*"

Jennifer could briefly feel her sister's doubt again—was that one of the parts arguing with the others?—and then she felt the surge of rage return as Evangelina sprang from the darkness and bore down like the predator she was.

She had no time to react. The collision was fierce. As they rolled over each other on the pavement, Jennifer felt blood trickling from her temple. Dark legs, wings, and claws wrapped themselves securely around her. Even before they stopped rolling, Jennifer could feel the probing mouth brushing against her scaled wing and shoulder. Whatever came out of her sister's jaws did not feel like a forked tongue or anything else she knew dragons to possess. Now it was at her neck, and her snout . . . soon it would be at her bloody temple, and the draining would begin . . .

In a flash she was back to her smaller, human shape. Before Evangelina could adjust, Jennifer had slid out of her sister's grasp and hacked at the flickering tail.

Standing up, she pulled both daggers up, kissed them, and began to battleshout before Evangelina was even up. Light shone. Sound echoed. The entire parking garage became a cavern of beaststalker fury. At least ten car alarms went off simultaneously.

And in the midst of it all, Evangelina stood up, regained her composure . . . and smacked Jennifer across the head with her tail.

I'm sorry, sister . . . did you say something? I'm afraid I can't hear you very well.

The realization hit Jennifer almost as hard as the tail had. Evangelina was blind. And deaf. Martin Stowe's vision problems were obvious, of course; and Angus Cheron had "explained" the deafness of Delores at the beaststalker trial. Those "weaknesses" combined to make Evangelina invulnerable to the beaststalker's shout. *That's why my mother had such a hard time with her!*

Correct

came her sister's voice.

> *I do not need to see or hear what I can feel. I felt our grandfather's excitement the last night he was with you, and your own mother's fear when she realized her first weapon was useless against me. And now, I can feel your despair. Your hopelessness. You're going to die tonight, Jennifer. You'll fail, like your mother before you, and your father after you. And then . . .*

"And then what?" Jennifer knew now her voice wasn't necessary, but shouting felt better. Plus, it was easier to hear herself over the wail of the car alarms. "You'll go back to your old dimension, since it was such a fabulous place? Or you'll stick around in our world, killing people when you feel like it and hiding when you don't?"

> *I'll worry about the future once I settle the past.*

"Sis, you don't *have* a future."

She ran straight at Evangelina, counting on the element of surprise. But her opponent stepped to one side, taking only a small swipe of one blade to the ribs.

> *Surprise won't work anymore, Jennifer. Tonight you're not the unexpected distraction. You're the prey. Your thoughts are your scent. I will read and track them.*

An idea came to Jennifer like a lightning bolt—and it did not bother her one bit that her sister could hear it as well. Holding her blades high, she swung around, traced a circle in the air, and then brought them down to strike the cement surface of the parking lot.

What came out astonished her. It was her mother's twin golden eagles. Like feathered bullets, they dove straight for Evangelina and dug at her face with razor claws.

"Read *their* thoughts!" Jennifer dared. She switched into dragon form, stomped the ground, and brought a stream of serpents to her aid. "And read *theirs*!"

Evangelina teetered back, flailing at the enormous raptors and obviously wary of the slithering mass approaching her feet. She had only one escape. The shadow around her extended . . . and then she was gone, the shadow retreating quickly after her.

Jennifer gritted her teeth and flexed back to human form. Her animal friends clustered around her protectively. The cars stopped wailing, perhaps silenced by the unnatural scene before them. Eagle eyes and snake tongues were all around her, but she knew none of them could tell where Evangelina had fled.

"Stay close. She's around here somewhere."

With the birds gliding ahead and the serpents wriggling on either flank, Jennifer made her way up each aisle of the parking ramp. Back and forth through the massive levels they went, named after states, themes, and colors for parkers' convenience: Arizona's green cactus, blue dice for Nevada, and the purple mountains of Colorado.

As they came within sight of the first few white Alaskan husky signs on the ramp to the top level, Jennifer wondered if Evangelina hadn't just fled altogether. Maybe summoning animals was something new to her, like beaststalkers had been.

The piercing cry of one of the eagles answered her question. It circled above something crawling down the ramp toward them. Jennifer couldn't make it out, but it was small and moved slowly.

The other eagle gave a cry as well. It had spotted another one. The small, shadowy shape struggled to catch up with the first.

Another cry—another one.

Still another cry.

Soon, the eagles were calling out repeatedly, and a small army of indiscernible shapes was making its way down the ramp. Some of the creatures were clinging to the walls and restraining wires between levels.

There were hundreds of them. But what were they?

I can summon an army as well, sister.

The mob sped up a bit. Suddenly, instead of crawling, some of them were jumping. One latched onto the talon of an eagle. A few others launched themselves into the bed of snakes Jennifer had arranged around her. The mambas hissed at the unearthly creatures and struck, as she finally got a good look at them.

They were spiders . . . almost. Black and hairy, with gray bellies, they had ten or so legs, several bright blue eyes, and short tails that suggested slugs more than anything else. One opened its mouth, revealing a set of clicking mandibles, and screamed.

Creatures from my own dimension . . .

Jennifer backed up in a hurry. These things were already swarming over serpents, paying little heed to the small fraction that got devoured. Poison seemed to have no effect on them. The eagles had shaken off the more aggressive jumpers, but were sailing back to her. They could not hold this ground.

Recalling the oreams of Crescent Valley, she raised her daggers and let out a battleshout. The nova of light and sound knocked back the advancing swarm, curling their legs into hundreds of miniature death spasms.

Out of this maelstrom, the invincible shadow of Evangelina swooped. Jennifer ducked just quickly enough to get nothing more than a claw to the head, which was still enough to send her reeling. She somersaulted backward until her shoulders slammed into a parked sedan. The impact knocked her breath away. She felt the metal dent beneath her.

Do you know what it was like?

The voice in her head purred with certain victory. She couldn't see her sister but knew she was close.

To grow up where I did?

Jennifer gasped for breath and struggled to her knees. The sound of something climbing on the sedan behind her motivated her to shuffle away a few feet. Then the sounds of claws on the asphalt warned her of something right behind her. Darkness curled around her. *This is it. I'll be whispering like Mom, "No daughter." Dad, I'm so sorry you'll find me like this.*

Everything there survives by sucking the life from something else.

Evangelina loomed over her.

There was so little left in that barren world when my brothers and I arrived. What a feast we must have seemed! What—

The sudden sound of an engine accelerating surprised them both. Jennifer turned just in time to see her predator knocked back by two tons of metal and a screech of tires. Like an explosion, Evangelina burst into five screaming pieces, casting black swirls across the pavement around them.

Before Jennifer could piece together what happened, Susan was out of the assault sedan, wielding a tire iron and shrieking at what was left of Evangelina.

"Stay away from my friend! I'm not afraid of you anymore!"

"Susan!" Jennifer panicked for a moment—*she hasn't been gone long enough to make it back to Dad!* But then she saw the device hanging from her friend's belt, and realized what Susan must have understood once she had driven away for a while and her head was straight. Jonathan Scales was reachable by phone at the hospital. *So he'll be here, maybe in fifteen or twenty minutes. He's flying as fast as he can.*

Susan Elmsmith.

Evangelina was plainly disoriented from the hit.

Friend of . . . Jennifer Scales. Goes to our geometry class.

One of the silhouettes on the ground wriggled and twisted into a new form—the shape of Gerry Stowe. His beautiful face was bruised, and there was blood in his golden hair. He looked up at the iron-wielding Susan, freezing her in surprise.

We do not need to fight, you and me.

"Gerry?" She almost dropped the tire iron. "How did you get here?"

"Susan, no! He's not our friend! He's—"

Gerry staggered to his feet, palms up. He didn't even seem to see Jennifer. "Wait! I can . . . I can stop this. I can . . . I can be a friend. Like I was at your school. I can tell Sister . . ."

Get her out of the way!

The other four pieces of Evangelina were rapidly recovering, moving toward each other and reforming into their more powerful outline.

Get her out of the way or we will kill her.

"No, we don't have to—" but the boy's protests were swallowed with the rest of him as Evangelina wrapped him in darkness and then advanced upon Susan.

Back on her feet, Jennifer ran at them both. "Susan, get back in the car!"

She took a claw in the teeth and fell back to the ground, but this gave her friend the time necessary to climb back into the sedan.

The engine revved and the car leapt forward, but this time Evangelina was ready. She hopped over the car, twisted to face up, and clung to the deep contours of the cement roof. Untrained and surprised, Susan drove right past her—and into a bright yellow support pillar.

"Susan!" Jennifer screamed as she watched the airbag deploy in the sedan. It caught her friend's flailing head, but blood still splattered onto the driver's side window.

Over the still-running engine, she could hear Evangelina slither and advance behind her. Jennifer had no time to check on her friend. She rolled out of the darkness, spotted the parking ramp railing and the wide-open evening beyond, and scrambled for it.

She cleared the railing right before the predator pounced for her. She felt the vast shadow pass over her as she plummeted toward the earth, flexed herself into the proper shape, and then sailed on dragon's wings a foot or two above the ground.

Her thoughts went to Susan, Eddie, and Skip just quickly enough for her to decide to pull Evangelina away from them.

I will follow you, sister. I have no interest in your friends, and I don't need them for bait. You cannot outrun me.

"Sure of that, are you?" Jennifer whispered, straining her wings and rocketing away from the ramp. Glowing headlights raced beneath her on Interstate 494. "You've never seen me fly, sis."

She could feel Evangelina taking wing and pursuing her.

Your friends are loyal.

She could feel the creature's doubt, could almost put it in words: Here, once again, a Scales was leading danger away from loved ones.

"Oof!" Evangelina slammed into her so hard, she spun into a stalled car on the shoulder of the highway. The highway Susan hated because of all the cars. *Oh, boy. All the cars.*

People don't see us, her grandfather's voice reminded her from long ago. She felt a chill at the memory of that day, up at the cabin, as she first learned about her dragon heritage. *They don't see what they don't understand.*

And, in fact, beyond this single car there were no wrecks. Nobody was honking. The drivers were all staring west through their windshields. Or yakking into cell phones. Or eating salad out of plastic bowls precariously balanced on their steering wheels.

Jennifer clawed over the car wreckage and scrambled along the highway shoulder. *Come on, you. I've got plenty left.*

Your youth is intoxicating. And tasty, no doubt.

"Bite me." She sensed her sister's movement—could she learn to anticipate the other, just as Evangelina anticipated her? Yes, she could. She took to the air just in time to hear a claw smash the pavement behind her. Triumph at the near miss made her almost dizzy. Her shape streamed over the rapid traffic. "Can I ask you a question, sis? I mean, you've been studying languages in this world for a while, I gather. So how does 'fat, slow cow' translate into your own world's language?"

She quickly realized she had spoken too soon. A blinding pain struck the middle of her back, and then another claw struck her belly as she spun off a car that had to be going at least eighty miles an hour. The car skidded into the ditch and screeched to a halt. Regaining her flight sense, she just barely cleared the bridge that jumped out at her. She heard Evangelina curse.

"A lame try," she sang, almost meaning it. She turned sharply as Evangelina followed her under the bridge and led her back. She wanted to check on the car in the ditch—was the driver all right? Yes, it appeared so. She hoped Susan and the boys were still all right, too. *Maybe I should go back for them.*

Again, she felt Evangelina's confusion . . . go back for the reckless girl? For the impulsive boys? For the random driver she didn't even know?

Why?

"I can't explain this to you while you're trying your best to kill me," she hissed with forked tongue. "But if you spared my mom, maybe part of you *does* get it. Have a small chat with yourself, why don't you?"

She arced through the air, turning a circle like the coolest roller coaster at Valley Fair, and headed back to the mall parking lot. *Dad will be looking for me there.*

He will be too late to save you, even if he could. And then I will finish him.

"Yes, yes. Your master plan. Your twelve-point plan for avenging . . . I'm sorry, could you explain this again?" Jennifer whipped past cars going the other way, saw the lights of the parking lot loom ahead, saw the bright yellow Ikea sign flash by on the left. "How does hurting people get your life back?"

I don't want . . . I don't want a life back.

But Jennifer heard the pause. More important, she heard Gerry's voice—not the voice of Evangelina, but the voice of Susan's friend—arguing in that short space.

He wanted a life. He saw a future. Were there others inside who did?

No dissent! We finish . . . we finish this!

But there was dissent, and it was growing stronger. She heard the voice of Martin Stowe joining Gerry's, and then the voices of two others—Angus and Rune, she guessed—pushing the dissent away, supporting their sister.

She soared into the western parking ramp, deftly maneuvering between the cement fixtures and parked cars on the Colorado level. There, a few rows away, was Susan's car, still crashed against the pillar and Susan was . . . there she was! Her friend was sitting up with the door open and holding a cloth up against her nose.

She'll be okay. She'll look after Skip and Eddie.

That was all she needed to see. Sensing the confused voices closing in behind her, she darted for the open air outside the confines of the ramp. With a surge of confidence, she saw her mother's eagles—her eagles—flying directly at them both. In an instant, she knew exactly what to do. As soon as she was clear of the ramp, she pulled up sharply, waited for the hulking shape of Evangelina to emerge beneath her and engage the large birds . . .

. . . and morphed back into a girl.

Without wings, she dropped like a stone onto her sister's scaled back. In one smooth motion, her daggers were out of their sheaths and into dark flesh. The stabs were deep—far deeper than she had managed at the cabin, and close to the spine.

Evangelina convulsed, knocking Jennifer off without her weapons—and in midair. She shifted quickly back into dragon form and lifted herself to the top level of the parking structure. Alaskan huskies stared at her from the shiny directional signs, and she saw a few small, strange corpses in the center of the ramp—some of the otherworldly creatures overwhelmed by her earlier battleshout. They had fallen—and she was sure, so had Evangelina. She lit onto the pavement with the blood pumping in her ears.

I did it! I won!

A tangle of black legs and wings surged over the railing, quick as thought, and knocked her down. Evangelina backed off long enough to split again—the large outline of Angus Cheron pulled away briefly, reached behind him, and pulled the blades out of his own back. He howled in pain but held the daggers firmly as he plunged back into the shadow surrounding his merged siblings.

This is not over.

And like that, the monster was standing tall again, rearing up on hind legs, and screaming loudly enough to shatter the glass in the car windows nearby. She drew forth two new front legs—two incredibly long and sharp front legs, not unlike the limbs Jennifer had when she morphed with her weapons drawn.

Time to go, Jennifer urged herself. She tried to get up, but Evangelina pounced on her and held her ankle down with a back leg. The weight twisted the muscle and pinned Jennifer—she could hiss and squirm, but she couldn't get out from under. Once again, shadow clouded her vision, and she could feel the sticky breath of imminent death.

No escape, sister. You lose.

Blood dripped off her sister's body and onto her chest, but Jennifer knew the wounds were not keeping Evangelina from finishing her work. She squeezed her eyes shut and forced her mother's words to the front of her mind. *There is always hope. Dad will come for me now. He will save me.*

Evangelina's scythelike right front leg came down through Jennifer's right bicep.

The agony was incredible. Jennifer screamed.

Again.

Somewhere in the darkness, Jennifer heard the second weapon come down.

"Stop, child!"

The predator paused, blow held in midair, thoughts and

memories suddenly swirling. Through her, Jennifer could feel the presence of someone new—someone vital.

Father?

The claws released her, and Jennifer saw Evangelina turn around. Jennifer rolled to the side and looked up. Jonathan Scales stood there, indigo scales shimmering under the lot's lights. His reptilian features looked sick for what he saw before him.

"Dad! Be careful! Evangelos . . . I mean Evangelina . . . I mean, he's a she! Or, um, actually, a she and four he's."

"You hurt, ace?"

"Um . . . hard to say." Jennifer scanned her twisted ankle, the bruised hip, and the gouge in her arm. Her sleeve was dark and wet. Wincing at the pain everywhere, she looked up at her sister's seething form. "Help me out, sis. This blood here . . . is this you or me?"

"Hang tight, Jennifer. Your sister and I need to talk."

Talk?

Evangelina appeared amused.

Whatever will we talk about, Father?

"About the life you spared earlier," Jonathan spread his wings in what looked more like a bow than anything else. "My wife, Elizabeth."

Jennifer felt the memories again move through Evangelina—

it was strange to see her mother through her sister's bitter eyes. She saw the hospital as if from across the street, the doctor walking in the front door on her way to surgery, then their house and the yard where Wendy Blacktooth lay under healing hands. Then inside that house, where a mighty warrior showed mercy, laid down arms, and offered peace.

Father's wife is still alive?

The question came out earnestly, but a rush of anger immediately followed, as if one voice was overriding another.

"She's still alive," Jonathan answered. "There's still hope."

For a few seconds, the stream of thoughts and memories from Evangelina subsided into blank confusion. Her father, feeling it, too, seized the opportunity.

"Please," he called out. "Stop what you're doing. If you have to hurt someone, hurt me. That's why I came here."

Jennifer felt Evangelina's thoughts flicker briefly to her, and then to the dragon before them.

You want me to show mercy again.

"To her," he agreed, indicating Jennifer. "Not to me. I know what I've done—"

You can't know!

She rose up on her hindmost legs and let the gloom spill down toward him.

You can't have any idea! Where she left me . . .

For the first time, Evangelina let the memory of that other place out onto Jennifer and her father. Jennifer reeled at what she saw, and heard, and smelled there.

That world—where Mother put us—it was dying. Even as newborns, we could tell. We aged rapidly, learning to see and walk within seconds of our arrival. But there was nothing to see, and nowhere to go. Almost nothing was left to this world. We must have been the first children there in centuries.

Without wanting to see it, Jennifer witnessed their arrival: A swarm of offspring, half-dragon and half-spider, struggling to make their way in a world full of charred rock, burnt vegetation, and eternal gloom. Only the sliver of an eternal crescent moon gave them any light to see each other and their surroundings.

I was the eldest, and the only female. My brothers—there were dozens of them—knew this. Their instincts told them to stay close. They sought safety and direction, like a hive from its queen. But we were hunted from the moment we arrived.

And then Jennifer saw the predators—or what was visible of them. They were too fast to define, other than by their voracious hunger. Her heart beat faster as she saw one coming for her. She squeezed into the smallest crevice she could find, and still the breath and the claws were behind her. She felt brothers torn away from her side, heard their screams, and tasted the scent of their blood on the air. Like an oak tree split again and again by repeated strikes of lightning, she felt her heart break with each loss.

So many of them died, food for predators that were at death's door themselves. I could not protect them. I could only hide, and learn, and collect those few brothers who survived. We grew quickly, and adapted.

Now the vision and emotions shifted. Jennifer felt the hunger of the predator, knew that she was aging rapidly . . . perhaps dangerously so. Desperate, she smelled prey on the air. *Youth.* Swifter than a falcon, she was out of the crevice, running a frightened shadow down into the ground, and feeding herself. Every bite of the meat made her feel younger. The world around them was ancient and dying; this was the only way to slow down her own aging and remain alive.

Hours stretched into days, and then into weeks and maybe years. I don't know how much time went by in that place— every feeding made time stand still, a little bit. The hunt became my life. Sometimes, I wonder. I wonder if my prey . . . maybe sometimes, they were my own brothers.

The memories went dark again. Evangelina was on her haunches, claws and wings listless. The dark corona around her head was fading, and her body heaved with sobs.

I could not protect them. I was supposed to protect them. They had no one else . . .

"How did you get out?"

Her father's voice was plainly an irritation.

Does it matter? I came here. To find you. And I did.

"Yes, you did." The three of them sat there for a while. An airplane roared overhead, unfolding its landing gear like claws ready to snatch prey from the runway. "What do you mean to do now?"

What?!

Memories leaked out again—the murder of Jack Alder, the fatal encounter with Crawford Scales, the assault on Elizabeth Georges-Scales.

Isn't it clear why I'm here? Haven't you figured it out?

"I know why you started doing what you did," Jonathan explained. "But I'm not asking you that. I'm asking you: What do you mean to do *now*?"

Evangelina turned from father to daughter, and back to father again.

You deserve to die.

His silver eyes were wet. "If I could have gone there in your place, I would have. For any of Dianna's children."

Not just her children! Your children!

The shadow deepened.

We were pushed away into a place of death! I was alone! And instead of coming to find me, you went on with your life! You forgot me! And you had HER!

A stray claw waved back vaguely toward Jennifer, who felt her cheeks redden.

"I never forgot you," Jonathan promised quietly. "I just couldn't imagine how you would have survived. Even if I had known Dianna still had hope, I would have thought her search fruitless."

At least Mother tried. Would you try for this one?

Another motion toward Jennifer.

He bowed his head. "You know you're asking an impossible question. I can't travel like your mother can. Like you can. Besides, I told you: I thought you were dead."

Evangelina was so swift, Jennifer didn't realize what was happening until she was within the shadow, with legs and claws wrapped around her throat.

This one's dead, as far as you're concerned. Will you still try to save her?

Jennifer could not see her father through the darkness, but she could hear him. His voice was full of shock, rage, and helpless desperation. "Let her go!"

No daughter, Father. No daughter!

"You let her go or I'll kill you!"

Ah. So I thought.

The claws pushed Jennifer away, out of the darkness and onto the ground. Her two daggers followed behind her as Evangelina discarded them in disgust. Jennifer's lips and teeth struck the pavement, and the copper tang of blood ran down inside her cheeks.

You made your choice, Father. Long ago, and again today.

Then something remarkable happened: Evangelina withdrew. The shadow receded, and the dark scales swirled, and the head that Jennifer had recognized as so similar to her own bowed down and away from them. The voices in their head went silent, and Jennifer knew, as sure as she was of anything, that Evangelina could not tell what either of them was thinking. She was blind and deaf to them both, turned inward, for just one moment.

It may have been the boldness that comes with seeing an opportunity, or the lingering taste of her own blood. It may have been the way her sister forced her into helplessness, or the rage she had heard in her father's voice, or all of these things. She darted forward, scooped up a dagger, and jumped, bloody teeth bared.

"No, Jennifer!"

At her father's words, Evangelina extended her awareness immediately, sensed her sister's approach, and spun around with dark corona in full bloom. The burst of defensive thought, however, was not nearly enough to slow the attack. Jennifer was going to deal a crippling blow upon landing. Even through the shadow, she knew now where the throat was. There would be no missing it. She felt the exultation of victory. *Is this what a successful hunt is like? Is this how she felt, in that other world, right before the kill?*

Before she could land, her father rammed into Jennifer's side and knocked her back, sending her dagger flying. As she hit the ground and grunted, a deep chill—something colder than November—settled in over them all. Jennifer couldn't place it, but it was unnatural . . . and familiar.

Jonathan ignored it. His wings fluttered in frustration. "Not like that, Jennifer! That's not what we're going to do!"

"She wants to kill you, Da—" She choked on her own words, because she saw just how right she was. Her other dagger was still close to Evangelina. A claw reached out for it, snatched it into the darkness, and then re-emerged—twice as long, with a sharp black edge and deadly point. It hovered behind the spikes on Jonathan Scales's head.

Jennifer was on the ground, looking over his left wing as he looked down at her. He was unaware of the death dangling behind him, and she couldn't find the words to speak. Nor could she possibly move fast enough to do anything.

He's dead.

All she could do was scream as the scythe came down upon him.

The chill worsened and dipped deep into her flesh. Clouds of vapor covered the ground. The scythe wavered in midair, and Jennifer felt Evangelina recognize the change around them.

Yes, it was familiar—Jennifer could place it now. The feel of a winter chill upon the lake by the cabin.

Grandpa Crawford's cabin.

What she saw behind the shadow of Evangelina made Jennifer scream again. It was pale lavender in color, dragonlike in shape—but nothing less than a vision of death. The venerable Crawford Thomas Scales was terrible to behold, moving in silent and relentless fury, reaching out with deadly violet smoke supported by a skeleton of cool and shining stone. He passed through Evangelina entirely, sending the black-scaled body into a seizure, and leaving a cascade of shadow in his wake. The venerable spirit swam swiftly over Jonathan and Jennifer, careful not to touch either of them, and then faded behind them.

The wail of Evangelina shattered any thoughts Jennifer had about her grandfather, where he came from, or where he went. The four dark twists that had come together in the mall parking lot fell from the center like rotting flesh, and where one voice had once been on the air, there were now five.

Kill Father!
No, enough! I'll stop you!
Do as she says or die!
We're done fighting them!
They are the enemy!

Loosed upon each other, the shapes were soon at each other's throats. Some of them began to shift into human form: Jennifer thought she could see Gerry wrestling the largest shadow, which gave the general shape of Angus

Cheron. Elsewhere, the shadow of Rune Whisper was struggling toward the center of the fray—was Delores in there?—in an attempt to darken it, while the elderly features of Martin Stowe clung to its backside.

"No, please!" Jonathan waded into the midst of the turmoil, heedless to his own safety. "Stop! Please! You'll kill each other! Jennifer, help me! Help them!"

"Dad, no!" But Jennifer had no choice, she had to go in to help him. And he was right: They were her brothers, and her sister. She picked up the dagger that Evangelina hadn't claimed and tried to separate the fighters.

It was like grabbing slippery snakes. Neither of them could get a true hold on anything happening around them, and half the time they couldn't see a darn thing—but they could still feel the sting of an occasional stray (or intentional) blow. Jennifer felt a great disturbance toward the center. It was her sister, she knew. She wasn't fighting.

She was crying.

No! Stop! Please!

The same voice that had ordered the death of her father was now using his very words.

You'll kill each other!

Her brothers, Jennifer realized, had spun out of control. They slashed harder at each other, tasting each other's blood, thrilling in the hunt and battle. She had to stop them. Before her father could stop her, she waded into the melee.

"Jennifer!" He clutched at her and followed her into the swirling shadows.

No!

They fought harder, tearing at each other and Jennifer, pushing aside Jonathan as though he were an afterthought. Rune Whisper dissembled into darkness again, casting a shroud over them all. Jennifer hardened into dragon skin and flailed away with her wings and feet, stomping snakes into existence and trying anything at all to organize the chaos. Someone landed on her already twisted ankle, then something jabbed into her side, and then someone else was pulling at her horns— her father, she was reasonably sure, since the effect was removing her from the worst of the fighting. Then she was out again.

The struggle went on for some time, as Jennifer and her father looked vainly into the warring gloom. At one point she got up to try to separate them again, but he stopped her.

"Don't." His voice was ragged with tired desperation. "Listen to them. This isn't about us anymore."

Ingrate!
Predator!
Weakling!
Murderer!

"We can't stop what they'll do," he told her as the voices raged on. "Any more than you or I could have reached into that dimension and plucked them out to safety."

Jennifer lay down and let her father hold her close. A horrible vision rose in her mind—the shapes of warriors, dragons, and spiders fighting to the death. *Was this what it was like?* She asked herself. *Centuries ago, when the first ones fought each other? Will it still be like this, centuries from now?*

The sounds of fighting were now interspersed with exclamations of anguish. The thumps slowed down, but were more forceful—killing blows, Jennifer guessed. Finally, there was the sound of two such blows landing at once. Slowly, like a last breath fading away, the darkness dissipated.

Four bodies lay dead on the ground. Among them, the veiled form of Delores Cheron—the last part of Evangelina—was sobbing uncontrollably.

I failed them. Again. Now they are all gone.

Jennifer and her father remained on the ground, protecting each other with their wings. They felt her senses extend across this strange world, and then retreat in fear.

I'm alone.

"Not alone," Jonathan corrected her. He got up and took a tentative step forward, reaching out with a wing claw.

Father. So much pain. So much death.

He took her under his wing. Jennifer felt a chill again and shivered.

I'm sorry. So sorry for what I've done to you.

"I'm sorry I couldn't save you."

You won't leave me alone again?

"You won't be alone, child." Jonathan was looking over Jennifer's shoulder. "Ever again."

The cold crept down Jennifer's spine: She knew who was behind her without turning around. The voice in her mind was no longer Evangelina, but a warped echo from her own past, distant but still kindly.

Step aside, Niffer. Step aside, son.

She relaxed back to human form and stumbled out of the way. Jonathan backed off, drawing Evangelina to her feet before separating. The shrouded face turned to the deathly presence that approached, and her right hand came up to pull back the veil.

Jennifer drew in a quick, cold breath. The hair was dark, there were ten more years at least in the high cheekbones, and this woman was definitely shorter . . . but there were the gray eyes, the pale skin, and the same curve of the mouth Jennifer saw when she looked in the mirror each morning. For the first time, she heard nothing of this woman but a shared heartbeat.

Evangelina stood tall under Crawford's pale shadow. She glanced over to Jennifer for the briefest moment.

Sister.

Then the wraith descended, and she collapsed. Her grandfather's phantom pulled her clear spirit upward and out. Jennifer saw it strain momentarily, unsure of its destination—then it reached out itself, to the four bodies around them, and plucked out four companions to tow behind her.

Her grandfather's spirit paused and turned slightly.

I'll take care of them, son.

She watched her father nod, unable to speak. His claw grabbed her hand.

"They'll be all right with him, ace. Come on, let's go check on your friends."

The spirits ascended into the starlight, and the largest one in the lead sent one thought back to Jennifer as delicate as a whisper:

Your mom's waiting, Niffer.

CHAPTER 17

The Return to Crescent Valley

Grandpa Crawford was true to his word. After carrying her friends' unconscious or woozy bodies to Eddie's car, cautiously driving them back to Winoka alongside her father's flying shape, and leaving them at the emergency entrance, Jennifer limped straight to the intensive care ward . . . in time to see her mother open her eyes.

"Mom!" Jennifer flung herself on the bed, heedless of the resulting *oomph* from the patient and her father's surprised warning. She knew her mother would be all right, now. Grandpa had said so.

"Jennifer! Oh, Jennifer. You're hurt!"

She looked down at herself. "Er, right. Well, *some* of this blood isn't mine . . ."

"Jonathan, you've got to make her go down to the emergency ward!" Elizabeth turned to him. "You're not hurt, too, are you?"

"Just a scratch here and there." His face glowed to see his wife awake. "Liz, if you think you can make our daughter do a damn thing, you haven't been paying attention lately."

"Well, I can't do a thing from this bed! *Somebody's* got to . . . Susan? What happened to you?"

They all looked at Susan, who was framed in the doorway with a bandaged nose and the beginning of a glorious black eye. She waved weakly. "Hey, Bissus . . . I bean, Dr. Georges-Scales. You would not eben *believe* the day I'be had. The bedics downstairs gabe be dis gwick bandage, but I wanted to bake sure you were okay."

"Susan . . ." Jonathan wrapped the girl in his wings. "How can we thank you?"

"By not bentioning *any* of this to by dad. Eber. Helb be think ub a really good lie for what habbened to the car. And by nose. You're, uh, looging good, Dr. Georges-Scales."

This was a rather large lie, Jennifer thought. Her mom looked *terrible*. Worse than she felt herself. And older. Much older. It was the silver in her hair . . . and the new wrinkles by the eyes.

"Will you forgive me if I leave now?" her father asked her mother.

"Only if it's to take our daughter downstairs."

"Dad, where are you going?"

"I should let Winona Brandfire and the others in Crescent Valley know what's happened. I can drop Susan off at home on the way. Jennifer could stay here with you."

Jennifer began to argue, but the floor suddenly rocked beneath her feet. She reeled. "I really want a nap." *Is this what a concussion feels like? Or is it the blood loss?*

"Jonathan! Our daughter! Emergency room! Now!"

Her father leaned up against her, as Susan took her by the elbow. "Okay, ace. Easy now. Susan, let's take her downstairs. I think they'll just want to fix her up quick and observe you for a few hours."

"And once you've got her settled," her mother's voice carried down the hallway after them, "you will drag your scaly butt back here and spend the night. Your friends can wait! For heaven's sake, Jonathan. You and your secret lizard club. Susan, mark my words: Boys are sad . . ."

Things were almost getting back to normal the next afternoon, when Jennifer came back from Susan's house and ran into her mother at the newly repainted, resanded, and now crimson painted front door of their house.

"What are you doing home? Where's Dad?"

"I don't need to be at the hospital. I told your dad he could go to Crescent Valley, since the crescent moon's almost over with."

"Hmph. And what are you doing *leaving* home?"

"I'm heading out," Elizabeth told her with a nod to the interior. Jennifer spotted—and heard—at least six construction workers within, all refurbishing the walls and floors from the scars of battle. "All the hammering's driving me nuts. Come with me?"

She examined her mother suspiciously. "The doctors told you it was okay?"

"Honey, *I'm* a doctor. *I* say it's okay."

"The doctor who treats herself has a fool for a patient."

"That's lawyers, dear. The lawyer who represents herself has a fool for a client."

"Hmmph. I'll bet it works for doctors, too. I'd better come along."

"Yes, I'm hoping you will!"

The minivan was moving at a fair clip out of town before Jennifer finally asked, "Um, where are we going, exactly?"

Elizabeth would only shrug.

"More secrets, eh?"

"This one can be between you and me, for a while."

It didn't take long for Jennifer to figure out they were headed for the Scales family farm. A couple of hours later, they were driving up gravel road past the beehives. The swarms of unusual insects braved the November chill to investigate the minivan's arrival. Recognizing the occupants, they dissipated quickly.

They parked well past the right edge of the driveway, rolling for a bit on pine needles and shriveled leaves before stopping. There were dragons on and about the farm. Jennifer could make out Joseph Skinner's beastly shape trying to soothe a pair of her grandfather's stallions to the west. Some tramplers were chasing sheep in the wildflower fields southeast of the house, and a few dashers were laughing out over the surface of the lake. She soon realized they were playing tag with a pair of golden eagles, under the barest sliver of a crescent moon.

"Help me get this out of the back, will you? It's heavy."

Her mother wasn't kidding. Whatever it was, wrapped in heavy burlap, it nearly dragged Jennifer's shoulders out of their sockets.

"Over here, nice and quick." Holding the other end, Elizabeth shuffled hastily around the minivan and toward the denser foliage close to the lake. Not having much choice, Jennifer kept up with her own end. "All right, set it down, honey. And get the shovel from the barn, please? I need to go inside and check on something. Thanks."

Jennifer came back in time to see her mother sticking an envelope in her jacket pocket and wiping away a tear. She didn't ask about it, and they set to work.

The ground had not frozen yet. It only took a few minutes to dig a hole deep enough to hold up what her mother had brought with them—a gravestone.

"I commissioned this a few weeks ago," Elizabeth explained. "So there would be a marker of him in this world. For us. Me, I guess."

Together, they stood the stone up in the narrow hole and removed the wrappings. The dark granite edges were square, and the polished surface had one carving: a large horse on its hind legs, a single horn protruding from its forehead, two strong feathered wings spread wide. Below that, the simple inscription:

CRAWFORD THOMAS SCALES
BELOVED FATHER-IN-LAW

"He spoke to me," her mother told her after they were done settling the stone and had sat down for a moment. "While I was asleep. He told me to come here and look inside. In the night-stand, by his bed."

She sniffled again, pulled the envelope out of her jacket, and handed it to Jennifer.

"I have to admit, when I first met him, I wouldn't have seen this coming."

Fingers shivering from the cold and the anticipation, Jennifer reached into the envelope and pulled out the contents. It was a sheaf of legal documents, the top one of which had CERTIFICATE OF TITLE at the top in bold words and a small note clipped to it. The writing was her grandfather's:

> *Lizzard,*
> *Look after the place for me, will you? Joseph and the others will help. Please keep them safe.*
>
> *Love,*
> *Crawford*

Before her grandfather's gesture had really sunk in, Jennifer heard a voice on the crisp air. Softly sung, the words barely carried to her cars.

> *Through many dangers, toils, and snares*
> *We have already come;*
> *'Tis grace hath brought me safe thus far,*
> *And grace will lead me home.*

She leaned over and rested her head on her mother's shoulder, shivering. "It's strange. I don't think I've ever heard you sing before, Mom."

Elizabeth put an arm around her to protect her from the cold, but didn't say anything.

"How come? You've got a great singing voice."

Finally, the answer came. "Some things, I just save for when I'm alone."

She looked up. "But you're not alone now."

Elizabeth smiled. "Our secret, then."

The moon elms of Crescent Valley shone a soft, pale blue when she landed at the Brandfire's cave. Catherine and her grandmother were there, along with her father and a dragon Jennifer definitely hadn't expected: Xavier Longtail.

Winona Brandfire's olive lips pulled back to reveal a toothy smile. "Right on time, as your father promised. He told me a full Blaze wouldn't be necessary—and frankly, I think we've had enough meetings lately." Jennifer noticed the twinkle in her crimson eye, so similar to the one Catherine had when she was laughing.

"Eldest, perhaps we could get this over with," Xavier suggested. His tone was polite but terse. His golden eyes regarded Jennifer with something between fatigue, respect, and fear.

Winona clicked her forked tongue. "Very well. Jennifer Scales, the Blaze has passed unanimous judgment upon you for the events before and during the hunt of September 20th. We absolve you of all wrongdoing, assign no penalty to you, and welcome you fully among us as an adult member of the Scales clan."

Jonathan's shimmering scales strained with pride.

"Furthermore," the eldest continued, "I hereby assign to you the role of Ambassador to the Beaststalkers."

Xavier's head snapped around. "We never spoke of this."

The aged trampler did not turn to look at him. "Nevertheless, it is done. Ms. Scales, you will be the first such ambassador in our people's known history. Your role is to reach out to those beaststalkers you feel have peaceable intentions, so that we can begin talks that may end hostilities between our people. Do you accept this mission?"

Jennifer nodded, suddenly feeling a cloak of responsibility wrap around her shoulders—and, it seemed, her throat. "I accept."

"Take this, then." Winona held out a wrinkled wing claw and opened it. In the scaly palm was a plain silver ring. The jewelry glowed with a soft inner light.

"Eldest!" Xavier seemed caught between awe and horror. "You can't just *give* that away!"

The trampler ignored him. "This is the Ring of Seraphina, one of our most revered dragon legends. Our kind's eldest has passed this down for centuries. It lets the wearer come into this world without waiting for a crescent moon. It also protects those who travel with the wearer from misfortune. It should help ease the passage of anyone who enters this world with you."

Jennifer bowed her head and took the ring, slipping it gently on her right forefinger. Catherine winked at her. "I coulda used *that* the first time you brought me here."

"With whom will you start?" Xavier had recovered his composure and kept an even tone—but his attention was fixed on the ring Jennifer now wore. "I mean, when you try to talk with these beaststalkers?"

"I . . . I'm not sure yet." Her mind raced as she realized she was now on the job—a job she had no idea how to do. "I'm open to suggestions, Elder Longtail."

Xavier gave a snort, but for once it was not entirely unfriendly. "A good answer, Young Ambassador Scales. Very well. If you really want my opinion, I'll give it to you." He looked at each of them in turn, speaking slowly and carefully. "I think your mission is a well-intentioned effort to stop people from dying. And I think you will make some friends on both sides, and no small number of enemies, before you fail."

Jennifer searched his expression, but saw no threat there— just anxiety. He gave her a solemn wink.

"I pity your gecko. In the meantime, do not trust the people who tell you what you want to hear. Trust the people who are honest enough to tell you the truth."

With that, he stretched his rich golden wings and took flight.

"Always the optimist, Xavier Longtail." Winona Brandfire sighed as they watched the dasher disappear into the dark air. She turned to Jennifer. "Naturally, your mother will have some insights on who you can start with. Once you have a group you can trust, you may bring them to Crescent Valley. Consult with your father, your clan's elder, in choosing those who may come here."

"Okay." Jennifer turned to Catherine. "Will you help, too?"

The young trampler's eyes widened. "Who, me? Um, yeah, I guess. But why? It's not like I know much about beaststalkers. I've never even been to Winoka before."

"Why you? To show you off, of course! You're my best

friend here. Also, that car of your grandmother's sounds infinitely cooler than my parents' minivan. Swing by next Saturday morning around nine, and I'll show you around town."

"Oh! Well, sure." At her grandmother's nod of approval, Catherine gave a nervous smile. "You sure it's safe?"

"You'll have this beaststalker's protection," Jennifer promised.

It was later, under the slowly turning crescent and deepening blue moon elms, that Jennifer and her father finally talked about Grandpa Crawford.

"So the venerables are the ghosts of weredragons?"

" 'Essence' would be a more accurate word," he answered. He sighed at the crescent moon. It was a gentle, not impatient, sound. "A dragon properly laid to rest at the stone pyre, like we did for Grandpa, will release his or her essence to the crescent moon. From there, the venerables watch over this valley and remind us of our obligation to the next generation."

With her thumb, she gently rubbed the Ring of Seraphina, spinning it around her forefinger. "And Evangelina is up there now."

"Yes. With your grandfather."

"Will we see Grandpa again?" Jennifer felt a thrill of hope at the idea.

"To be honest, Jennifer, I had never heard of a venerable coming down from that place before, much less crossing through the lake into our everyday world. How it happened once, I have no idea—much less how it would happen a second time."

"I guess Evangelina was unique enough that Grandpa thought he had to come down for her," Jennifer guessed.

He took her wing claw in his own and smiled at her. "Well in that case, ace, he might very well come down again someday. Because you're unique, too."

Winoka City Hall seemed much smaller to Jennifer than it had during the trial. She walked into its council chamber alone the next afternoon, brushing aside her irritation about the ceiling decor and her nervousness about the lone figure who waited in that room for her.

"Mayor Seabright," she greeted the woman as calmly as she could. "Thanks for agreeing to see me."

The old woman, standing as straight as ever in her flowing white dress robes, gave her a faint smile that did not reach her white eyes. "You're welcome. Your mother isn't here?"

"Mom dropped me off," Jennifer explained. "She has a follow-up appointment at the hospital."

"I see." The disappointment in the mayor's voice was clear, but it seemed more wistful than disdainful. "I am glad she's better, of course."

She raised her head, and it seemed to Jennifer that the mayor had suddenly grown seven feet tall. "So what can I do for you, Ms. Scales? Are you here to—how did you put it—'kick this crazy loon's ass and burn this building down?'" For the first time, Jennifer saw the sword at Glorianna Seabright's side, sheathed but very much there.

"Well, uh, no." *Awkward!* She took a deep breath. "I'm sorry I said that in the hospital. I was upset." Looking around, she found herself impressed. "You thought my mother and I would be here to fight you . . . and you came alone?"

"Do you believe I would need help?" The woman stared at her with such an inscrutable expression, Jennifer couldn't help but think of her own mother. Did all beaststalkers practice that look? Did others think she looked like that, sometimes?

"Er . . . no. Of course not. I'm not here to fight, Your Honor. I'm here to . . . to . . ." She stopped herself, realizing with a red face how little she knew what to say next or how the mayor would respond. "I'm here to make a friend, if you want one."

"A friend." The mayor's face did not change.

"Yeah. After all, we did what you told us. Evangelina is gone, and there's no threat to the town anymore. You said you'd—"

"I know what I said at the trial. I am not a fool, Ms. Scales. My mind is as good as my vision."

Glorianna Seabright turned slightly and walked a few steps away, her left hand rubbing her forehead. Jennifer realized something, and the shock was like cold water.

"You knew all along."

"Pardon?" But the mayor did not seem confused at all.

"You knew who Evangelina was. Every piece of her."

Those mysterious white eyes with their small, dark pupils turned to focus on Jennifer. "Well, yes. Now that you mention it. I did. I'm blessed to see a great deal, Ms. Scales. Especially beasts. I saw you and your father for what you were when you moved here nearly ten years ago. And I certainly spotted Evangelina. All five of her."

"That's why you called those people to the trial. You were going to kill Evangelina right here."

"I was debating it," the beaststalker chief admitted. "Certainly we had the numbers to overwhelm your half sister, had she chosen to reveal herself to the gathering. But truthfully, my intentions were less violent, at least for that night. I wanted to get a measure of this monster, find out what made her tick, and assess her strength."

"And then you let my mother take on the job of getting rid of her."

"Yes." Mayor Seabright's elderly features curved into a deep-grooved smile. "It was definitely in this town's interest to have Evangelina gone—and I knew your mother was up to the task. At the same time, I found an opportunity to remind Winoka of your mother's heritage and skills. Getting her away from the surgery table and back in the field was the best way to re-establish her reputation in this town."

"So you think you were doing us a favor? Then why not tell her—tell us—what you knew? That might have helped us!"

"Your mother," the mayor pointed out wryly, "did not need my help. I'm a big believer in self-reliance, Ms. Scales. People who learn on their own strengthen their souls. Certainly, you've had enough experience with that!

"In any case," she continued, "Dr. Georges had Evangelina beaten, before she extended a hand of mercy and paid dearly for it. Had she finished the job properly, she would have come through the entire ordeal with nothing more than a few scratches."

"She was reaching out to Evangelina," Jennifer pointed out. "She was looking for a better way. You know, like heroes do."

"And did she find it, Ms. Scales?" The question was clearly rhetorical. "While she was drifting away helplessly in a coma induced by her assailant, did your mother find this magical path to friendship and peace?"

Jennifer sighed. "I'm wasting my time here, aren't I?"

"That depends on what you came for, doesn't it? You say you want to be friends, but friendship can mean all sorts of different things. If you came to ask me to leave beasts alone, the answer is no—though I will make an exception for your father in deference to your mother, and an exception for you in deference to . . ." The mayor's voice trailed off, and those unnerving eyes seemed to smile. "Well, let's just say, in deference to what you may become someday.

"But if you came here for friendly advice—and I think you need it, Ms. Scales—then you may count this visit a success after all."

She stepped forward again and put her hand gently on Jennifer's shoulder. "Mohandas Gandhi once said, 'Human nature will only find itself when it finally realizes that to be human, it has to cease to be beastly or brutal.'"

There was a pause for Jennifer to answer, but she did not.

"You have something beastly inside of you, Ms. Scales. One day, you will have to fight it—and defeat it—to attain your true human nature."

Jennifer licked her lips thoughtfully. "I've heard that quote, Your Honor. *In Search of the Supreme.* My mother taught it to me, months ago." She gently took the mayor's hand off her body. "It's a great saying, and I believe in it. But I don't think it means what *you* think it means."

On her way out of the council chamber, she remembered

something and paused. "Your eyes can't be as good as you say, can they? After all, you brought Mr. Slider to the trial, too. But he was innocent. You made a mistake."

She felt the mayor's stern stare bore through her platinum locks and send a chill down her spine. "I made no mistake, Ms. Scales. I still have business with Edmund Slider."

She had walked nearly all the way to the hospital to catch up with her mother when she saw Skip coming the other way. He looked unsure of what to do as she crossed the street and approached him. A cold autumn wind suddenly blasted them both, her in the back and him in the face, and they both winced as brown leaves whipped past.

"Skip. You're okay."

"Yeah." He rubbed the back of his head. "Just took a couple of stitches and a day or two of observation. My aunt can't exactly drive me home, since it's not a new moon until late tonight. But I could use the exercise."

"You know what happened?"

"Susan filled me in."

"Skip, I—"

"I don't want to talk about it," he interrupted grimly. "Or us. Telling me anything now . . . it's just too late, Jennifer."

She felt her heart slip down. "No more secrets, Skip. I promise. There's nothing else to know about me."

He scanned her up and down. "No, I guess not. Just that you're the combination of my people's sworn enemies—beaststalker and weredragon."

Persisting through his efforts to avoid her grasp, she eventually caught his arm. And is that so much different from last year, when I was only a weredragon and you saved my life?"

He wrenched his arm away. "That was before you lied to me."

"You're such a *jerk*!" She felt herself shift within, but suppressed the Ancient Furnace's urge to change. "I said I was sorry! When you apologized for lying, I forgave you. But you won't do the same for me. Why not?"

He could only stare at her from under his bangs. There was no hatred there, no anger—just a lost boy. Again, the thought occurred to her: *Boys are so sad.*

"Ugh. Listen, Skip. If you can't handle me as a girlfriend, just say so! But stop with the lousy excuses, okay? All this dragon and spider crap is just a smokescreen for you being scared. Fine. Be scared. Ditch me if you have to. But be honest."

He stared a little longer and then began to chuckle. She felt her face start to burn.

"Great. You're laughing at me. Again."

"I'm sorry. I think. No, I'm not sorry." He began to laugh again, but it sounded kinder this time. "Jennifer, I'm not laughing to get you angry. I'm laughing because you're absolutely right. I can't handle you for a girlfriend." He wiped his hands on his cheeks. "It's too much—my mother, my father, my aunt, my half sister, and put you on top of all that— I can't handle it. I just can't. And if I've made it sound like it's anyone's fault but my own . . . okay, I'm sorry for that, too."

Her mouth hung open for a moment before she remembered herself. "Um, okay. Apology accepted. Wow. I've never heard you talk like that before. To anyone."

"Yeah, well, you're pretty special."

"Thanks. You are, too."

They moved closer together, feeling the warmth of each other's breath as tiny snowflakes began to fall. She pushed a stray stalk of chocolate hair away from his face, revealing a tear. She felt one of her own slide down to the corner of her mouth. "You're sure you don't want to be together? I'd miss you."

"I'll miss you, too. I just need time, Jennifer. There's too much . . . too much happening right now. It's not fair to you."

"Okay." She felt around her throat for the necklace he had given her, but he stopped her before she could take it off.

"No, Jennifer. Keep it. I need you . . . I need you to have that. Please."

"Why?" She was touched, but couldn't imagine why he would want her to have his mother's old necklace anymore.

He leaned close and whispered a single word in her ear, and then he was gone. Fingering the Moon of Fallen Leaves just under the base of her throat, she watched him walk away into the thickening snow and tried hard to stop the tears. Her mother put so much faith in that word, and right now Jennifer struggled to feel the same way.

Hope.

She was still wiping away the tears when she entered the hospital. The first person she saw in the lobby was Bob Jarkmand, the largest sophomore in the history of Winoka High. He saw her and his huge features immediately turned very serious.

"Oh, crap," she muttered. *Come on, then. Make my day perfect, you freaking behemoth.*

"Jennifer." He was suddenly right there, his chest right in front of her runny nose. *Ugh, what did he grow since Halloween, six inches?*

"What?" she muttered at his letter jacket.

"You remember last year, when you punched me?"

"My goodness, was that you?" She tried an innocent tone, but then gave up and slouched again, resigned to her fate. "Yeah. I remember that."

He was cracking his enormous knuckles; they made sounds like small cannons. His face was getting red, and his jacket smelled like raging sweat. "And the way you threatened all of us at the Halloween dance?"

"Well, *threatened* is a strong word . . ." Jennifer braced herself for the assault. *At least we're already in a hospital.*

"Yeah, well. Um. That was really hot. I mean, I think *you're* really hot."

"Huh?" Jennifer tried to translate the words. *Hot?*

Then she looked up into his face and saw Bob *was* sweating. In addition, he kept cracking his knuckles nervously, even though they couldn't possibly make any more sounds. His thick lips struggled around the next words. "Do, um, do you wanna go out for burgers later tonight? Maybe see a, er, movie?"

"Oh . . ." She examined his face for signs of jocularity, then spun around to check the room for giggling football buddies. There were none of either. She looked desperately for help from the only other person in the room—a nurse throwing a tan cardigan over her pink scrubs—but the woman was plainly hurrying off shift, possibly under the impression that this personal hell of Jennifer's would soon spread and then freeze over. "Jeez, Bob, I . . ."

"I know you probably like that guy Skip." The word "Skip" came out like a command. "I mean, I've been passing you notes in Mr. Slider's geea—gom—geometry class, but you don't answer them, and you hang around with Wilson a lot . . ."

"Oh!" So Bob was the note writer? *But why didn't he sign his name?* Jennifer carefully examined the boy's Neanderthal jaw that had worked so hard around the word "geometry." Perhaps a cursive signature was asking too much.

". . . but I was just talking to Eddie upstairs, 'cause he knows you, and he said he figured you and Skip might be having problems, so maybe I should ask you out. So I'm askin'."

"Yes, you certainly are." *Eddie!* She stifled a chuckle of admiration as she thought of the fun he must have had siccing Bob on her, in revenge for his humiliation in the parking lot. *Kid fights better from a hospital bed than on his own two feet.*

"So, um . . . you wanna?"

This broke her train of thought. "Do I wanna . . . oh! Go out! Um . . ."

It occurred to her that this boy was a young beaststalker—one who knew she was a dragon, and who admired her anyway. She was the Ancient Furnace, Ambassador to the Beaststalkers, pledged to bring together her two peoples. *He* was reaching out to *her*. Could she accept the offer? For world peace?

And he was a football player. Football players were cute, weren't they? They were in all the magazines she read. If she looked at him—*really looked* at him, mind you—she could see the softness of those blue eyes instead of their dullness, and the firmness of his jaw instead of the warped shape. Couldn't she?

Ugh. "No, I can't. Bob, I'm sorry. I gotta go with my gut

here—it wouldn't work out between us. You're too . . . you're too . . ." She searched for the right word, scanning the enormous spread of letter jacket. "You're just too much for me."

Rejected, his eyes narrowed, entertaining a specter of the hostility she had seen at the Halloween dance. "Too much, huh? Yeah, I guess you can't handle me, after all."

"That's it exactly," she agreed as she patted his chest and deftly maneuvered around him, aiming for the stairs.

World peace could wait for a more appealing guy.

She passed Wendy Blacktooth's room on the second floor. The door was slightly open, and she could make out the woman's shape in bed. A few feet away, the doctors had thoughtfully placed Eddie's bed. The boy looked bruised from Skip's beating, but he was sitting up and smiling at his mother, who was smiling back at him.

He looked up first and caught her eye. His grin faltered for a moment, but returned when Jennifer waved and winked.

Hey there, he mouthed.

Jennifer stiffened a bit as Wendy Blacktooth followed her son's gaze. The woman's smile disappeared—but there was no frown, no look of cold hatred. In fact, was that a nod of greeting?

Heaven help her, it was. Smile frozen in place, she wiggled her fingers at Wendy Blacktooth in response, terrified to do much more.

"What are *you* doing here?!"

She jumped at the horribly familiar voice behind her, and lost the smile immediately.

"Nothing, Mr. Blacktooth," she hissed, starting down the corridor without bothering to look at him. A corner of her mouth twitched up as she felt his glare on the back of her head. "Shame about your sword."

All she heard in response was a door slam.

She turned a corner and ran into Edmund Slider's wheelchair.

An impolite word escaped her as she held her shin. Then she added, slightly more politely, "And who are *you* visiting today, Mr. Slider?"

"No one," her geometry teacher replied with ironic amusement, rearranging the blond strands of his hair. "I simply enjoy rolling around the hallways, ramming my students' shins when I get the opportunity. Makes the chair work better or so my doctors say."

"Very funny. So you're here by yourself? Are you okay?"

Two different emotions passed over his face so quickly, Jennifer wasn't certain of them both: frustration and gratitude were her best guesses. "I'm fine, Ms. Scales. Thanks for asking. I have physical therapy sessions here; sometimes I need a full weekend, as is the case this time. I checked in a couple of days ago, after . . . well, after seeing you at the mall. Before running into you just now, I was rolling around for some exercise. My room is right here." He motioned to a door, just slightly ajar, next to Jennifer. The lights were off inside.

"Oh. Um, Mr. Slider, about that night at the mall . . ."

"No need to apologize, Ms. Scales. You and Skip had my safety in mind, as well as that of the others. It was . . . most kind." He said this last with a mysterious smile. "Perhaps I can return the favor in the future."

"Do you, um, need help getting back? I mean, into bed? I could—"

"Thank you, Ms. Scales, but I have help." He rolled over to the door and opened it quickly enough that Jennifer could spot a large, bulbous shape scuttling out of the light and into a dark corner.

"Edmund, you're back already! Was your exercise rewarding?" The voice from within was unmistakable. Jennifer didn't need to see the source to recall the maniacally wide smile and spindly frame of Tavia Saltin.

Mr. Slider nodded to the unseen woman with a small sigh. "Yes, dear. I'm back." From the doorway, he turned to Jennifer with a dry smile. "Since I am sure rumors will now swirl around the hallways of Winoka High within minutes of your return to school, let me inform them appropriately: Yes, I am dating your boyfriend's aunt."

Any impulse to correct Mr. Slider's outdated view of her relationship with Skip was overwhelmed by a wave of embarrassment. "Oh, sir, that's really none of my—"

"I find her," he continued, oblivious to Jennifer's intense desire to hear no more, "exhilarating."

My ears! I think they're bleeding! "Listen, Mr. Slider. I, um, okay. Here it is. I really need to change the subject. Besides, you should know I was talking to Mayor Seabright earlier, and—"

"Yes, I know. She has her eyes on me." Mr. Slider suddenly adopted a much more ominous expression than Jennifer had ever seen grace his sallow features. "Her creepy, all-seeing, totalitarian eyes."

The hairs on the back of Jennifer's neck wouldn't stay down. "Mr. Slider?"

"The woman plagues me," he spat out. "And someday, she will regret it."

And with a quick *whrrr,* his wheelchair went through the doorway and into the darkness beyond.

After carefully checking a few more corners before walking around them, Jennifer finally found her mother in an examination room, fully dressed. She was thanking a colleague and picking up her jacket and pocketbook.

"Hey, honey!" Elizabeth's face shone through the new wrinkles she had inherited from Evangelina. "Clean bill of health. You ready to go?"

"Am I."

"How did it go with the mayor?"

"My chat with Mayor Seabright," said Jennifer pointedly, "was the *least* disturbing of those I've had since you dropped me off."

That night, lying in bed, Jennifer thought of Bob Jarkmand and the forgone burgers and movie date. *Maybe I can hook him up with Susan,* she thought with a wicked smile on her face.

The waxing crescent moon shone just outside her window. She stared at it for a long time, delving deep into its shape. As she scanned the craters and mountains on its surface, she felt a small *snap* inside. Though she couldn't see it, she knew the crescent phase was over, and another change had come. *In this world at least,* she thought to herself.

Without knowing why, she rolled over and began to cry for the sister she had barely gotten to know.

Even though it was a Saturday, Jennifer woke up and got dressed early so that she would be ready for Catherine. Today the two of them would just drive around Winoka, she decided over breakfast. Maybe visit Eddie in the hospital, if his father wasn't around and his mother didn't mind. Or was that too fast? The memory of Ms. Blacktooth in her hospital bed, solemnly nodding, intrigued her.

"Mom?"

Her mother was at the new kitchen table, serenely chewing oatmeal while sitting in the midst of buckets of plaster, cans of paint, and rolls of plastic. *Right there,* Jennifer thought briefly. *That's where she drove her sword into the floor.* She took a quick step forward as she realized she was standing on the spot where she had found her mother's unconscious body.

"Yes, honey?"

"Do you ever think things might be right again, between you and Mrs. Blacktooth?"

Elizabeth chomped her oatmeal thoughtfully—her mother's cooked oats were frightfully chewy—before answering, "If I didn't think so, I wouldn't keep living next door."

"Huh. Do you think maybe she feels the same way?"

Her mother could only shrug.

Maybe we can start there, Jennifer told herself. It seemed strange to begin with the woman who had nearly sliced her apart last spring. But such was life in Winoka, it seemed.

Lost in ambassadorial thought, she jumped at the sound of the doorbell, five minutes before Catherine was due to arrive.

It wasn't Catherine. It was Susan. The nose bandages were gone, the black eye was brownish-yellow, and the perky smile was back in those flushed cheeks.

"Good, you're up. Let's go do something!" The brunette curls bounced as her friend leapt through the doorway. Jennifer could barely keep up with her as she glided past the construction work in the hallway and picked an orange out of the bowl on the kitchen counter. "Only problem is, my dad's back, and of course the car's wrecked, so I'm in trouble. Though I think the bandages and black eye were good for a little sympathy."

"So suffering severe injury is your new way of avoiding trouble? Brilliant."

Susan gave her a sour look and stuck out her tongue. "Anyway, he says I can't use *any* car for a month now; and I have to clean the basement, which is the spookiest pocket of cement you've ever seen. I'm certain zombies live there. Ugh, it'll be so cool when I *just have a real license!* Hey, the little dragon guy!" She pointed at the spot on the windowsill where Jennifer's birthday present kept silent vigil. "It looks good there! So anyway, what do you want to do? We could—"

The doorbell rang again.

They opened the door to what appeared at first glance to be a young Egyptian queen. Definitely older than Jennifer or Susan, the young woman had a mahogany complexion, jet-black hair pulled back in a bun, and the highest cheekbones either of them had ever seen.

It wasn't until Jennifer spotted the blue Mustang convertible in the driveway that she gasped in recognition. Of course, she had never seen this girl or her family as anything but a trampler dragon before.

"Funny," she chuckled while tossing her own platinum hair. "I had you pegged for a blonde."

Catherine stepped up and gave Jennifer a hug. "I'm glad I made it! I was so freaked out when I reached the city limits. Grammie Winona told me not to stop, not even for the police, until I had you with me in the car."

"Winoka's not that bad!" Jennifer protested. "You've just got to get to know it."

"Which we can all do together," Susan interrupted quite seriously without breaking eye contact with the driveway, "in this wonderful, wonderful girl's beautiful, beautiful car. Whoever the heck she is."

Jennifer introduced Catherine to Susan, and then to her mother.

"So," Catherine asked as they sat down together at the kitchen table, "what do you want to do today? I think . . ."

The doorbell rang a third time.

"Eddie!" Jennifer took an astonished step back. "You're out of the hospital!"

"Got clearance this morning." The left side of his face was one big bruise, and he was favoring his right leg, but his sparrowlike frame stood tall in the doorway. "I, er, huh." He shook his head and gave a rueful glance across the yard to his own house. "I'm kinda here to see your mom. And you, of course. Can I come in?"

"Sure." She followed him down the hallway, smelling the faint odor of unshowered boy. Once they were in the kitchen, she answered her mother's shocked expression with a confused shrug of her own.

"Hey, Dr. Georges-Scales." Jennifer couldn't help noticing her mother's warm smile at the proper address. Eddie was one of the few people who had always gotten it right. He looked nervously at Susan, who gave him a half-hearted smile. "Hey, Susan. Um, hi . . ."

"Catherine." They shook hands.

"Nice to meet you, Catherine. Um, Dr. Georges-Scales, there's no easy way to ask this."

Elizabeth stood, face lined with concern. "What do you need, Eddie?"

He took a deep breath. "I need a place to stay. For a while."

"My goodness, Eddie. Sit down. Tell me what's wrong."

Catherine and Susan diplomatically gave up their seats and retreated to the living room as Eddie and the Scales women sat down. Within a few moments, Jennifer heard the stereo playing brass quintet music, which she knew Susan hated but no doubt afforded some sort of privacy to their kitchen conversation.

"It's Dad," Eddie explained tersely. "He's thrown me out. Or maybe I left. It doesn't really matter which."

Jennifer reached out and gently took his hand. "Was it because I stopped by your room yesterday? Or because of the sword I broke? Or because of Evangelina? Because I could try to—" She stopped. What? Apologize? Unlikely.

He smiled grimly. "All of that and more, but this has been a long time coming. Ever since . . ." He choked on the words. "Ever since I betrayed you last spring, we've had problems. It was just a matter of time before things got out of hand. Last night at the hospital, he and I finally engaged in open hostilities, right in front of my mom. I can't believe I let that happen," he added quietly, as if to himself. "She's still pretty fragile, and it hurts her to move. She actually had to sit up and scream in pain to get me to stop. And even then, Dad wouldn't quit. He went on and on about how I was a failure, and how I'd lost his precious sword, and how I had shamed the Blacktooth name. He told me if I had been worth anything, I would have helped my mother and she wouldn't have gotten hurt."

"But you saved her!" Jennifer felt the bile rise into her throat. "And he just stood there on the—"

Her mother's hand on her elbow was signal enough. *Everyone here knows this already, honey. Let him talk.*

"He finally left, after my mother yelled at him to get out. But not before he forbade me from coming home. I told him I wouldn't live under the same roof with him again if dragons burned down every other house in town—no offense, Jennifer."

She waved the comment away. "So you stayed at the hospital last night?"

"Yeah, in a sleeper chair. I didn't feel right leaving Mom after all that, anyway. This morning, she told me I should report here." He looked up at Elizabeth. "She told me to stay at a friend's house, and she said that's what this was. She made sure to have me tell you that.

"So," he finished nervously, scratching the back of his long neck with dirty fingernails. "What do you say?"

Elizabeth bit her lip and communicated silently with Jennifer: *He can stay, right? For my friend?*

Of course he can, Mom.

"We're so glad you came here, Eddie." Elizabeth stood up and gave Eddie a hug. "You stay as long as you like. I'll make up the guest room, and you can call your mom and tell her not to worry." She spared a glance at the kitchen clock. "Heck, I'll tell her myself when I go on shift in an hour."

"Thanks, Dr. Georges-Scales."

Susan appeared in the kitchen, bouncing up and down on her toes. "I see people hugging! Can I play?"

Eddie chuckled, wiping his face. "Sure. I'm sorry we argued at school, Susan. And I'm sorry for what I said."

"Forgiven. I'm sorry I hocked a loogie in your face." She laughed, holding him tight.

Looking at Eddie, Susan, and now Catherine in the kitchen together, Jennifer suddenly realized what she wanted to do today.

"Come on," she said. "Let's get in that car."

They opened the door just in time to catch Skip ready to ring the doorbell.

There was a tense moment as he and Eddie stared at each other, but then Skip shook himself and offered Eddie his hand. Jennifer sighed in relief as Eddie took it, thinking of her mother's words: *There is always hope.*

"Okay," she declared. "Let's make sure we all know each other. I'm Jennifer Scales and I'm half-dragon, half-beast-stalker. This is Skip Wilson. He's my ex-boyfriend, he's super smart, and he can turn into the ugliest freaking scorpions and spiders you've ever seen. This is Catherine Brandfire. She's a trampler dragon, and she can't hunt or fly to save her own life—"

"Hey!"

"—but she has a Ford Mustang convertible and a driver's license, so she is a goddess unto us. This is Eddie Blacktooth. He's a beaststalker and his father would like to see all of us dead, but Eddie's the best kid you could ever hope to grow up with. And this is Susan Elmsmith." She turned and placed her hand on Susan's arm. "She's incredibly loyal, and the most special friend I have. I owe her so much."

Susan blushed furiously through a wicked grin. "You're right. We'll start with dibs on the front passenger seat."

"We're all going to hang," Jennifer announced, looking at each of them in turn. "We're going to get along. And we're not going to keep secrets from each other anymore. Right?"

"Right."

"Right."

"Right."

A pause. "Right."

Jennifer didn't catch the hesitation: She had turned to call back to her mother down the hallway.

"We're going out now."

"Where?" Her mother's voice sounded serene over the sound of rinsing dishes.

Her gray eyes twinkled. "We're all going to Crescent Valley."

The crash of a glass shattering on the kitchen floor made Jennifer smile. Her mother's head appeared in the hallway, laced with an expression of awe and admiration.

"Are you serious, honey?"

Jennifer flexed the finger that wore the Ring of Seraphina. There was a new moon in the sky, but the gateway would always be open to her now. "Yep. We're definitely going. I'll get Dad's approval once I'm there."

Elizabeth bit her lip anxiously, longing filling her emerald eyes. Jennifer knew exactly what she was thinking.

"We'll be back soon," she promised. "You should go to the hospital. You have your own friend to catch up with. In a day or two, maybe you and I can go back to Crescent Valley to see Dad together."

Her mother rewarded her with a brilliant smile—and to Jennifer's delight, all of the years Evangelina had stolen came tumbling back in a youthful instant. "Thanks, honey. See you later. Love you!"

"Love you, too." She turned back to her friends. "I hope you all can swim!"

The five of them held hands as they walked down the sidewalk and plunged together into a waiting world.

EPILOGUE

Rebirth

The eternal crescent moon was dark and silent. Only the reflection of an unseen sun off the lunar surface gave Evangelina any sense of bearing or direction.

Even without this light, the path was clear. The venerables moved in only one direction, and their numbers stretched as far as she could sense, both before and behind.

Brothers. Sisters. Fathers. Mothers. Cousins. They were all there, a family of nearly infinite size, dating back thousands of generations. Evangelina still had bittersweet memories of her own brothers, but those were not the only ones she had any more. It would take Evangelina an eternity to absorb the new and sundry recollections that surrounded her—lives full of happiness and grief, fear and passion, and above all . . . hope for those still below.

She thought of Father's new wife again and felt some of her own sorrow and guilt slowly strip away.

The shape closest to her reached out, with his thoughts and memories. Evangelina took it all in, but lingered over the joy. She felt her first genuine smile as she recognized the memories of a child, and a child's bride, and a child's child. There was so much within that future to look forward to.

Suddenly, the host caught fire, their sign to new arrivals in the valley below. A sheet of flame swept through them all, each spirit adding their own breath to the conflagration.

Family! Friends!

She exulted in the thought.

Easing closer to her grandfather's shape as they flew together, she let him feel her own joy.

She would never be alone again.